BY THE OPEN SEA

August Strindberg, born in Stockholm in 1849, was the author of more than fifty plays, as well as novels, short stories, poems and an autobiography. Few of his earlier plays are remembered, but from the 1880s his writing took on the intensity which characterizes such plays as *The Father* and *Miss Julie*. He went on to write historical dramas based on Swedish history and a series of plays dealing with similar themes to those of his middle period, including *Easter* and *The Dance of Death*. He died in 1912.

•

Mary Sandbach taught in various language schools in Cambridge for six years and translated Strindberg's *Inferno* in 1962. Other Strindberg works followed: *From an Occult Diary* in 1965, *The Cloister* in 1969 and *Getting Married* in 1972. In 1974 she received the Swedish Order of Vasa for her services to Swedish literature.

AUGUST STRINDBERG

BY·THE·OPEN·SEA

Translated with an introduction
by Mary Sandbach

PENGUIN BOOKS

Penguin Books Ltd, Harmondsworth, Middlesex, England
Viking Penguin Inc., 40 West 23rd Street, New York, New York 10010, U.S.A.
Penguin Books Australia Ltd, Ringwood, Victoria, Australia
Penguin Books Canada Limited, 2801 John Street, Markham, Ontario, Canada L3R 1B4
Penguin Books (N.Z.) Ltd, 182–190 Wairau Road, Auckland 10, New Zealand

First published in Great Britain by Secker & Warburg 1984
Published in Penguin Books 1987

Reproduced, printed and bound in Great Britain by
Hazell Watson & Viney Limited,
Member of the BPCC Group,
Aylesbury, Bucks
Typeset in Bembo

Introduction

Strindberg was forty when he started to write *By the Open Sea* in 1889. He had behind him five intensely productive years, over-productive he would have said. During these years he had written his autobiography, *The Son of a Servant*, the three great plays by which he is best known outside Sweden – *The Father*, *Miss Julie* and *Creditors* – and a host of other works. Among these were some stories about the people of the islands of Stockholm's archipelago, the best-known being *The People of Hemsö*. No one previously had written about the archipelago as he did and these books were warmly received. No wonder his publisher's son, Karl Otto Bonnier, was pleased when in January 1889 he announced that he was going to write a continuation to *The People of Hemsö*. What he actually produced was a very different book.

The People of Hemsö is a genuine novel. It has a plot, plenty of incident and humour, and fully drawn characters who, if they are erring are also likeable. *By the Open Sea* has incidents too, but it is in essence the study of the development and decline of a single human being, and is as such a masterpiece, but almost every event in it is seen through his eyes alone, and the other people in the book are there only to illuminate various aspects of his character.

Strindberg's mood had changed; from being in principle the champion of the masses, he was now antagonistic to what he called the 'small people', and in *By the Open Sea* he attacks them furiously. They were the cause of the downfall of Inspector Borg, the hero of the book, whose mission it was to help them. Strindberg still loved the archipelago as much as ever, and the book contains many magnificent descriptions of scenery, but its inhabitants were anathema to him.

As a rule Strindberg wrote fast and well, but *By the Open Sea* took him more than a year to finish and is full of what he himself called 'inadvertencies'. He began it in Denmark in April 1889, and had only got as far as chapter VII by November of that year. He had spent the summer in his beloved archipelago, but in November he returned to Stockholm where he endured five unhappy months, during which no work at all was done on his novel. In April 1890 he once more retreated to the islands and inspiration returned. The last seven chapters of the book were written rapidly, and Bonnier received the whole manuscript on 7 June 1890.

There were several reasons for this delay in completing the book. Strindberg had found it difficult to decide whether it should be a collection of short stories like his popular *Lives of the Men of the Skerries*, or whether it should be a novel. He was also uncertain which island he should choose for the setting. He had used so many of them in earlier books that they were 'spoiled' for him.

Then there was his love of science and nature-study. A desire to know how things worked, and why, had been with him from his schooldays and this, combined with his recurrent feeling that there was something immoral about imaginative literature, also played a part. In *By the Open Sea* he could combine his love of science and nature-study with literature, but preparation for this involved a tremendous amount of reading. His letters to Bonnier and others in 1889 are filled with requests for books and complaints about his difficulties in writing. 'My great creative udder is beginning to run dry,' he wrote to Bonnier in September 1889. 'It runs now and then but the long intervals between are occupied with learned plodding, unproductively alas. At any rate it beats belles-lettres out of me and can therefore be used as a cane. All the same the prospects of printing by the autumn look dark . . . All efforts to hurry me on only delay matters as forced work makes me ill.'

The results of this 'learned plodding' can be found in many parts of the book, chiefly in chapter III, but also to some extent in chapter VII when Borg is trying to train Maria to experience nature with the eyes and ears of a scientist. She complains that he is spoiling nature for himself, and he replies that his approach makes him intimate with nature. Chapter III contains many examples of this intimacy in the wonderful descriptions of seascapes and the fauna and flora of the sea. The sea was always of enormous importance to Strindberg. Most of his paintings are of it – sometimes turbulent, sometimes calm. To his hero Borg it was a way of escape, a comforter, a restorer. No wonder that he fled to it to help him to end his life.

Bonnier's fears that chapter III was too learned were hardly justified. It is the centre-piece of the book, the key to Borg's character and to the whole course of the work. The only time in the book where learned speculations appear tiresome are the passages of pseudo-ethnographic research in chapter XIII and the wild suggestions for improving conditions in Sweden in chapter XIV, but these are introduced to illustrate Borg's mental deterioration and are not meant to be taken seriously.

Strindberg's 'learned plodding' was by no means the only reason for his delay in finishing the book. The unhappy circumstances of his life were equally responsible. He was desperately poor, his marriage to his first wife, Siri von Essen, was breaking up, and they were living in both discomfort and disharmony in miserable lodgings. However, a letter he wrote in January 1890 to Ola Hansson, a fellow Swedish writer resident in Germany, shows that life in Stockholm had a few advantages: 'The situation: social surroundings, diet, have given me a sort of lethargic calm, but the return to stages long past, inhalation of bad air, association with mean minds tear me apart and oppress me so that I cannot write. While still on Sandhamn and alone a new idea came to me every other hour, but town life upsets me and makes me sterile.'

Strindberg was always torn between a need for solitude and a desire for company, and in *By the Open Sea* he explores the effects first of contact with 'mean minds' and then those of complete isolation. However, it is a mistake to regard the book as an autobiographical work as some critics have done. Inspector Borg in no way resembles Strindberg, though some of his experiences do reflect aspects of his creator's life. His upbringing as we shall see in chapter III was quite unlike Strindberg's. It was much more like that of John Stuart Mill, who was certainly brought up to be a man, not educated to be a child by being given fairy-tale books to read. Indeed, much of Borg's upbringing suggests that Strindberg had read Mill's *Autobiography*, though there is no direct evidence for this.

Borg was quite unlike Strindberg in another respect: Strindberg survived the many trials and tribulations of his life; Borg succumbed. Strindberg retained and even enhanced his mental capabilities through a period of enormous strain; Borg disintegrated and took his own life. *By the Open Sea* is a study of the effects of frustration and isolation on a hypersensitive intellectual aristocrat, not, as some people have claimed, the portrait of a Nietzschean superman. Strindberg himself at the time he wrote it declared that the book was a 'modern novel written in the footprints of Nietzsche and Poe'. Some years later, when he was planning to write *Inferno*, he said it would be on the same theme as *By the Open Sea*, 'the ruin of the individual when he isolates himself'.

That Nietzsche did exert some influence on Strindberg is undeniable. Strindberg was first introduced to some of his works by Georg Brandes, the Danish critic, in 1888. He was at that time an uneasy atheist and Nietzsche's anti-Christian stance appealed to him. He had also written his two *Vivisections* – *The Small* and *The Great* – in which he denounces the baleful effects small people can have on great ones, and for this too he found sympathetic echoes in Nietzsche's works. But he himself believed that in holding these views he had anticipated Nietzsche, not followed him, and it was Nietzsche's decline into madness rather than his philosophy that inspired *By the Open Sea*, in particular Borg's tragic end.

It is clear right from the start of the book that Borg is no superman. He achieves his feat of navigation not by brute strength but by means of his superior intellect and sensibilities and, let it not be forgotten, by the magic of his bracelet. This bracelet is never displayed except when Borg has some special feat to perform: the direction of the successful voyage to Österskär, the curing of Maria's feigned illness, and finally her seduction. When his personality is described in chapter III it is not that of a superman. He is a nervous, hypersensitive human being, always in need of renewing himself by periods of isolation after exceptional strain. Borg is in fact a 'modern man' as Strindberg conceived him in his essay 'Deranged Sense Impressions' where he says: 'am I deranged because I have involuntarily been forced to live too rapidly in this era of steam and electricity . . .? Am I casting my skin? Am I turning into a modern human being?' This was written in 1894, but Strindberg says much the same thing of Borg in 1889:

> . . . having been brought up in the era of steam and electricity, when the pace of life had quickened he, like the rest of his generation, was inevitably afflicted by bad nerves . . . These symptoms of illness were an expression of increased vitality, the result of extreme sensitivity, like that of the crayfish when she changes her shell, or the bird when it moults. It was the creation of a new race, or at least of a new type of human being. (pp. 40–41)

This gives us a clue to what Strindberg means when he talks about a 'modern novel', i.e. a novel about a modern man, a being far removed from Nietzsche's superman.

Borg's personality as it is presented to us in chapter III reflects more of Mill's teaching than Nietzsche's, for instance in the attitude he has been taught to adopt to instinct versus nature. It is known that Strindberg read Mill's essay 'Nature' in 1885, and Borg's father's arguments about the need to suppress or control what he called his 'ganglia conclusions' stem from Mill. This author's influence is also clearly visible in Borg's belief that the freedom of the individual should never infringe the rights of others. This doctrine undoubtedly derives from Mill's *On Liberty* which Strindberg possessed. His notes and underlinings clearly indicate the importance he attached to it. He would not have found in Mill anything to support his attitude to Christ, whom Mill admired but he despised, but he probably approved of Mill's opinion of Christian doctrine.

More important to Strindberg than either Nietzsche or Mill was his obsession with the act of creation. It runs through the book like a red thread. The word 'create' and its derivatives crop up all the time, particularly in chapters II and III. This has been pointed out by Sven Delblanc in his essay 'The Demiurge' (1979). Borg himself is an artist and a creator when he transforms his room from a naked waste to a pleasing interior. He is again a creator when he makes an Italian landscape on a desolate island, and last of all, when he nears his tragic end, in his attempt to create a living being.

In chapter II, man is the creator as will be seen from the following passage:

> Inspector Borg did not worship nature . . . On the contrary, as a being conscious of himself, and of standing highest in the chain of terrestrial creations, he entertained a certain contempt for the lower forms of existence. For one thing he fully understood that the products of the conscious mind were much more ingenious than those of unconscious nature, and for another he realised that they were advantageous to man who, when he invents his creations, pays particular attention to the usefulness or beauty these will have for their creator. (p. 20)

Or again, in chapter III, when Borg, after his investigations of the sea-bottom, becomes aware of the wonderful spectacle around him and we are told that:

> . . . when he sought the cause behind the tremendous impression this landscape in particular had made upon him, and found the answer, he experienced the great joy that must be felt by nature's highest creation when he lifts the veil from a secret; the bliss which follows every act of creation on the long road to clarity and which is perhaps the motive force that drives us forward from dreams to knowledge, a bliss which must resemble that of a supposed conscious Creator who was aware of what he was doing. (pp. 29–30)

Here Borg is still clinging to the idea that man is the creator, but can anyone doubt that God lurks behind, even if he is referred to as a 'supposed' Creator? There is another backward glance at God on p. 30 when it is said of Borg that 'he used such moments as a substitute for the departed pleasures of religion'.

The longing for these 'departed pleasures' is even more evident in one of the final passages of chapter III where he says: 'Over this repeat performance of the creation . . . Here hovered the God of the story of creation. He who divided light from darkness, as if to give a sensory reason for His searching mind.' This passage seems to anticipate the great passage in *Inferno* written eight years later when Strindberg had found his very individual God. He was visiting the Jardin des Plantes in Paris and he says:

> I made my way through the vegetable and animal kingdom and came at last to Man, behind whom I found God, the Creator. The Creator, that great artist who himself develops as he creates, who makes rough drafts only to cast them aside, who takes up abortive ideas afresh, who perfects and multiplies his primitive conceptions. Most certainly everything is the work of His hand. (p. 177; Penguin edn, 1979)

Borg's longing for God in the person of the Creator reaches its height in the scene in chapter XIV with the preacher when he says:

> Do you know what God is? He is the fixed point outside ourselves, desired by Archimedes, with which he would have been able to lift the world. He is the imaginary magnet inside the earth, without which the movements of the magnetic needle would remain unexplained. He is the ether that must be discovered so that the vacuum may be filled. He is the molecule, without which the laws of chemistry would be miracles. Give me a few more hypotheses, above all the fixed point outside myself, for I am quite adrift. (pp. 180–81)

Borg never found his fixed point and took his own life. Strindberg had to pass through many harrowing experiences before he found his God, but *By the Open Sea* shows clearly that when he wrote it his search had already begun.

I

One May evening a herring-boat sailed out with a following wind into the straits of Gåssten. The Rök islands, notorious throughout the archipelago for their three pyramids, began to turn blue, and in the clear sky clouds were forming as the sun started to sink. The sea was breaking round the headlands, and the unpleasant jerking of the square sail indicated that the land-wind would soon encounter newly awakened currents of air from above, from beyond, and from behind.

At the tiller sat the customs officer from Österskär,[1] a stalwart with a long black beard, who seemed now and then to be exchanging glances with his two coast-guards. They were sitting forward, where one of them was managing the boat-hook that kept the big square sail in the wind.

Now and again the steersman cast a questioning look at the little gentleman sitting crouched by the mast, who seemed both frightened and cold, and who, from time to time, drew his shawl closer about his stomach and lower body.

The customs officer must have found him ridiculous, for every few minutes he turned leewards, as if to spit out his impending laughter with his tobacco juice.

The little gentleman was wearing a beaver-coloured spring coat beneath which protruded a pair of wide trousers made of moss-green tricot, and below them a pair of crocodile shagreen boots with rows of black buttons on the uppers of a brown material. You could see almost nothing of what he was wearing underneath, but round his neck he had wound a cream-coloured foulard handkerchief, and his hands were protected by a pair of salmon-coloured *glacé* gloves with three buttons.

The wrist of the right-hand glove was encircled by a thick gold bracelet in the form of a serpent biting its tail.[2] Under the gloves there were lumps on his fingers that seemed to be made by rings. What could be seen of his face was lean and deathly pale, while a pair of small thin black moustaches, trained to turn upwards at the ends, enhanced his pallor and gave him an exotic appearance. His hat was pushed back, revealing a black, evenly cut fringe that looked like a bit of a skull-cap.

The things that most seemed to engage the helmsman's untiring attention were the bracelet, the moustache and the fringe.

During the long trip from Dalarö[3] this man, who was a great humorist, had tried to open a merry conversation with the Inspector of Fisheries whom he had been instructed to sail out to his headquarters on Österskär. But the young gentleman had shown a wounding lack of receptiveness for his intrusive witticisms, and this had confirmed the customs officer in his view that the 'instructor' was stuck-up.

The breeze freshened as they passed Hansten to windward, and the dangerous sail began to flap. The inspector, who had been sitting with a naval chart in his hand, occasionally making notes after throwing out one of his questions, now put the chart in his pocket and addressed the helmsman in a voice more like a woman's than a man's.

'Be so good as to sail with a little more care.'

'Are you afraid, Instructor?' was the helmsman's scoffing response.

'I'm afraid for my life, for I care about it,' answered the inspector.

'Not for the lives of others?' was the man's second reprimand.

'At least not as much as for my own,' retorted the inspector. 'And sailing is a dangerous occupation, especially with a square sail.'

'Indeed, then you've sailed a lot with a square sail before, sir?'

'Never in my life. But I can see where the wind applies its force, I can calculate what measure of resistance the weight of the boat can produce, and I am well able to judge when the sail's aback.'

'Well then, take the tiller yourself,' half-snapped the customs officer.

'Oh no, that's your place; I don't sit on the coachman's box when I'm out on Crown business.'

'Can't sail, of course.'

'If I can't it must be pretty easy to learn since every other schoolboy and every single customs official can, so it's no disgrace that I can't. Just sail carefully now, for I don't want to get wet, and I'd rather not spoil my gloves.'

That was an order, and the customs officer, though cock of the roost on Österskär, felt somewhat put out. After a movement of the tiller the sail filled again, the boat got well under way, and steered out past the island, whose white customs house shone brightly in the direct light of the setting sun.

The inner archipelago faded away and they felt that all protection and safety was left behind as they set out across the great expanse of water that now opened up before them without bounds, darkly menacing in the east. No prospect here of creeping into shelter behind the islands or skerries, no possibility, in case of storm, of lying up and reefing the sails. Headlong into destruction they must go, out over the black abyss, out to the little island that looked no bigger than a buoy thrown into the sea. The inspector was uneasy. As we have seen, he was strongly attached to his one and only life, and was intelligent enough to be able to calculate the insignificance of his own ability to oppose the mighty forces of all-powerful nature. At thirty-six he was far too clear-sighted to overestimate the helmsman's knowledge and courage. He did not look with confidence upon the man's brown face and full beard, nor did he believe that a muscular arm was a match for a wind which blew with a force of thousands of pounds against an unstable expanse of sail. He saw through the sort of courage whose only base was imperfect judgement. What folly, he thought, to risk your life in a little open boat when there are vessels with decks, and steamships. How silly to hoist such a sail on a pine mast, that bent like a drawn bow when the wind blew most strongly. The leeward shroud hung limp, likewise the forestay, and all the pressure of the wind was taken by the windward shroud which, moreover, looked rotten. He decided he would not abandon himself to such an uncertain fate as the greater or lesser durability of a few hempen ropes, and consequently, at the next gust of wind, he turned to the coastguard who was sitting by the halyard and in an abrupt but penetrating voice ordered: 'Take down the sail.'

The man looked aft, awaiting the order of the helmsman, but the inspector's command was immediately repeated, and with such emphasis that the sail sank. Now the customs officer in the stern began to yell:

'Who the devil is in command of my boat?'

'I am,' answered the inspector, upon which he turned to the coast-guards with a new order:

'Put out your oars.'

The oars were put out and the boat lurched a few times, for in his rage the helmsman had left the tiller with the words:

'Well, then, take the tiller yourself.'

The inspector immediately took his place in the stern, and the tiller was under his arm before the customs officer had finished swearing.

The seams of the kid gloves immediately split at the thumbs, but the boat proceeded at a steady pace while the customs officer sat jeering to himself, with an oar at the ready to right the boat's course. The inspector had no attention to spare for the sceptical mariner. He was staring fixedly to windward, and was soon able to distinguish between rollers, with their troughs many metres long, and the white horses with their short cascades. After a quick look aft to gauge the leeway, and to observe in the wake the set of the current, he was quite clear about the course he must steer to avoid being driven past Österskär.

The customs officer, who had long been trying to meet those glowing black eyes, and to show them his scorn, soon grew tired, for it looked as if those eyes would not accept anything from him, as if they wanted to keep themselves free of any contact with things that might disturb or contaminate. So, after his looks had gone a-begging for a time, the customs officer grew depressed and absent-minded, and took to watching the handling of the boat.

The sun was now down on the horizon and the waves were

breaking, purplish black at their base, with walls of a deep green, and crests at their highest point the shining green of grass. The spray splashed and spluttered, rosy-red in the sunlight, the colour of pink champagne, while the boat and its crew were down in the dusk. Then, up on the ridge of the wave again, their four faces would be lit up for a moment, only to be extinguished immediately.

But not all the waves broke; some only rolled onwards, gently rocking the boat, lifting it and sucking it forwards. It seemed as if the little helmsman could judge at a distance when a breaker was coming and, with a light touch on the tiller, held his course, gave way, or slipped past the frightful green wall that sprang forward threateningly, wanting to cast its vault over the boat.

Taking down the sail had really increased the danger, for their power of propulsion was reduced, and they had to do without the lifting action of the sail. Consequently the customs officer's amazement at the incredibly fine manoeuvring began to change to admiration.

He saw, by the varying expression on the pale face and the movements of the dark eyes, that behind them quite intricate calculations were taking place and, after sticking out his oar in order not to seem superfluous, he considered that the time had come to give his recognition before it was wrested from him.

'You've been to sea before, you have!'

The inspector did not answer. For one thing he was deeply engrossed, and for another he wanted to avoid any form of contact which might, in a weak moment, surprise him into being fooled by the seeming superiority of the giant's physique.

His right glove was split down to the base of the thumb and his bracelet had slipped down. Now that the fiery crests had faded and the dusk was falling he took out a single eyeglass with his left hand, stuck it into his right eye, and turned his head rapidly towards a number of points as if seeking landfall where no land could be seen; whereupon he threw out an abrupt question forward:

'You've no lighthouse on Österskär?'

'Not that I know of, worse luck,' answered the customs officer.

'Are there any reefs?'
'Clean water.'
'Have we any sight of Landsort or Sandhamn lighthouses?'
'Not much of Sandhamn, rather more of Landsort,' answered the customs officer.
'Just sit still where you are, and we'll find a way,' ordered the inspector, who seemed to have taken a dead reckoning by the heads of the three men and some unknown fixed points in the distance.
The clouds had gathered, and the May twilight had been replaced by semi-darkness. It was like rocking forwards in some thin but impenetrable material, without light, and with waves that rose up like dark shadows against the half-shadows of the air, stuck their heads under the boat, took it on their backs, and popped up on the other side where they rolled themselves out flat. But to distinguish friend from foe was now more difficult and his calculations less certain. Two oars were out on the leeward side and one on the windward, and by applying more or less power at the right moment he would keep the boat afloat.
The inspector, who could see practically nothing but the lighthouses to the north and south, now had to substitute his ears for his eyes. But before he could accustom himself to tell by the thunder, soughing or hissing of the waves the difference between a breaker and a roller, water had got into the boat, so that he had to save his fine boots by putting them up on the thwart.
He soon taught himself the harmonics of the waves and he could even hear when danger was approaching by the tempo of the swell. He could tell by the pressure on his left eardrum when the wind was blowing hardest and threatening to whip the water up higher. It was as if he were improvising nautical and meteorological instruments from his delicate senses, to which cords passed freely from his large brain-battery concealed behind the absurd little hat and the black dog's bang.
The men, who for a moment had muttered rebellious words when the water came in, fell silent when they felt the boat shooting forwards and knew from each word of command – windward or leeward – on which side they were to pull.

The inspector had taken his bearings from the two lighthouses and was using the quadrangular lens of his eye-glass to measure the distances. But what made holding a course so difficult was that no lights shone from the windows of the cottages on the island, since the houses had been built in the shelter of rocky knolls. Now, when their dangerous journey had lasted for an hour or more, he began to be aware of a dark eminence against the horizon. Not wanting to receive dubious advice which might upset the intuition in which he put more trust, he steered silently towards what he took to be the island or one of its outlying rocks, comforting himself with the thought that to reach a stationary object, whatever it might be, would be better than continuing to float between air and water. But the dark wall approached with a speed greater than that of the boat, and this began to awaken in the inspector a suspicion that they were not on the right course. In order to discover what the dark shape was, and simultaneously to send out a signal in case it should prove to be a vessel that had failed to hoist its lantern, he took out his box of fusees, struck the whole bunch at once and rotated them so that they lit up a few metres round the boat. The light only penetrated the darkness for an instant, but the magic-lantern-like picture that appeared remained before the inspector's eyes for several seconds. He saw a block of drift-ice upended on a shoal with a wave breaking over it like the vault of a grotto over a gigantic lump of calcspar. He saw too a flock of long-tailed duck and black-backed gulls lift and then drown in the darkness from which all you could hear was a chorus of shrieks. The sight of this breaker affected the inspector as the sight of the coffin in which his dismembered body will lie affects a man condemned to death, and in the moment of apprehension he experienced a mortal dread both of cold and suffocation. This paralysed his muscles but, on the other hand, it roused all the hidden powers of his spirit. He was able in a split second to estimate exactly the extent of the danger, and also the only way of avoiding it, and instantly yelled out the word of command 'STOP!'

The men, who had their backs to the breaker and were therefore unaware of it, rested on their oars. The boat was sucked towards a wave which must have been three or four metres high. It broke high above the boat like a cupola of bottle-green glass and the whole watery mass came down on the other side. The boat, half-full of water and with its passengers nearly suffocated by the terrific atmospheric pressure, was spat out, so to speak, on the far side of the foam. Three shrieks, like those of nightmare-ridden sleepers, were heard simultaneously, but from the fourth, the helmsman, nothing at all. He only made a gesture with his hand towards the island where a glimmer of light a few cable-lengths to leeward could now be seen. Then he sank down against the stern-post and remained lying there.

The boat had ceased to rock for they were now in smooth water, but the rowers sat as if drunk, dipping the oars they no longer needed, as the boat was being driven ashore by a following wind.

'What's that you've got in the boat, my friends?' asked an old fisherman, who had hailed them with a 'good-evening' that the wind had swept away.

'It's supposed to be a fishery instructor!' whispered the customs officer as he drew the boat up behind a boat-house.

'Indeed, it's one of those is it, come to pry into our nets. He'll get on fine, he will, as he seems to be ill into the bargain,' opined fisherman Öman, who seemed to be the spokesman for the sparse poverty-stricken population of the island.

The customs officer was waiting for the inspector to show signs of going ashore, but feeling uneasy when there was no movement from the little bundle lying in the stern, he climbed back into the boat, put both his arms round the crumpled body, and carried it ashore.

'Is he done for?' asked Öman, not without a note of hope in his voice.

'He's not up to much,' answered the customs officer and carried his wet burden into the cottage.

The scene was rather like that of Tom Thumb and the giant [4] as the big customs officer entered his brother's kitchen, where his sister-in-law was standing by the stove. And when he put the little body down on the sofa an expression of compassion for the weakling radiated from the big beard under the low forehead.

'See here, Mari, here's the Inspector of Fisheries,' was his greeting to his sister-in-law, as he put his arm round her waist. 'Help us to get something dry on him and something wet into him, and then he can go to his room.'

The inspector cut an absurd and miserable figure as he lay on the hard wooden sofa. His white stand-up shirt collar was twisted round his neck like a dirty rag. All the fingers of his right hand projected from his tattered glove, and his sodden cuffs hung down, stuck together by dissolving starch. His little crocodile-skin boots had lost their shine and shape, and it was with the greatest difficulty that the customs officer and his sister-in-law dragged them off his feet.

When his hosts had removed most of the clothes from this piece of wreckage and thrown some blankets over him they brought some hot milk and spirits, and after each had shaken one of the sick man's arms the customs officer raised the little body on his arm and poured the milk slowly into the open mouth beneath the closed eyes. But when the sister-in-law was about to pour the spirits after it the smell seemed to act like a strong poison. With a gesture of his hand the inspector pushed away the glass, opened his eyes and, as wide awake as if he had just emerged from a refreshing sleep, he enquired about his room.

Of course it wasn't ready, but they'd get it done in an hour if he'd just lie where he was and wait.

So there the inspector had to lie and spend an intolerable hour letting his eyes rove round the furnishing and the inhabitants of the uninteresting room. It was the official residence provided by the State for the customs officer at the little customs house on Österskär. Everything was on the mean side, put together just to be a roof over his head. The white, unpapered walls were as abstract as the conception of the State, four white rectangles, enclosing a space covered by a white rectangle. Impersonal, unrelenting as an hotel room, which is not intended as a habitation, only as a lodging. Neither this customs officer nor his predecessor had had the heart to paper it for his successor or for the State. In the middle of this dead whiteness were dark pieces of manufactured furniture of semi-modern design. A round dining-table of knotty deal, stained with walnut and full of white plate-rings; high-backed chairs of the same wood and design that rocked on three legs at a time; a sofa-bed that, like ready-made mens' clothing, was made out of the least possible material at the cheapest price. Everything was unsuited to its purpose, and seemed unable to provide the rest or comfort required of it. Consequently it was unsightly, in spite of the papier-mâché ornaments that were glued to it.

When the customs officer sat his broad bottom on the cane seat of a chair and leaned his vast back against its support, the manoeuvre was followed by an ominous creaking and a testy admonition from his sister-in-law to be careful of other people's possessions, to which the customs officer responded with an insolent pat, followed by a glance that left no doubt as to the nature of their relationship.

The depressing effect that the whole room had on the inspector was increased by the discovery of this discordancy. As a naturalist he did not share the current view of allowed and disallowed, but on the other hand he had a strongly developed instinct for the practicality of certain of nature's fixed laws, and he was inwardly pained when he saw these laws being transgressed. For him it was like finding in his laboratory an acid which, since the world began, had only been combined with one base and was now, against its nature, combining with two.

It confused his conception of the development from universal intercourse to monogamy, and he felt he was back among the wild hordes of primaeval days, living in colonies like the polyps, before selection and differentiation had succeeded in establishing individual personal existence and lineal descent.

And when he saw a two-year-old girl with too large a head and fish-eyes going about the room on cat's-paws, as if she was afraid of being seen, he soon realised that her doubtful parentage had sown the seeds of discord and was working to disrupt and disturb, and he was easily able to foresee that the time would come when this living piece of evidence would have to pay the price for all the involuntary sins of a dangerous witness.

As he was thinking these thoughts the door opened and the man of the house entered.

He was the customs officer's brother who had stayed on

for the present in the subordinate office of coast-guard. Physically he was even better endowed than the customs officer, but he was fair-haired, and had an open, endearing, and trustful appearance.

After wishing them a cheerful good-evening he sat down at the table beside his brother, took the child on his knee, and kissed it.

'We've a visitor!' the customs officer informed him, pointing to the sofa where the inspector was lying. 'The fishery instructor, who's going to live upstairs.'

'So that's who it is,' answered Vestman, rising to his feet and preparing to shake hands.

With the child on his arm he approached the sofa, thinking that, in as much as he was the host and his unmarried brother only a lodger, it was his duty to wish his guest welcome.

'We live simply out here,' he continued after a few welcoming words, 'but my old woman isn't too bad at cooking, for her was in service in better-class homes before her married me three years ago, but since we had the child here her's had other things to think about, well children come when you get a helping hand – that's to say – not that I needed any help, as you might say.'

The inspector was surprised by the sudden change in direction taken by the long sentence and asked himself whether the man knew anything, or whether he only had a feeling that things were out of joint. He himself had seen how matters stood in ten minutes; how then was it possible for an interested party not to see anything in two years?

He was overcome by revulsion for the whole affair and turning towards the wall closed his eyes so that his own visions, of a pleasanter nature, would while away the remaining half-hour.

Even so he could not make himself deaf, but against his will overheard a conversation which, though it had been lively, was now stumbling along as if the words were being measured by a ruler before being uttered. When a silence did occur it was filled by the husband, who seemed to dread it, fearing to hear something he did not want to hear, and unable to be calm unless intoxicated by the stream of his own words.

When at last the hour was up and nothing had been said about his room the inspector got up and asked if it was not ready.

His hostess thought it was in a sense, but . . .

In a tone of command the inspector requested that he should be taken to it immediately, reminding them in carefully chosen words that he had not come to live as one of the family, that he was not a guest, but on official business, and that he was only asking for what was his by right, and which he intended to have in accordance with the memorandum that the Minister for Civil Service Affairs had sent to the customs officer at Dalarö via the Board of Customs and Excise.

The matter was thereby put right and, with a candle in his fist, Vestman led the severe gentleman up a flight of stairs to a gable room where nothing in the arrangements could explain the hour's delay that had been requested.

It was quite a large room with walls as white as those in the living-room, and with a large window opening up the middle of the long wall like a black hole through which the darkness streamed unhindered by any curtains.

There was a bed, made up as simply as if it were merely an elevation in the floor to avoid draughts, a table, two chairs and a wash-stand. The inspector, who was used to having his eyes sated by impressions, cast a despairing look about him when he saw only these utilitarian objects planted out in a vacuum, in which the candle-light battled with darkness, and where the large window seemed to consume every gleam of light produced by the burning tallow.

He felt as lost as if, after a life-time of effort upwards – towards refinement, a good position, and luxury – he had sunk into poverty and moved down into a lower class; as if his spirit, that loved beauty and wisdom, had been shut up in prison, been deprived of nourishment and incarcerated in a house of correction. These naked walls were those of the cell of a mediaeval monastery where visual asceticism and an empty environment drove a starving imagination to gnaw at itself, to conjure up brighter or darker images merely to escape from nothingness. The white, formless, colourless nullity of these lime-washed walls dragged to the surface a pictorial urge which primitive man's cave or arbour has never evoked, which the forest, with its ever-changing colours and mobile contours has made unnecessary – an urge never produced by either the plane or the moor with their rich iridescent skies, or the sea, of which we never tire.

All at once he felt a feverish desire to instantly paint the walls full of summery landscapes of palms and parrots, to stretch a Persian carpet across the ceiling, to lay the skins of animals over the floorboards, that ran in lines like a ledger, to put sofas in the corners, each with its little table before it, to hoist up a ceiling-lamp over a round table covered with books and periodicals, to set a cottage piano against one short wall, and fill the long wall with bookcases; and in the corner of a sofa to place a little female figure, never mind whose! Like the candle on the table fighting out its struggle against darkness his imagination worked on the arrangement of the room, but then it gave up. Everything disappeared and his horrible surroundings frightened him into bed, whereupon he put out the light and drew the quilt over his head.

The wind shook the whole attic, the carafe of water rattled against the tumbler, draughts blew through the room from the window to the door, and sometimes raised wisps of hair, dried by the sea-breezes, so that he imagined someone was passing a hand over his head. Between the gusts of wind great breakers broke against the rocks of the island's southern promontory like the beats of a kettle-drum in an orchestra. And when at last he had got used to the monotonous sounds of the wind and the waves he heard, just before he fell asleep, a man's voice in the living-room below, saying the words of an evening prayer for a child to repeat.

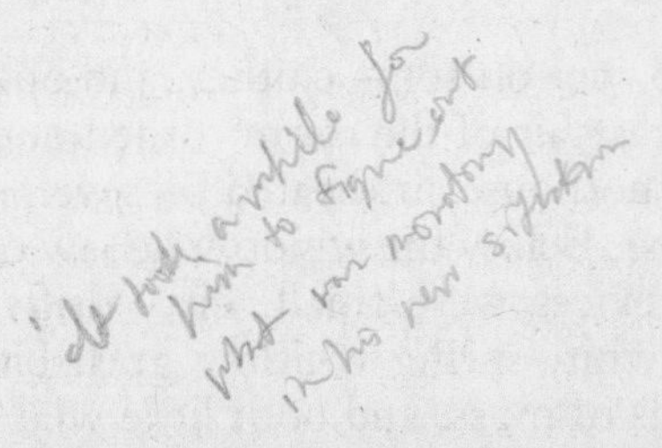

II

When the inspector woke the next morning after a heavy death-like sleep, induced by the exertions of the previous day and the strong sea air, he looked across the quilt and the first thing he noticed was an inexplicable silence. He observed that his ear was catching tiny sounds of which he was usually unaware. He heard every little movement of the sheet as it rose and fell with his breathing: he heard the hairs of his head rubbing against the pillow-slip, the throb of the pulse in his neck, the faint reverberations of his heartbeats from the rickety bed. He heard the silence, for the wind had dropped completely, and the pounding of the waves against the compressed air in the hollows of the cliffs was repeated only once every half-minute. From his bed, which was placed opposite the window, he saw in the lower pane something like a blue half-blind that was bluer than air and moved towards him gently, as if it wanted to come in through the window and flood the room. He knew that it was the sea, but it looked so small and it rose up like a vertical wall instead of spreading out like a horizontal expanse. In full sunlight the long swells had no shadows by which the eye could form a picture in perspective.

He got up, put on some clothes, and opened the window. The damp, raw air of the room rushed out and from the sea came warm hothouse air, heated by several hours of brilliant May sunshine. Below the window he saw only broken rocks, in whose crevices were small, dirty drifts of snow. Beside these, little white spring whitlow grass bloomed, well protected in beds of moss, and poor little wild pansies, pale gold from hunger and bluish-mauve from cold, hoisting the poor colours of their poor country in the first spring sunshine. Further down crept ling and crowberry, peeping over the cliffs below which lay a bank of white sand that the sea had pulverised and into which a scattering of lyme-grass plants had been stuck. On the white sand lay a belt of last year's seaweed like a dark scarf or hem in which shells, pine-needles, twigs and fish-bones had fastened. Furthest up the beach it was almost ebony black, but on the sea's side it was soft-soap brown with the last fresh skeins of seaweed whose curves and knots formed a lace edging along the shore. Inside the seaweed, on the path of sand, lay the dead top of a fir tree, stripped of its bark, skinned, scoured by the sand, washed by the water, polished dry by the wind and bleached by the sun, looking like the thorax of a mammoth's skeleton. Round about it was a whole osteological museum of similar skeletons or fragments of them. Here lay a stranded spar-buoy that had indicated the channel for years; now its thick lower end looked like a thigh-bone and socket-joint of a giraffe. There lay a whole juniper bush like the carcass of a drowned cat with the thin, white roots spread out like a cat-o'-nine-tails.

Off-shore there were rocks and reefs, which at one moment shone wet in the sunlight and at the next were drenched by swells. These went over them with a thud or, if lacking strength, broke up, rose, and heaved a cascade of foam into the air.

Beyond these the sea was smooth. It was here that you got out to 'the great flatness' as the fishermen called it, and now, at this morning hour, the sea stretched out like a blue cloth, unwrinkled, but swinging like a flag. It would have been tedious, that great, circular expanse, had it not been for a red buoy that was anchored off the reef and whose splash of red lead sat like a seal on a letter, brightening up a monotonous surface.

This was the sea, no novelty to be sure for Inspector Borg who had seen a good many parts of the world. But this was the desolate sea, met as it were in a *tête-à-tête*. It did not alarm as did the forest with its dark hiding places, but had a soothing effect like a wide-open, steadfast, large blue eye. Everything could be seen at once: no ambushes, no nooks and crannies. The onlooker felt flattered when he saw about him this circle of which, whatever his position, he was the centre. This great expanse of water was like the embodiment of something emanating from the beholder, and only existing through him. As long as he stood on land he felt intimate with this now harmless force, superior to this immense source of power now that he was out of its reach. When he remembered the mortal danger he had been in the previous evening, and the rage and anguish he had suffered in his fight against a brutal enemy whom he had nevertheless outwitted, he smiled generously at his vanquished and prostrate foe, who had only been a blind tool in the service of the winds, and who now stretched itself out to take its rest in the sunshine.

. . .

This was Österskär, classical Österskär, because it has had a long life, flourished, and decayed. Old Österskär in the Middle Ages was a great fishing ground, where that important commodity the Baltic herring had been caught, for which a separate charter had been drawn up and is still preserved today. The Baltic herring has the same function in central and northern Sweden as the herring has on the west coast of Sweden and in Norway. It is simply a herring – adapted to and the product of the poorer conditions of the Baltic – and is much in demand when herring is rare and expensive, and less so when it is plentiful. It has long been the winter food in central Sweden, so much so that the complaint of the Frenchmen – beguiled into settling here by Queen Christina – about the everlasting hard bread and the eternal herring, is preserved in a rhyme. Only a generation ago the great landowners paid dues to their tied labourers in herring, but when herring fishing declined, this payment in kind took the form of salted Baltic herring. The price rose, and the fishing, which had formerly been practised in moderation and for domestic consumption, now assumed a fiercely competitive character. The fishing grounds of Österskär, the richest in Södermanland's archipelago, began to be fished in a big way. The fish were disturbed in their spawning season, and the mesh of the herring-boat nets grew progressively smaller. The natural result was that the fishing declined, perhaps not so much because the fish were being eliminated, as because they had fled from their usual spawning grounds and taken refuge in deep waters, where no fisherman had yet been resourceful enough to seek out his fleeing foe.

Learned men, investigating the reasons for the decline in Baltic-herring fishing, disputed over them at length until the Ministry of Agriculture and Fisheries took the initiative, and decided that, by installing a knowledgeable Inspector of Fisheries, they would discover the reason for these adverse circumstances and find a means of curing them.

This then was Inspector Borg's immediate mission for the coming summer on Österskär. The place was not a lively one as the island does not lie on one of the main channels into Stockholm. From the south the large vessels usually come in via Landsort and past Dalarö and Vaxholm. From the east, and in certain winds even from the south, vessels make their way in via Sandhamn and Vaxholm, while from Norrland and Finland merchantmen approach via Furusund and Vaxholm.

Österskär's channel is an emergency entrance, chiefly used by Estonians, who usually approach from the south and east, and by others who are compelled by wind, current or storm, to set a course to the windward of Landsort, and to the leeward of Sandhamn. Consequently the place is only provided with a third-class customs house, manned by one customs officer, and a little pilot station, controlled from Dalarö.

This was the end of the world – quiet, peaceful, deserted, except during the fishing seasons of autumn and spring – and if a single pleasure yacht arrived there in the height of the summer, it was greeted as an apparition from a brighter and happier world. But Borg, the Inspector of Fisheries, who had come on another errand – 'to spy' the inhabitants called it – was greeted with marked coldness, shown first in the indifference of the previous evening, and now by the wretchedly cold coffee brought up to his room.

Blessed with an extremely sensitive palate he had nevertheless acquired, by severe training, the ability to suppress unpleasant sensations. He therefore swallowed the beverage without blinking, and then went downstairs to look at the place and to get to know the people.

When he passed the customs officer's kitchen, silence fell and those inside seemed to want to make themselves invisible. To avoid giving themselves away, doors were shut and conversations cut short.

With the unpleasant feeling that he was unwelcome he proceeded on his walk along the island and came down to the harbour. Here stood a collection of small cabins of the simplest possible construction, looking like random collections of stone splinters stacked together with a bit of mortar smeared on here and there. Only the chimneys over the fireplaces were of brick. At one corner of each a wood-shed had been added, at another a shed made of coarse boughs and twigs to shelter the pigs brought out here to be fattened when the fishing was in progress. The windows looked as if they had been taken from wrecked ships, and the roofs were covered with anything that could be spread out in several directions and would soak up rain, or let it run off: seaweed, lyme-grass, moss, turf and earth. These were the quarters, now deserted, each of which could be used to accommodate twenty sleepers when the great catches were being made, and every cabin was an unlicensed gin-shop.

Outside the most decent-looking of these cabins stood the big man of the island, fisherman Öman, cleaning out his flounder net with a twig. Since he could by no means regard himself as the dependent of a fishery inspector, yet at the same time felt that the latter's presence was bringing pressure to bear on him, he bristled up and prepared to give some sharp answers.

'Is the fishing going well?' was the inspector's greeting.

'Not yet, but it probably will now that the government's taking a hand in it,' answered Öman rather rudely.

'Where are the herring grounds?' asked the inspector, leaving the government to its fate.

'Well now, we thought that you, sir, knew that better than we do since you're being paid to teach us,' retorted Öman.

'Yes, you see, you only know where the grounds are, but I know where the herring gather, and that's going one better, isn't it?'

'Indeed, so if we have a go at the sea we'll get fish,' bantered Öman. 'So, that's how it is. Well one's never too old to learn.'

His wife now came out of the cabin and began a lively conversation with her husband, and the inspector, seeing that there was nothing to be gained by trying to resume negotiation with the antagonistic fisherman, directed his steps further along the harbour.

Some pilots sitting on the jetty, engaged in languid small-talk, became increasingly animated and did not seem inclined to greet him.

Not wanting to turn back he continued his walk along the shore. But very soon the inhabited area came to an end and only the naked rock remained, desolate, without a tree, without a bush, as anything that could be consumed had been burnt. He walked beside the water, sometimes on fine soft sand, sometimes on stones, and after he had walked for an hour turning always to the right, he found himself back at the place from which he had started, and a feeling of being shut in came over him. The rocky heights of the little island pressed him down and the circular horizon tightened round him. It gave him the familiar sensation of not having enough room, and he climbed up the rocks until he reached the plateau at the top, which was probably about fifty feet above sea-level. He lay down on his back and gazed up into space. Now that his eye could no longer catch sight of any hint of either land or sea, and all he could look at was the blue dome above him, he felt free, isolated, like a cosmic sliver floating in the ether, obeying only the law of gravitation. It seemed to him that he was entirely alone in his den, and that the earth was merely a vehicle, by which he was travelling along its orbit. In the soft soughing of the wind he heard only the current of air set up by the passage of a planet through the ether. In the roar of the waves he perceived only the splashing to and fro of liquid thrown about as the great container turned on its axis. Now that he could no longer see the fragment of earth to which he was bound, all reminders of his fellow men, of the community, of laws and customs were swept away, and he allowed his thoughts to run riot like calves let loose in spring, leaping, tail in air, over all enclosures, all restrictions. By these means he intoxicated himself to the point of unconsciousness, like the Indian who gazes at his navel and forgets both heaven and earth in the contemplation of an unimportant external part of himself.

Inspector Borg did not worship nature any more than the Indian worships his navel. On the contrary, as a being conscious of himself, and of standing highest in the chain of terrestrial creations, he entertained a certain contempt for the lower forms of existence. For one thing, he fully understood that the products of the conscious mind were much more ingenious than those of unconscious nature, and for another he realised that they were much more advantageous to man who, when he invents his creations, pays particular attention to the usefulness or beauty these will have for their creator. But he gathered the raw materials for his works from nature, and though one can produce both light and air with machines, he preferred the unsurpassable ether waves of the sun, and the inexhaustible source of oxygen in the atmosphere. So he loved nature as a helpmate and an inferior, who was there to assist him, and it amused him to be able to trick his powerful adversary into putting its strength at his disposal.

Meanwhile, having lain for an unknown length of time experiencing the great peace of absolute solitude, the freedom from influences, from pressure, he rose and climbed down to return to his room.

When he entered the half-empty chamber which echoed with the noise of his footsteps, he felt imprisoned. The white squares and rectangles of the space in which he must dwell reminded him of human hands, but those belonging to a lower order of being who only operated with the simple forms of inorganic nature. He was enclosed in a crystal, a cube, or something of the sort. The straight lines, the uniform size of the surfaces converted his thoughts into squares, ruled lines through his soul and, by simplification, turned the freedom of its organic life into a pattern and brought the rich, primaeval forest vegetation of his brain, full of varying impressions, back to nature's first child-like attempts at organisation.

After he had called the servant-girl he asked for his chests to be brought in, and immediately started upon the transformation of the room.

His first care was to regulate the entrance of light with a couple of heavy, flesh-coloured Persian blinds, which at once tuned the room to a softer note. This done he raised up the two leaves of a big dining-table, and the emptiness of the large white floor-space was immediately filled. But the white surface of the table-top still distressed him and he concealed it with a piece of oilcloth of a warm moss-green, which harmonised with the blinds and had a soothing effect. He then put up his bookcases against the worst wall. This did hardly anything to improve it, it only divided it into columns like a so-called 'ready reckoner', and the white plaster screamed even louder against the walnut-coloured wood, but his only aim was to sketch out the whole before attending to details.

He hung his bed-curtains from a nail in the ceiling, which made a room within the room, as it were. The place where he slept was now separated from the rest of his study as if he had put it under a tent.

Over the long white floor-boards, whose black parallel cracks had been filled with dirt from shoes, dust from furniture and clothes, tobacco ash, and waste from scrubbing and sweeping, forming hot-beds for fungi and hiding-places for woodworms, he now threw down here and there pieces of carpet of different colours and patterns and these floated like flowery, verdant islands on the great white expanse.

Now that he had introduced warmth and colour into the vacuum he turned his attention to refinements. First of all he must create a hearth, an altar to work – the centre round which everything would be grouped, and from which everything would radiate. Consequently he began by standing his large lamp on the desk. It was two feet high and rose like a lighthouse above the green table-cloth. Its painted porcelain foot with its cheerful kaleidoscopic arabesques and flowers – an ornamentation reminiscent of animals, though admittedly unlike the ordinary ones – showed the power of the human spirit to violate the fixed, monotonous forms produced by nature. Here the painter had changed a stiff, carline thistle into a creeper, had forced a hare to stretch out like a crocodile and, with a gun between the tiger's claws of its front paws, had made it take aim at a huntsman with the head of a fox.

Round and under the lamp he placed his microscope, his diopter, his scales, his deep-sea sounder, and his dip-sticks, the varnish and brass of which cast a warm sun-gold light about them.

His inkwell, a large, glass cube cut in facets, shone with the pale blue light of water on ice. His porcupine-quill pen-holders, with their oily, indeterminate colours, produced a suggestion of animal life. The loud vermilion of the sealing-wax, the variegated vignettes of the pencil-box, the cold brilliance of the steel scissors, the varnish and gold of the ash-trays, the bronze of the paper-knife and all the small objects for use or ornament soon filled the large table with a patchwork on which the eye could rest for a moment and receive an impression, a memory, an impulse, so that it was continuously in action and never wearied.

It was now a matter of filling the bookcases and blowing a living spirit into the vacuum between the dark boards. And soon these were in place, row upon row of the motliest collection of works of reference and handbooks, from which their owner could obtain information on all past and present happenings. Encyclopedias which, like a radio telegraph, responded when you pressed the right letter, textbooks on history, philosophy, archaeology and the natural sciences, travels to all the countries of the world, and even all the Baedeker guides. These enabled their owner to sit and plan the shortest and cheapest mode of travel to this or that place, to decide on an hotel, and even to know how much he ought to give in tips. But, as all these works had in them the inescapable seeds of decay, he had manned one shelf with an observation corps of technical periodicals which instantly gave him reports on the smallest advances made in even the most unimportant discoveries. Last of all a collection of skeleton keys to all the knowledge of all the ages in the form of bibliographies, publishers' catalogues and booksellers' lists so that, sitting in his room, he could tell how high or how low were the barometers of all the sciences that concerned him.

And now, when he looked at the wall with the bookcases, it

seemed to him that at last the room was inhabited by living beings. These books were like individuals, for no two works had the same outward appearance. One would resemble Baedeker, and wear scarlet and gold, like a man who, on a Monday morning, puts sorrow behind him and escapes from everything. Others were ceremonious, a whole procession clad in black, like the *Encylopaedia Britannica*. Then there were the paper-backed journals in bright, cheerful, light-weight summer coats: the salmon-pink *Revue des deux mondes*, the lemon-yellow *Contemporaine*, the rush-green *Fortnightly*, and the grass-green *Morgenländische*. From their backs great names greeted him like acquaintances present in his room, where he got the best out of them, much more than they would have given a traveller paying a visit that disturbed their midday nap or their lunch.

With the arrangements of his writing desk and his room completed he felt restored after the unsettling effects of his journey, and now that he had his tools at hand his soul regained its strength. These instruments and books had grown to be a part of his being like new senses, other organs, stronger and finer than those nature had given him as his heritage.

The temporary attack of fear, the result of isolation, loneliness, and incarceration with enemies – for as such he rightly regarded the islanders – gave way to the calm which comes of being installed and, now that his headquarters were established, he sat down like a well-equipped general to draw up his plan of campaign.

III

During the night the wind had veered north-east, and had blown drift-ice down from Åland, but the inspector set out in the flat-bottomed boat to make a preliminary investigation of the nature of the sea-bottom, the depth of the water, and its fauna and flora.

The pilot, whom he had taken with him as an oarsman, soon got tired of imparting information when he saw that by means of a lead-line, and various other instruments, the inspector was finding out about things he had never thought of. The pilot knew where the shallows were, he knew too over which you should position your herring-boats. But the inspector was not satisfied with that. He dragged different depths, and pulled out small fish and mucilage, upon which he believed the herring fed. He dropped his lead to the bottom and got up specimens of clay, sand, sludge, mould and gravel, which he sorted and numbered and put into small glasses with labels on them.

Finally he took out a large telescope, that looked like a speaking-trumpet, and peered down into the sea. The pilot had never dreamed that you could peer into the water and, in his surprise, he asked if he might put his eye to the glass and gaze down into the secret places.

The inspector, who for one thing did not wish to play the magician, and for another was reluctant to arouse false hopes of a result by giving a too hasty explanation of what he was investigating, confined himself to agreeing to the pilot's request, and told him a few simple facts about the living pictures that were unfolding themselves in the depths.

'Do you see the bladder-wrack on the reef?' he began. 'Do

you see that it is soapy-yellow at first, turns liver-brown lower down, and ends up red when it reaches the bottom? That is because of the decreasing amount of light.'

He rowed a few strokes from the shallows, still keeping within the shelter of the island and thus avoiding the ice.

'What do you see now?' he asked the man, who by this time was lying on his stomach.

'By Jesus! No, I believe it's herring! And they're as close as cards in a pack!'

'Do you understand now that herring don't keep to the shallows? Do you realise that you should be able to fish them in deep water? Do you now believe me when I tell you that one should never fish them in the shallows, where they only go to lay their roe, which the warmth of the sun can reach better there than in deep water?'

The inspector rowed on until he saw that the water had turned grey-green because of the clayey nature of the bottom.

'What do you see now?' he resumed, and rested on his oars.

'Upon my soul, I believe there are snakes on the sea-bed. There are actually snakes' tails sticking up out of the mud, and there are the heads!'

'Those are eels, my boy,' the inspector informed him.

The pilot looked incredulous, for he had never heard of eels in the sea. But the inspector did not want to play his best card in advance, nor did he want to squander his resources by long-winded explanations of obscure matters. He therefore relinquished the oars, took back his telescope, and leaned over the edge of the boat to resume his observations.

He seemed to be searching for something with unwonted eagerness, searching for something that must be there, on one shallow or another, but which he had of course not seen before, as he had never investigated those waters.

For two hours they rowed around as the inspector directed. At times he dropped down his dredge and his lead alternately, and after each test he lay prone with his telescope. His pale face was wizened with exertion, his eyes had sunk into his head. The hand holding the telescope shook and his numbed arm seemed as stiff as a post. The cold, damp wind that had penetrated the pilot's thick jacket did not seem to bite the slender figure, wrapped only in a half-buttoned spring overcoat. His eyes were filled with tears caused by the sea-breezes and his efforts to see clearly into this half-impenetrable element, three-quarters of the earth's surface, about whose life the last quarter generally knew so little and guessed so much.

Through his marine-telescope, not invented by him but picked up from things heard said by bridge-builders and other workers engaged in underwater blasting, he gazed down into the lower world from which the great creations of terrestrial life had developed. The forest of seaweed which had recently crossed the boundary between inorganic and organic life. Swaying in the cold sea-bed current it looks like freshly curdled egg-white that has borrowed its shape from rippling water, and reminds one of the plant-like patterns formed by water when it freezes on the window-panes. Down there it was spread out in great gardens of golden leaves among which the inhabitants of the sea-bed dragged themselves along on their bellies, seeking darkness and cold, hiding their shame at having been left behind on the long journey towards sun and air. Furthest down in the clay rests flounder, half-buried in the mud, lazy, immobile, lacking the ingenuity to develop an air-bladder that would lift it.[1] It is awaiting a lucky accident which will lead its prey past its nose, and has not the initiative to manipulate chance to its advantage. From pure idleness it has wriggled and stretched, so that for convenience' sake its eyes have come to rest on the right-hand side of its twisted head.

The blenny has already put out two oars in the stem, but it is trimmed by the stern, and reminds one of the first attempts to build a boat. Its architectonic gargoyle of a head, with the whiskers of a Croat can be glimpsed between the heraldic foliage of the seaweed. It raises itself from the gravel for a moment, but instantly sinks down again into the slime.

The lump-sucker, with its seven backs, moves upside down. The whole fish is one vast nose, going about sniffing out food and females. For a moment it lights up the blue-green water with its rose-coloured belly which radiates a faint morning-glow in the dark depths, but soon fastens its sucker firmly to a stone again, to wait for the millions of years to elapse that will bring redemption to the backward creatures in the endless chain of evolution.

The horrible angler-fish or sea devil, the embodiment of fury, its rage expressed by the spikes on its face. Its fins have turned into claws, more for instruments of torture than for attack or defence. It lies on its side, sensually caressing its own body with its slimy tail.

But in the brighter, warmer water higher up swim the beautiful, contemplative perch, perhaps the fish most characteristic of the Baltic. Well-built and firm, yet all the same a bit bulky, like a cutter, he has the strange blue-green colour of the Baltic and its Nordic temperament. A bit of a philosopher and a bit of a pirate, a gregarious solitary, a shallows creature that seeks deep waters, and sometimes reaches them. An idle eccentric, who pauses and stares at the stones of the shore for long minutes together, until he awakes and shoots forward like an arrow. A tyrant to his own kind, but soon tame, he returns willingly to the same place and is host to seven intestinal parasites.

And so to the eagle of the sea, the king of the Baltic fish, the slenderly built, cutter-rigged pike, who loves the sun, and who, as the strongest, does not need to shun light colours. He lies with his nose on the surface of the water, and sleeps with the sun in his eyes, dreaming of the flowery meadows and groves of birches up above, which he can never visit, and of the blue dome that stretches above his watery world like a vault. In it he would suffocate, though birds, with their hairy chest-fins, swim in it so easily.

The boat had got in amongst the drifting ice, and over the gardens of seaweed on the bottom the shadows of the floes trailed like fleecy clouds. The inspector, who had sought for several hours without finding what he was looking for, now lifted his telescope out of the water, dried it and laid it aside.

Then he collapsed on to the after-thwart, put his hand to his eyes, as if he wanted to rest them from further impressions, and seemed to fall asleep for a few moments, after which he indicated to the pilot that he should row on.

The inspector, whose attention had been concentrated on the depths all morning, seemed at last to become aware of the splendid picture that had unfolded itself on the surface of the sea. The segment of water that was spread out some way ahead of the boat was ultramarine-blue, until the drift-ice took over and the scene became completely arctic. Islands, bays, creeks and sounds were outlined as if on a map. Where the ice had mounted a reef, mountain-tops had been formed by one block pressing down the first, and another, in its turn, climbing upon the second. The ice had also struggled up the rocks, formed vaults and grottoes, built up towers, church ruins, casements and bastions. The magic of all these shapes was that they seemed to have been made by a gigantic human hand. They were not like the accidental shapes created by nature, but awakened memories of human inventions that had been made in past periods of history. In one place the blocks had piled up into Cyclopean walls, or laid themselves out like an Assyrian-Greek temple. In another, by repeated blows, a wave had dug itself a Romanesque barrel-vault and gnawed a rounded arch that had settled into an Arabian horseshoe, out of which sun and spray had bitten stalactites and honeycombs. Here the whole length of a wave had eaten a vaulted passage out of a piled-up wall, thus making a Roman aqueduct, while over there stood the foundations of a mediaeval castle, which bore traces of fallen pointed arches, ornamental gables and pinnacles.

This oscillation between ideas associated with an arctic landscape and those associated with the history of architecture put the beholder into a vacant mood, from which he was aroused by the boisterous life that flocks of birds were leading on the floating islands of ice and the pure blue water. Eider ducks, floating here in flocks of hundreds upon hundreds, were resting as they waited for open water towards the north. The insignificant russet-brown ducks were surrounded by gorgeous drakes with their snow-white backs who, riding high on the water, sometimes took a brief flight to display their sooty-black bellies. Divers were there in smaller flocks, showing their minever breasts, their snake-like necks and, when their wings were closed, the chessboard-like squares of their specula. Legions of lively long-tailed duck, wearing black and white, were swimming, diving and stretching themselves. There were smaller bands of guillemots and puffins, gloomy coal-black scoter scouts, standing out against the brighter parties of goosanders and the red-breasted mergansers that have tufts of feathers on the backs of their heads. And over the whole of this diving, flapping army of birds, pursuing their amphibious life, hovered various kinds of sea-gulls, who had already chosen the air as their element and only used the water as a fishing-ground and bathing-place.

Into this world of ceaseless activity a solitary hooded crow had sneaked, and was sitting half-hidden on the island. His low brow, suspect colour, thievish bearing, criminal demeanour and whole water-shy, grubby aspect made him an object of hatred to the industrious, who recognised in him the nest-robber and egg-sucker.

From all this winged world, whose throats set the air vibrating above the heads of the dumb creatures in the water, could be heard a chorus of sounds, ranging from the reptile's hiss, that first weak effort to express rage, right up to man's harmonic instruments. For there were eider ducks, that hiss like adders when the drakes seize their necks and try to trample them under water, mergansers croaking like frogs, terns screeching, gulls cackling, herring-gulls screaming like children, eider caterwauling like tom cats in rut, but above them all, highest and therefore most beautiful, the wonderful music of the long-tailed duck, that is not quite song. A major common chord, but out of tune, resounding like a herdsman's horn. And however and whenever it chimes in, mingling with the three notes of the other birds it makes a complete chord, a canon for a hunting-horn, without beginning or end – a reminiscence of the childhood of man, of the days when the herdsman and the huntsman first appeared.

It was not with the dream-like imagination of the poet, or with vague and consequently disturbing emotions and confused perceptions that the beholder enjoyed this great spectacle. No, it was with the calm eyes of the scholar and conscious thinker that he detected order behind this apparent disorder. He was able with his great store of accumulated memories to arrange all his observations in relation to each other. And when he sought the cause behind the tremendous impression this landscape in particular had made upon him, and found the answer, he experienced the great joy that must be felt by nature's highest creation, when he lifts the veil from a secret; the bliss which follows every act of creation on the long road to clarity and which is perhaps the motive force that drives us forward from dreams to knowledge, a bliss which must resemble that of a supposed conscious Creator, who was aware of what he was doing.

This landscape took him back to primaeval ages when the earth was under water, and the highest mountain-peaks were beginning to appear above the surface. In the skerries the primaeval formation was still preserved in the bed-rock which was directly exposed to the light.

But under the water, co-existing with the algae of the cooling-off period who were there already, swam the fish of primaeval days, and among them their oldest descendant, the herring; while up on the skerries the ferns and club-mosses of the Carboniferous era were still growing. Further in towards the mainland, in the first place on the larger islands, you will meet with the coniferous trees and reptiles of the Secondary era, and still further inland the deciduous trees and mammals of the Tertiary era. But out here, where the formations are primaeval, capricious nature seems to have hopped over the era of stratification and thrown the seals and otters back into the far past, tossing them into the ice-age this very morning, right in the middle of the Quaternary period, like top-soil on primaeval rock. Borg himself was a representative of the historical period and, unperturbed by the apparent confusion, he rejoiced in this living picture of the creation, and his pleasure was enhanced by the feeling that he was, on the whole, the highest link in the chain.

This was the secret fascination of this landscape. It and it only reproduced creation using the methods of the historians, eliminating and abbreviating, so that you could travel through a pictorial history of the world in a few hours and end up with yourself. In it you could refresh yourself by experiencing again sensations that led your thoughts back to your origins. You could rest in past stages of development, relax from the wearying tension of struggling to reach a higher step in the cultural ladder. You could fall back as it were into a healthy trance and feel at one with nature. He used such moments as a substitute for the departed pleasures of religion, since thoughts of heaven were no more than another form of the urge to go forwards, and feelings of immortality were a disguised expression of the surmise that matter is indestructible.

How soothing it was to feel at home on the earth. In his childhood it had been described to him as a vale of tears, through which you wandered on your way to the unknown. How secure and comforting to have gained a knowledge of what had previously been unknown, to have been able to look upon and see through all God's hitherto 'secret plans', as they were called, those phenomena which had been regarded as unfathomable because, up to now, they had not been fathomed. Now man had reached clarity about the origins of human beings and their purpose. But instead of tiring and settling down, as one civilisation after another had done when they had destroyed themselves by thinking, the present generation had made their choice, accepted the fact that they were the highest animal, and had set to work in a sensible way to realise heaven upon earth. Consequently, Borg thought, this present era was the best and the greatest of all eras, and had carried mankind further forward than the previous centuries had succeeded in doing.

After communing reverently for a while with thoughts about his origins and his destiny, the inspector allowed his memory to run through the story of his personal development, as far back as he could trace it. He did this to find his way back to himself as it were, and to read his probable future in the course taken by his past.

He saw his deceased father, a major in the Royal Engineers. One of the indeterminate type of the beginning of the century, mixed like a conglomerate blend of cemented splinters and refuse from preceding periods, gathered at random after the great eruption at the end of the last century. He believed in nothing, since he had seen everything lapse and then be re-adopted, had seen all forms of government tried, greeted with rejoicing when first accepted, then discarded after a few years and later brought forward again as new and again greeted as universal discoveries. Finally, Borg's father had settled for the existing state of affairs as being the only tangible one. It might have emanated from a directing will, which was improbable,

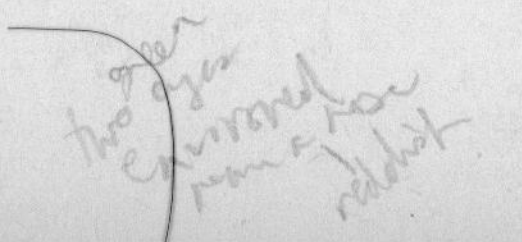

or from a series of accidents, which was pretty certain but a dangerous thing to say.

Through his university studies his father had come into contact with the pantheism of the Young Hegelians and things took an ingenious turn and were then carried to extremes. The individual became the one reality and God was reckoned to be the personal element in humanity. This lively conception of the intimate bond between man and nature, with man himself as the highest link in the chain of world development, created an élite corps of persons who silently despised the repeated efforts of the political enthusiasts to place themselves outside the reigning laws of nature – enthusiasts who tried by artificial systems of philosophy and decisions of parliament to put together a new world order. This élite continued to press forward unnoticed, useless to either high or low. Above them they saw mediocre people collected by natural selection round a mediocre monarch. Below they met ignorance, gullibility and blindness, and in between, in the middle classes, such a marked interest in trade that, not themselves being businessmen, they were unable to work with them. But they could not join any party, and had no wish for ineffective individual opposition. They were not numerous enough to form a pack and, as strong individualists, would not follow a bell-cow. Thus they remained relatively mute, kept their discontent under lock and key, smiled like soothsayers when they met at the council table, or in the Hall of the Nobility,[2] and left the world to its own devices.

The aristocracy to which his father belonged was certainly not very old. It had won honour by civilian services such as the improvement of mining, not by doubtful deeds of valour in war, executed with the help of natural accidents or the mistakes of the enemy. For his services he had been rewarded with a coat of arms, and some quite moderate privileges such as wearing the uniform of a nobleman, and fruitlessly participating with a fourth part[3] in the heavy work of government. Consequently he reckoned that he belonged to the deserving aristocracy, and the consciousness of having sprung from talented forefathers acted like a spur all the way down to their now-living representative. The possessions he had rightfully acquired through the ability and work of his forefathers had also put him in a position to educate himself for his profession. He became a distinguished topographer and took part in the building of the Göta Canal and the first railways. This preoccupation with a whole kingdom, which he was accustomed to have spread before him on the maps laid out his table, taught him to view it from above, to survey it in a moment, and by degrees this developed in him a capacity to see things on a grand scale. There he sat, and with a ruler opened a new means of communication which would transform the physiognomy of a whole district, obliterate old towns, create new ones, change the prices of commodities and search out new sources of production. The map had to be altered, old waterways forgotten, and the straight, black lines of the new railways had to become the deciding factors. The uplands had to be made as fertile as the valleys, the struggle over the rivers had to end, and the boundaries between kingdoms and countries rendered unnoticeable.

A strong feeling of power resulted from this manipulation of the fates of countries and peoples, and his father had not escaped being gradually affected by the tendency to overrate his own ego, a thing which often follows the acquisition of power. He began to take a bird's-eye view of everything. Countries became maps and people tin soldiers. When the topographer ordered a hill which it would have taken thousands of years to erode to be levelled in a few weeks, it made him feel like a creator. When he had tunnels blasted, ridges of sand moved into lakes and swamps filled up, he could not help feeling that he had taken in hand the reshaping of the globe, and overthrown higgledy-piggledy the laws governing geological formations. Consequently his regard for his own personality swelled unbelievably.

Added to this there was his position as an officer with a whole community of subordinates, with whom he communicated only by issuing orders. Thus he had come to regard them as muscles serving his volitional cerebrum.

As he had the decisiveness and physical courage of the soldier, the thoroughness of the scholar, the reflectiveness of the thinker, the calm of the financially independent and the dignity and self-respect of the honourable man, Borg's father represented a type of a high order, in which beauty and wisdom combined to produce a moderate and harmonious personality.

This father was to his son, whose mother had died early, both an example and a teacher. To spare his son the bitterness of miscalculations, and disapproving of the current methods of education which, with fairy-story books and cautionary tales, bring children up to be children instead of men, he immediately drew aside the veil of the temple of life and initiated the child into the difficult art of living. He taught him the intimate connection between man and the other forms of creation, among which man, on his planet, certainly stands highest. At the same time he continues to be in the thick of things, and is able to modify to some degree the effects of natural forces, though still ruled by them. In a word, a sensible worship of nature – if by 'nature' we mean all that exists, and by 'worship' a recognition of our dependence on natural law. By so doing he got rid of the megalomania of Christianity, of the fear of the unknown, of death and of God, and fashioned a wise man, conscious of what he was doing and personally responsible for the results of his actions.

He found the regulator for man's lower impulses in that organ which, precisely by its greater perfection, separates man from the animals, i.e. his cerebrum. Judgement, based on comprehensive knowledge, would direct and if necessary suppress lower impulses, and thus keep a man of this type on a high level. To nourish and to reproduce yourself were the lowest impulses, because you shared these with the plants. 'Feelings', as the lower, rudimentary thought-processes of the animals were called, since they are located in blood-vessels, spinal cords and other lower organs, must of necessity be subordinated to the cerebrum of a human being of the higher type. And those individuals who could not control their lower impulses, but who thought with their spinal cords, belonged to the lower forms of humanity. Consequently, the older man warned him of the danger of youthful eagerness and enthusiasm, which could as easily lead to crime as to virtue. This did not mean that great passions for matters of general benefit were to be excluded. These were not feelings, but tremendous expressions of a will for good. Everything that youth had to offer was completely worthless. It lacked originality and, as a rule, was no more than the distilled wisdom of those who had gone before, which their youthful descendants had adopted as their own and with grand gestures were now wanting to hawk around. In fact, originality could only arise when the brain was mature, and real reproduction, to which belonged the upbringing of offspring, could only occur when a man was mature and able to acquire the means wherewith to educate his children. A sure sign that the immature brain was incapable of judgement was the perpetual state of megalomania in which young people and women lived. People often say that the future belongs to the young, but how mistaken they are, seeing that mortality is greater among the young than among the mature. And the far-from-bright remark that if youth is a mistake, it is one that time will cure does not disprove the rule that youth is a defect, a deficiency, in other words a fault, the existence of which is admitted by the saying that it can be cured, since something that has never existed cannot be cured. All the attacks the young make upon the establishment are the hysterical outbursts of weak people who cannot endure pressure. They evince as little wisdom as the wasp when it attacks a human being and thereby goes to meet certain death. As a good example of youth's lack of judgement and inability to draw conclusions he cited the case of the book *Robinson Crusoe*. This had clearly been written with the intention of disparaging a state of nature and an isolated life but, for a hundred years, has been regularly misunderstood by the young as a hymn of praise to the life of the savage. This life is plainly described as a way of punishing the foolish young man who had, like a savage, misused the treasures of civilisation. Moreover, this little trait shows what a low ontological form youth is, revealing as it does his predilection for Indians and other rudimentary lag-behinds like the emotions. These will one day be discarded as the thyroid gland has been which, though no longer used by human beings, is still situated in its old position.

When the son could not refute these harsh truths with rational arguments and explained that his feelings, yes, his most holy feelings revolted against this dry doctrine, his father told him he was a wasp who still thought with his ganglia. He warned him against flights of fancy or conclusions based on insufficient evidence or lack of material. This was not to be confused with rapid scientific conclusions, which could sometimes produce fresh results from apparently few premises. These only seemed few because the intermediate processes had been forgotten. It was the same when a chemical combination through two older conceptions had merged to form a new thought. Ontogenesis had shown that a human embryo lived through all the earlier stages from the amoeba through the frog to the anthropoids. How then could youth doubt that the human spirit in a child must relive man's history from the animals and savages onwards as long as his body continued to grow, and that consequently the man stood much higher than the youth? In particular he warned him against letting his judgement be clouded by the lowest of all impulses, the sexual impulse. This, by reason of its strength, had long blinded common sense, so that enlightened men were still obsessed by the superstition that woman, as a type, stood as high as man, indeed, according to some, higher. In fact she is merely an intermediate form between the man and the child, as we know from the history of the embryo, which shows that at one stage man was a woman, but never that woman was a man. Warning the young man against allowing himself to be dominated by his sexual impulses was the same as casting a shadow over woman, and the son soon began to draw what his father called 'ganglia' conclusions. The first of these was that the Lieutenant-Colonel[4] was a woman-hater. And how could he do otherwise when he was continually being told stories of how some person or other had forfeited his future by affairs with women. How some gifted man had wasted his talent by engaging in the work of procreation, sacrificed happiness and energy for a wife who had been unfaithful and children who had died before reaching maturity. Breeding should be left to lower spirits, the great should live through their works, and so on.

It was under such direction that the son grew up. At birth he was an unusually delicate baby but with a harmoniously formed body. He had finely developed senses, comprehended rapidly and surely, and possessed keen understanding and a nobility of thought which showed itself in his deference for and accessibility to other people. He soon found out how to arrange his life, to suppress his vegetable and animal impulses and, after he had collected a large stock of observations and knowledge, he began to work these up. He soon showed that he had a fertile brain, that from a couple of known facts he could find the unknown quantity he was seeking, and that from old ideas he could produce new ones – in a word, that he possessed what is called 'originality'. He was a future pioneer and had the gift of seeing coherence in disorder, of discovering the invisible forces at work behind phenomena, and likewise the hidden and extremely complicated motives governing human behaviour. Consequently he was regarded with suspicion by his schoolmates, and his teachers saw in him a silent critic of what they communicated as incontrovertible facts.

His arrival at the university coincided with the great popular movement for parliamentary reform then in being, and Borg saw clearly what was lacking in representation based on the Four Estates, since the State consisted of at least twenty Estates, each with different interests and a varying ability to judge a matter as involved as representative government. On the other hand, he could not agree to a return to the rule of the masses and the clan, where everyone had just as much or just as little say as another. He recognised at once that this simplification of government whereby the 'masses were to decide' was not a reform suited to the needs of the times. He had seen that universal suffrage in France had produced an emperor and a mock representation composed of lawyers, businessmen and the military, from which workers, farmers, learned and scientific men were excluded – that is to say that only three classes approved by the emperor were represented. He had himself evolved a system of representation by class, based on proportional representation carefully balanced to accord with the needs of each class. It would be right to take into consideration the interests of the highest, that is the greater right of wise men to have the final word, since they were more likely to promote progress than the foolish. The authors of the bicameral system had already surmised something of the kind when they perceived the necessity of some questions being handled by committees and, where certain matters were concerned, by temporary committees or boards that would include experts.

In order to make the national assembly perfect – so that all interests were watched over, all points of view put forward, all information about the state of the country made available – it was necessary that all classes of society, from the highest to the lowest, must select delegates in proportion first to their numbers, and then to their importance for the good of the whole country. He would eliminate the Court which, along with the monarch, would come under the Department of Foreign Affairs where they belonged, as the monarch only represented his country in its relations with foreign powers. Then he would build up his advisory but not legislative parliament as follows:

Class I: Landowners and tenants, cottars, stewards and foremen etc.

Class II: Mineowners, millowners, manufacturers and workers.

Class III: Merchants, seamen, hotel proprietors, porters, hauliers, the personnel of banks and customs offices, and postal, rail, telegraph and pilot services.

Class IV: Civil servants and the army, parsons and those who served them, caretakers and their staff.

Class V: Scholars, teachers, literary men and artists.

Class VI: Doctors, chemists, poor-law administrators.

Class VII: Houseowners, capitalists and rentiers.

What proportion of people should be chosen from each class was a question that could not be answered off-hand. Able men well-versed in the art of government must feel their way forwards, and consequently the ordinances governing representation must only and always be provisional. Over this advisory body there should be a cabinet of experts in political science, educated solely for their difficult calling, so that the most complicated of all arts should not come to be carried on by bunglers and enterprising amateurs, as had hitherto been the case. Before taking up office these politicians should be subjected to a thorough investigation of their previous lives, and their private financial and social positions. This last provision would spur youth on to self-discipline and watchfulness of their sayings and doings, and would create a stock of admirable men. On the other hand the so-called blameless life and negative virtues would not be, as hitherto, a short-cut to promotion. This élite would be the new aristocracy which would succeed the old civilian, military and Court aristocracy. And the fact that they would reproduce themselves by natural selection of the ablest, would guarantee that the country would be governed in the best possible way. By this means parliament, which would only be able to vote on an opinion, not on a decision, would become a large investigating body, and not an army of legionaries who were bribed and manipulated into using violence by their votes.

The young man was already too wise to air his views. The word 'aristocrat' had become the equivalent of 'degenerate', 'superfluous' and 'effete', and the masses were storming forwards so blindly that the industrial workers frequently played into the hands of the farmers, the class who would be their future enemies. At such times a wise man could only smile and wait. So he waited until he saw representation by Four Estates replaced by One Estate, and the country represented from now onwards by the Farmer's Estate only.

This historical event exercised a great influence on the young man's thought and development. He had come to appreciate the frightful muddle that prevailed in the thought-processes of the majority. As he read the reports of the Estate's proceedings and studied the speeches of the most influential orators, he noticed that what he called 'ganglia' arguments – the result of a contraction of the blood-vessels and congestion of the heart – exercised the greatest influence on the opinion of ordinary people. At times it seemed to him that there was no question of fatherland or progress. For those making the proposals it was simply a matter of getting their own way by faulty conclusions, the grossest blunders against logic and the most ruthless distortion of facts. His observations awakened in him the suspicion that it was all a struggle for power, for the gratification of using your brain to get other brains to ring in unison with yours, for the ability to set the seeds of your thoughts in the grey matter of other brains, where they would grow parasitically like mistletoe. Meanwhile, the parent stock could proudly shrug its shoulders at the thought that the creatures up there on the top of the tree were no more than sycophants.

Upon this he founded his ambition, and to satisfy it he acquired knowledge and experience by studies, journeys and the companionship of able men of good standing. In the midst of this ever-moving chaos of conflicting forces and interests, he sought in himself an anchorage for his existence, a central point in the circle which life had thrown round him. Unlike the weak Christian, who postulates a support outside himself in God, he grasped the tangible present in his own personality and tried to create out of himself a perfect type of human being – a man whose conduct and actions would not infringe anyone's rights and who knew that the fruits of a highly esteemed tree could not fail to be of profit and comfort to others. He avoided all the confusion and absurdity present in the efforts of those who say they are living for others, but who in fact are living on others – on their gratitude, their opinions and their recognition. Thus he pursued his way straight forwards, aware that one single great, strong individual would involuntarily be of more use than these masses of thoughtless beings whose numbers were in inverse proportion to their usefulness.

By thus establishing his personality he obliged himself to set a norm for his behaviour. This resulted in a high degree of morality. Instead of leaving decisions to some uncertain future, he so ordered his conduct that he never left anything undecided, never pushed the blame from himself on to a suffering Christ, and consciously, and on his own responsibility, never did anything which might have awakened the need for a scapegoat.

In this way he learned to rely on himself, never to take advice, and always to weigh up the probable results of an action. But having been brought up in the era of steam and electricity, when the pace of life had quickened he, like the rest of his generation, was inevitably afflicted by bad nerves. And how could it be otherwise for one who had been obliged to destroy millions of old brain cells, to put into storage obsolete impressions, and to take care, when a new judgement had to be made, to reject old-fashioned axioms that tried to present themselves as premises? The thing that had produced this disorder of his nervous system was a whole new rebuilding. It was not, as some said, the result of the alcoholism of his ancestors, or their sexual excesses. These symptoms of illness were an expression of increased vitality, the result of extreme sensitivity, like that of the crayfish when she changes her shell, or the bird when it moults. It was the creation of a new race, or at least of a new type of human being. Consequently it appeared to the old type sick and unhealthy, because it was in process of being formed. This the old type was reluctant to admit. It wanted to be the healthy norm itself, though it was in fact in a state of disintegration.

The nervous sensitivity of the growing youth was increased by his abstemiousness in the matter of food and drink, and by the strict discipline of his sexual life. He considered it degrading to induce in himself the ungovernable state of the madman or the savage by means of fermented liquor, and he was too refined to dally in a momentary relationship with a prostitute. This resulted in an increased awareness and a sensitivity to unpleasant impressions which, at times, caused him to feel disgust where others with coarser senses would have experienced pleasure.

For instance, he was sometimes depressed for many hours if his morning coffee was not strong enough. A badly painted billiard ball and a dirty cue made him turn away and seek another hall. A badly dried glass turned him sick, and he could smell human odour on a newspaper someone else had read. He could spot traces of human grease left on the polished surface of unfamiliar furniture, and he always opened a window if a maid had been cleaning a room. But if he was abroad on a journey he could, as it were, shut off all the connecting links between his sensory organs and his brain, and make himself impervious to all disagreeable sensations.

When he had completed his university studies in natural science – the least humiliating of all studies, as opinions were less important than the collecting of material – he got a post as an assistant at the Academy of Science.

He had applied for the post with the idea that he would be able to survey in one place all the realms of nature collected and arranged there, and maybe find therein the great affinity – if it existed – or the universal disorder (which was more probable). But his intentions were soon discovered, chiefly because he was not long able to avoid the danger of being enticed into suggesting a way of re-arranging the birds on principles quite other than those currently in use. His superiors, who of course did not want to lapse into being mere collectors of material for a young man and who did not like the idea of their work being made to look out-of-date, conceived an instinctive aversion for the man who would have unmasked them. Their first defence against the intruder took the form of setting him to do routine work of secondary importance which was also repulsive to his senses. For six months he was made to change the spirits in the collection of fish. At first the horrible smell made him vomit, but when he had overcome his unpleasant sensations, he turned in fury to the study of fish and, as he worked quickly, before the six months were up he had made a thorough study of the material. By that time he had spent the whole winter in a cold, dirty, dimly lit kitchen, inhaling bad spirit, his hands freezing with cold. He had also contracted inflammation of the bladder, which proved difficult to cure.

He was then put to writing labels for the algae. As he had not been taught calligraphy at the university, and his handwriting was by nature weak and uneven, the labels were thrown away, and he was made to appear incompetent. He could not even write! But after two months, during which he attended a school of penmanship, and spent the evenings at home over his copybooks and examples, he had acquired a beautiful and legible hand. As well as learning the invaluable art of writing he had gained a much more complete knowledge of algae than previously, His superiors, who had believed that he would despise doing the work of a subordinate, soon realised of what stuff he was made and that he knew how to use every opportunity to his advantage. Thus he increased his knowledge, nimbly avoided blows and shook off showers.

But his growing gift as a calligraphist was to be a new source of humiliation. They now put him to writing fair copies of official documents and letters thus, as they thought, degrading him by stages to the mean role of copyist. However, he uncomplainingly accepted the job. It gave him the chance to learn foreign languages, and simultaneously the opportunity to gain an insight into all the secrets of the great men, which they thought would be worthless in his hands. He was thus able to see all the correspondence that was being carried on about the controversial scientific questions of the day. He discovered the path leading to the secret meeting-places of the learned community. He became aware of the underground channels to honours, and the opportunities of making your researches bear fruit. As a result he was unassailable, and when they thought they had trampled him underfoot he came up head first.

It was in his dual capacity of nobleman and independent thinker that he was made to feel isolated. His name did not sound like a learned name, and his manner of dressing himself with modish elegance was regarded by those who remembered Berzelius's[5] ragged trousers as an indication of an unscholarly temperament. His patience and apparent submissiveness was mistaken for inferiority, and his reflections on natural science as poetic effusions. They now regretted that they had let him into their secrets and, in order to crush him again, they decided to put him to work on a new job which all the newcomers had rejected, and which was therefore known as the 'touchstone' or 'stumbling-block'. The fact was that up in the attic there was a miscellaneous collection of rocks and minerals, acquired partly through gifts and testaments and partly through world-wide voyages and expeditions.

At a time when geology was in its infancy most of these had been discarded as duplicates, but now, with the increase of knowledge they had to be re-assessed and consequently needed sorting. Space had been found for them in a lumber-room under a metal roof where they lay in one great heap, considerably mixed with dust and cobwebs. Borg, who now had to stand in a bent position under the hot roof inhaling dust, very nearly gave up, but when, on the second day, he came upon a mineral that he suspected was unknown, he immediately set to work with a will, and began to put them in order. While doing so he had some experiences which shook his already weak faith in the doctrinal system. He realised for a start that it was not the stones which were by nature in an ordered state, but that it was the brain that arranged the facts. For that matter anything could be put in order if you only adopted a principle on which to base your classification, and he soon saw that the most common-sense principle of classification had not been adopted here. As the principle was itself an unproved hypothesis, i.e. that primaeval rock was the result of fusion by fire, in contrast to stratified rocks, which were regarded as having been formed by water, it was simultaneously held that primaeval rock was stratified like younger, sedimentary formations, and so the whole thing seemed to him like bits and pieces screwed together, hit upon by accident, and the system itself based on guesswork.

Meanwhile he analysed his mineral and found that it was unknown. He then took it to his professor, who sent it to the Berlin Academy, and got his name affixed to the new mineral. Borg received no thanks and no recognition, only a few taunts from his superior. This annoyed him and he himself sent the next unknown mineral he came upon to Lyell.[6] His thesis was read at the Geological Society, of which he was made a Fellow. His colleagues and superiors pretended to be unaware of his success, as it was in a way an insult to the professor, who had mistaken the unknown mineral for a duplicate. Dislike now changed to hatred which in its turn became persecution. But he kept out of their way, made himself invisible, and worked. As this collection of minerals came from all European countries, and as Borg was clever enough to make every discovery a matter of direct advantage for the study of mineralogy in each, he had, in a couple of years, so ordered his affairs, that he was a member of most of the learned societies of Europe. He was the holder of the Italian Order of the Crown, the French *Instruction publique*, the Austrian Order of Leopold, and the Russian Order of St Anna, second class. But nothing helped with those about him. Their scorn increased with every distinction, though these were founded on merit. If they could not deny the fact they minimised its value, or pretended to be unaware of what was going on. This did not prevent them from using for their own hunting the track that he had beaten.

When, after seven years of painful service, he inherited the estate of his father, who had just died, and resigned his post to travel abroad in a private capacity, he had to hear people saying that he had been a failure at his job, that it was a pity he had come to nothing or, alternatively, that he had been dismissed.

Consequently he left his country to pursue his studies abroad feeling the deepest disdain for mankind. In hotels and boarding-houses around Europe he saw many kinds of people and formed attachments that were soon broken by enforced separation. But everywhere he went he saw that people of the same generation expressed the same views on the same subjects, put forward the opinions of the majority as if they were their own and uttered platitudes instead of thoughts. This revealed to him that the masses were really only chewing over the thoughts of a few geniuses. For instance: he discoverd that all geologists repeated the views of Agassiz[7] and Lyell from the 1830s and '40s. That all religious free-thinkers delivered themselves of Renan[8] and Strauss,[9] that all active politicians lived on Mill[10] and Buckle,[11] and that all who talked brightly about literature disgorged Taine.[12] That is to say: only a few main batteries possessed annunciators which, having leads from their talents, set all these bells ringing. From this point he soon entered the territory of psychology, and visited spiritualists, hypnotists and thought-readers. Behind their fraudulent activities he saw a number of new discoveries which would certainly change mankind's thoughtless, bovine manner of life. They might perhaps help thought-processes to adjust to a recognition of the fact that the whole struggle being carried on about opinions was really only a struggle for the power to put other minds in motion and to force the masses to 'think as I do'. That was why he had seen learned conflicts which had ended in victory for false views only because the victor had had sufficient authority and support. And why he had seen political and religious feuds which had ended in law-making that went directly against sense and justice, laying the foundations for approved errors which were then inherited by succeeding generations as obvious truths.

No, it was only a question of getting your own way, and the whole motive force behind the vindication of opinions sprang from interest and passion. Interest which was no more than need, the need for food and love, and to win these you required a certain amount of power. The person who did not struggle for power was a weakling whose will to live was attenuated. Therefore you always heard the weak clamouring for their rights, the rights of the weak, while in fact the only right was a mathematical right, an arithmetical truth: to calculate that you needed a strong mind which could free itself from the false visions of interest and passion. When he ransacked his inner man and compared himself with the great majority of other people, he found that by strict self-discipline he had, to a great extent, emancipated his judgement. He found in himself a carefully cultivated inclination to seek for abstract right, for the heart of the matter – the truth that lies in the actual circumstance. For this reason he called himself a lover of truth in its highest sense, though this did not make him feel that he must blurt out all that he thought, or refrain, when need arose, from answering an impertinent question with an untruth.

In order to study more closely the way in which man the animal is organised, he devised individual studies on the mental ability of all the lower animals, and found his way through these up to man. Having done this, he set to work upon a ledger of all the people he had encountered in his life, from relatives, nurse-maids and servants, to schoolmates, university friends, social contacts and superiors – in a word, everyone who had come within his range of observation. He sketched out histories of their origins and backgrounds, and completed these by consulting biographical data, parish registers and the evidence of their friends. He drew up their equations, and tried to find a key to their problems in life. The material he amassed was enormous, and when he had reduced muddle to order, he realised that human beings could be classified like animals and plants in large classes, types and families, according to the method of classification used. By employing various methods he came very near to the truth, and was able to see the object of his investigations in the clearest possible light.

Among other things he made a chart of man with three sub-divisions: conscious, self-deceiver and unconscious. The conscious or dedicated stood highest. They had seen through the fraud, believed in nothing and no one, and were commonly called 'sceptics'. They were hated by the self-deceivers who recognised each other immediately, and usually parted by calling each other scoundrel, and with mutual accusations of evil intentions. Under the heading of 'self-deceiver' he put all religious believers, hypnotic mediums, prophets, Party leaders, politicians, do-gooders and all the swarm of ambitious weaklings who professed to be living for others. Under 'unconscious' he put children, most criminals, the majority of women and some madmen, all of whom were living at a semi-mammalian standpoint and were unable to distinguish between subject and object.

From another method of classification, which traced development ontogenetically from the foetus to its highest point, man, the result obtained was children, young people, women, and men.

In addition, he always looked for inherited racial characteristics in his fellow-countrymen, distinguished between midland Swedes and southern Swedes, was able to see the Norwegian in the people of Värmland and Bohuslän, picked out the Finn in some of the people of Norrland, and kept track of the immigrant Germans, Walloons, Jews and gipsies. This often provided the key to many features in an otherwise inexplicable character.

He had yet another way of classifying character by what he called its 'dominant feature'. He put food-addicts or gluttons, drunkards and the greedy into the lowest group; then sexualists or sex-addicts; then sentimental or emotional people; with the intellectual or thinking people placed highest.

He brought this science to a high state of perfection and, given sufficient time, he could judge a person and give him his equation.

In order to verify the rightness of his observations he used himself as a psychological specimen – cut himself up alive, experimented with himself, built fistulas and fontanels, subjected himself to unnatural and often repulsive mental diets – but when doing so carefully guarded against making personal mistakes in his observations and avoided laying down a norm for others based on himself and his habits.

When he finally tired of foreign travel and his body longed for its own milieu he returned home to find a sphere of activity. Not minding what he did for an occupation, he applied for a post as an inspector of fisheries and, as people did not want him near at hand, he was sent to be the chief man in the Stockholm archipelago.

. . .

At this point he awoke from this revision course in his making. He used it to regenerate himself by rapidly living over his life. By so doing he felt his way forwards to his standpoint and, after calculating his resources, his future course became clear, and he could see his probable objectives and his chances of achieving his purpose.

The pilot, who meanwhile had been rowing the boat inside the islands, sheltered from the cakes of ice, had already made up his mind that the doctor was a bit cracked, sitting there like a statue, with a vacant expression in his inward-looking eyes. He therefore took the opportunity to enquire whether they should return to harbour, to which the inspector nodded assent.

He once more ran his eyes over the splendid spectacle out to sea where the blocks of drift-ice were being driven forwards, split in two, packed, pushed together, piled one on top of another, stood on end, changed from their horizontal position into endless dislocations and faults that formed mountains, valleys and hills. It seemed to him that he was watching the earth's crust being born as, on the glowing sea, the first stiffening cake was broken asunder, driven forwards, up-ended and compressed into primaeval rock, making skerries, rocks and promontories, which yet were no more than tremendous blocks of pack-ice, icebergs, but still not the same mineral as water.

Over this repeat performance of the creation, the primitive, undivided white light of the ice shimmered beside the primaeval blue of the air and water, the first refraction of darkness. Here hovered the God of the story of creation. He who divided light from darkness, as if to give a sensory reason for His searching mind. And once again the first attempts at ordered, musical sounds came from the reptiles-turned-birds, and rang out from the circle of water that had become the limits of his self, that self which must be the central point, wherever he took his stand.

At that moment the boat drifted into the harbour where the smoking chimneys heralded dinner.

IV

On a Sunday morning, when early summer had set in, colouring the water a pale blue and the insignificant scraps of lichen and moss in the crevices of the rocks a faint green, the inspector sat by his open window. The flocks of birds had flown north and only a few pairs of eider duck swam two by two in the creeks. Today he was stirred by the 'great solitude' – his name for the Baltic – as he watched the odd vessel or two sailing south under their cheerful foreign flags which, perhaps accidentally, perhaps logically, were all more brilliant than the drab blue and muddy yellow,[1] so easily soiled. He saw the inflammatory tricolor on a brig that had brought wine and oranges, and was now on her way to golden, more populated coasts, carrying planks from Norrland. He saw the effeminate Dannebrog[2] on a butter-schooner, lying in the wake of a huge German mail-steamer's white sheet with mourning borders and the emblematic crown, like an ace of spades, above a bit of red; the English blood-red ensign, the Spanish canvas awning, the American King Cotton's mattress ticking. They were like many greetings from foreign peoples, with whom he felt more akin than with the strangers he was doomed to call his fellow-countrymen, and this because he had the right to wear all their colours on his ceremonial attire, but not those of his own country. Today it seemed to him that these reminders of his universal citizenship strengthened him more than usual since, for the past few days, he had been living in his place of exile in the midst of an outbreak of total enmity. The fact was that he had recently been taking steps to apply the law on the size of mesh allowed for seine and net, a law which had long been in existence though not observed. This had resulted in open defiance, which had obliged him to call the police and confiscate the nets. Before doing so he had explained in detail that the State had intervened solely out of consideration for the population's own good. He pointed out to them that, while they would not divide up a farm, preferring to see one prosperous son left to represent the family, they continued to fish so imprudently that their children would certainly be paupers. Nothing was of any avail; each measure or step he took was looked upon as the evil invention of a lot of idle civil servants, who were having their salaries paid by the people whom they then proceeded to persecute. It was useless for him to object that it was the Farmer's Party in parliament who had voted for the law, for at this the inhabitants simply poured their hatred upon both the farmers and the government.

It was then that he became aware that this fishing community really represented a remnant of primitive society, carefree, heedless, completely lacking the farmer's thought for the morrow and the coming year. They were like the savage who hunts for two days and sleeps for eight. Like the savage this group of people possessed a certain negative capacity for doing without and enduring, but not the positive capacity for improving their situation by inventions. Indeed they had an instinctive dislike for new things, thereby revealing their inability to adapt themselves to a higher form of civilisation. All these fishermen were the dregs of the population who had not been able to hold their own in the struggle for the fertile valley-bottoms and lakeside shores. Instead they had fled or been driven to the rocks where the fertile soil gave out and it was only from the unreliable water that there was anything to be won. And like gamblers they were as undependable as luck, never husbanding their resources, but always taking out small advances on the ever-expected big haul that a fortunate shipwreck could bring them. Consequently their hatred for the newcomer had been kindled instantly and, blinded by fury, they were incapable of seeing that he was only driven by an ambition to improve their position and relieve them from labour. To this end he had contructed an automatic wind-gauge for the senior pilot, who had to hand in the weather-reports. He had made it from an old log-drill and some sardine-boxes cut into pieces, but it had not been accepted, and was now in the attic. He had been willing to assist when there was illness, but his help had been refused. He had wanted to teach the women how to prevent their ranges from smoking by fixing an old herring-barrel on top of their chimneys as a cowl, but they had sneered at him and continued to whine about the incorrigible smoke. He had vainly attempted to teach a fisherman, whose potato crop always failed, to manure the shore-sand with seaweed and fish-offal as he had seen people doing successfully in coastal regions in England. And when he saw the left-overs from the big Baltic-herring catches of the spring lying rotting for lack of salt, he wanted to show how, when necessity arose, the Faroese had a method of salting down fish for their own consumption with seaweed ash, and how this ash was also used as a preservative when making cheese.

The result of his efforts to give them useful tips was that people nicknamed him Doctor Know-all, and regarded him as a fool. He became a standing joke at coffee-parties and drinking bouts, and even the children grimaced when he passed.

The disparity between what he was and what he was taken to be amused him at first, but by degrees, as coldness was replaced by antagonism, he noticed that it was having a deleterious effect on his mental health. It was as if a thunder-cloud, charged with electricity of a different potential, hung over him and irritated his nerve fluid, which it wanted to destroy by neutralising it. He felt that the thoughts of the many, directed upon him, had the power to drag him down gradually, and to depress his opinion of his own value. The moment would come when he could no longer believe in himself and his own spiritual superiority, and their view that he was the idiot and they the wise would take hold of his brain and force him to agree with them.

As he sat thinking this way and that, a new object appeared on the forty-five degrees of the horizon which he could compass from his window. A naval gun-boat sailed at half-speed into the lee of the island, struck sail and dropped anchor. Through his binoculars he could see the sailors moving about in apparent confusion, but without knocking into each other, for at the sound of the mate's whistle each man hurried to his cleat, his bit of rope, or his halyard. The narrow sides of the vessel, the taut stem – where the metal plates seemed to want to push apart, but united their combined strength in one direction forwards, as if streaming out into the bowsprit – the energetic cylindrical shapes of the steam-pipe and the funnels, the thrust of the masts and shrouds, the round mouths of the cannon, all indicated a combination of forces – orderly, exercising restraint upon each other, acting upon each other, co-operating with each other – the contemplation of which put him into a harmonious frame of mind. It seemed to him that strength and order streamed out from the wedge-shaped iron hull, where suitability, restraint, and moderation combined to produce perfect beauty, and that the sight of it conferred a deeper pleasure than the emotion usually felt for a beautiful work of art by the casual observer.

But, upon reflection, something more came to him from this little floating, sea-encompassed community. He felt strengthened, as if he had gained support from this display of power that was authorised by parliament and government and which, by the application of all the resources of knowledge and civilisation, protected the more highly developed from the encroachments of barbarism from below. He saw with satisfaction how a couple of the most knowledgeable, having passed a test, were able with a whistle to direct the hundred or so semi-savages, who did not dare to think they could comprehend what they did not understand. He had never been tricked into making the fashionable human mistake, based on faulty observation, of believing that the lower classes suffer from their subordinate position and coarser food. He well knew that they had advanced as far as they could, and that they suffered as little from their situation as the fish down there did from not being amphibious. And in the matter of coarse food he knew from the experience of inviting some of the fishermen to dinner how much they disdained anything which would not merely fill their stomachs. Why, he had seen them choose the poorer rye-bread from the basket instead of the finer wheat! He had never believed all that talk of starvation except in cases of real misfortune. And then it was only temporary, as there was poor-law relief, so often abused by idlers and artful dodgers, who feigned illness in order to force people to support them. He had never worshipped the small people, had never needed to bend the knee to the insignificant, in spite of the fact that he had himself been kicked down from above by a party which, during a period of general decline, had manoeuvred itself to the top on stolen reputations, and was now pressing down what should have come to the fore. Nor did he now allow himself to be duped by what was more or less an image of the upper crust, a man-of-war, which on the one hand inspired admiration, but on the other was simply a relic of a system of government that exercised violence over man's spirit with compressed gas and Bessemer cylinders.

Now came a bang from the door of his landlord's house below and tongues were set wagging by the entrance of Öman, who had lost his net. Schnapps glasses clinked and the bawling increased as the orgy of the day before started again.

'Idiots and wreckers who think they know more than wise fishermen. People who lie on sofas and read books costing two thousand crowns; ragamuffins who want to teach father how to fuck; gangs of thieves and fancy-cigarette heroes who have pigtails under their noses . . .'

And then a big wave broke over Vestman's factual information that had been collected aboard the ship, the *Jacob Bagge*, all about the inspector's family, his father's irregular sexual affairs, his mother's humble origins, hints about his own expulsion from previous posts, and so on.

The listener tried to make himself deaf and unconcerned as usual, but the words bit him, soiled him and hurt him against his will. His old doubts about his father's uprightness began to stir in him and his doubts about his own value started to awaken. He feared that it would be impossible to keep dry in this deluge of filth, or avoid a battle in which his refined choice of weapons would be his undoing.

The bell rang on the man-of-war, a roll of drums followed, and out across the water, borne on the summer wind, there came from a hundred throats the notes of a psalm – serious, rhythmic, ordered, submissive – while simultaneously the bawling and threats roared from below as if they came from cages in a menagerie. In a *fermata* in the psalm these increased to howls as disagreement broke out between the parties whether or not to recover the nets by force.

The inspector, who regarded churches as archaeological collections or interesting pagodas from past ages, involuntarily remembered a remark a young cleric had made one night when they were discussing the cult of Christianity: 'I don't care a damn about the divinity of Christ and all that, but mark my words, the mob must be intimidated!'

The mob must be intimidated, he thought to himself, but lost the thread when he heard a fight break out down below. Chairs were being knocked over, heels were bracing themselves against or kicking furniture. There was a bellowing like that of cattle mingling with the hissing of snakes, while under it all a woman's voice prattled on, uttering many hundred words a minute.

At that moment the steamship's whistle sounded, the anchor was heaved, the sail hoisted, and the funnel sent out a soot-black cloud into the early-summer sky. It was with a feeling of loss and anxiety that he saw the ship with her lovely cannon disappear southwards. He felt that he had lost a support, and as if hatred was closing round him like a sack. He wanted to flee, no matter where.

Then a child screamed, but whether from pain or fear he could not hear as, in the midst of the tumult, he had crept down the stairs, gone to the harbour, unmoored his boat, and put out from land as fast as he could.

The island he was leaving was the most easterly of a whole small archipelago which he had not noticed before, but now, in his need to be alone, he was intent upon investigating. He had never learned to row as he hated violent exercise, which he considered superfluous when there were means of transport and machines. He also thought it harmful for his nerves and mental life, as the delicate instruments enclosed in his brain-box could no more endure being shaken than a building in which the precision instruments of an astronomer were housed. But now his sense of rhythm, his well-balanced centre of locomotion instantly made him a capable rower, and his knowledge of physiology taught him how to improve on the ancient invention by raising the bench and thus sparing his arms.

When he saw the island receding behind the boat he began to breathe more freely, and not long after, when he had landed on the first rocky islet he met, he was seized by a feeling of indescribable happiness. It was a long, cheerful, low-lying islet, and the grey gneiss rocks along its shore formed a little harbour into which his boat had run. The water along the shore was as transparent as a flow of concentrated air, and the soft colours of the seaweed on the bottom shone as if they had been fused in melted glass. The stones of the shore lay washed, dried and polished, offering such a variety of colour that one never tired of them, for no two were alike. Between them hair-grasses and sand-sedge had sought anchorage for their tufts. Little hillocks climbed gently upwards and in the moss lay gulls' eggs, three by three, coffee-brown flecked with black, while the mother birds screeched and croaked above his head. He climbed higher, and up beside a cairn, raised by some hydrographer and painted white by black-backed gulls and terns, grew some juniper bushes, spread out like mats. Under them multitudes of delicate white chick-weed wintergreen had improvised a habitat, a combination of the mountain areas of Central Europe and the shade of the northern forests.

The little turnstone, daring and blithe, fluttered uneasily round this disturber of the peace, trying to lead him away from her nest.

Not a bush, not a tree protruded above the half-naked rocks, and this absence of shadow, of hiding places, put the visitor in a harmonious and happy frame of mind. Everything on these rocks was open, surveyable, sunny, and the water separating him from the home among the savages which he had just left seemed to surround him with an impassable barrier of pure transparency. This half-arctic, half-alpine landscape, with its primaeval formations, refreshed and rested him, and when he was completely restored he returned to his boat and rowed on. He passed three clean-scraped rocky knolls that looked like three petrified billows, naked as a hand and without a trace of organic life, but all they did was to arouse scientific geological speculation about their origins. He brushed past a flat islet of ruddy gneiss on the lee side of which stood a hundred-year-old rowan, solitary, moss-covered and gnarled. On its ragged trunk, for lack of roof-tiles or stone walls, a wagtail had bred. The coquettish little bird flew down to the stones by the shore, wanting to persuade the enemy that nothing like a nest and grey-white eggs was to be found.

The single rowan stood on a few square feet of greensward, so solitary yet, in the absence of competitors, so unusually strong, as if it was better able to defy storm, salt and cold than the scramble of envious equals for the bits of earth. He felt drawn to the lonely old fellow and, for a passing moment, longed to build a shelter by its trunk, but then rowed on, and as he did so the impression was blown away.

A dark cliff came into view on the headland of the last island. It was coal-black, made of the volcanic rock diorite, and as he drew near it he became depressed. The black crystallised mass seemed to have been spewed up from the bottom of the sea and then, as it had begun to petrify, had been involved in a fearful struggle with the water or some thunder-cloud. It had been split into eight parts and the rubble carried away by sea and ice or dragged into the deeps. The gleaming walls stood steep and straight as a die alongside the tiny harbour, and when the boat was anchored under them he felt as if he were in a coal-mine, or a sooty smithy. They squeezed and crushed him and when he had climbed up by the clefts a tall sea-mark post with a cask on top, painted white, rose up before him. This example of man's handiwork, out here, where no man could be seen; this reminder of gallows, shipwreck and coal; this crude contrast between the unblended colourless colours black and white of violent infertile nature, lacking organic life – for on the whole mass of rock there was no trace of moss or lichen – and this carpenter's work, without the link of vegetation between primitive nature and human activity, seemed shocking, disturbing and brutal. And in the great Sunday silence he heard under his feet, where a fallen rock formed a roof over a crevice, how the long swell was sucked in under half the islet, so that it thundered to a halt and then drew back sputtering with a hollow sigh.

He stood there for a moment relishing his depression and let himself be led back to earlier sensations that always brought with them feelings of discomfort. He was aware of the smell of coal; saw factories and dirty, discontented people; heard steam-engines, the noise of cities, human voices uttering words that wanted to eat their way through his ears into his brain, set seed, and like weeds, smother his own sowing and change his own laboriously cultivated arable land into a natural meadow like that of the others.

When he returned to the boat and had the mournful scene behind him, he rejoiced again at the infinite purity of the water, the empty blueness which, like a blank sheet, lay before him, soothing, because it could not arouse any memories, could not call forth any ideas, could not squeeze out of him any strong sensations. And when he approached a rather larger island, he greeted it as a new acquaintance who would speak to him of something else and erase the feelings he had recently experienced. New islands, new rocky islets floated past, each offering its own surprises, its own individual physiognomy made up of differences so small that only a sharp practised eye could detect them. And these little eminences, which looked so boringly alike from a boat sailing past, presented on closer examination the most varied spectacle, like variants of the same coin which only reveal their secrets to a numismatist.

He now landed on a rather larger island whose irregular, broken appearance tempted him, especially as sticking up above the brows of its hillocks he saw the tops of leafy trees. And when he climbed the northern headland, whose black base was polished clean by the sea, he saw that the island was a cluster of at least four others that seemed to have been driven together by different prevailing winds. This crowding together of various geological formations had produced a group of landscapes collected from all zones. The northern part consisted of a cone of hornblende-schist which, down by the shore, was cleft into huge blocks, hurled down from the wall of rock, and not yet polished by the sea. Sticking up between these black cubes, as if drawn there by some secret sympathy, there were, strange as it may seem, an unbelievable number of blackcurrant bushes, their dismal colour harmonising with that of the sparkling black stones. Finding these tidy deserters from a garden out here in the wilderness was so unexpected that they seemed like some jest on nature's part, perhaps put into the mouth of a wounded black-cock who had come out here to die, bringing with him seeds for the dawn of cultivation. Further up on the mound of stones was a grove of deciduous trees, bright green, but with their tops clipped and their trunks white, as if they had been lime-washed by a protective human hand. He tried to guess their species at a distance, but they were so unlike all the other trees he had seen in these latitudes that his thoughts raced between acacias, beech and the Japanese varnish trees so common in southern Europe, and he ended up hardly believing his ears when he heard the well-known rustle of the common poplar. Soon afterwards, having avoided an adder that slipped down between two stones like a jet of water, he drew near and saw that he had heard aright. They were the neat, stately poplars of groves and plantations which the north and the stony ground, the drift-ice and the salt had chastised and stylised into an unrecognisable variety. They had grown grizzled at the top, and had lost their crowns in their struggle with the stormy weather and the cold, and now they consisted only of frost-bitten shoots which had ceaselessly sprouted, ceaselessly renewed themselves, while the goats had stripped the protective bark and let the sap run away. There was eternal youth about these tender, pale-green shoots on the grey, shaggy trunk with no branches – old age without manhood, an abnormality that seemed refreshing, as it had by-passed the commonplace.

When he had climbed over the sharp stones and reached the top it was as if he had scaled a mountain in ten minutes. The region of deciduous trees lay beneath him, and on the plateau of the rock alpine flora were already in command, with the mountain variety of the juniper beside the true nordic cloudberry in the white moss of the damp crevices, and between them the very civilised dwarf cornel, perhaps the only plant that belonged to Sweden and the archipelago. He made his way slowly down the southern slope through cowberries and bearberries, hair-grass and sedge, cotton-grass and springy mosses, until he suddenly stood by a ravine where the island had split and formed a canal between the black walls of rock.

The impertinent razorbills flew up shrieking wildly while he crossed the shallow canal by a natural bridge of stones, climbed another rock-wall of a pleasanter formation, and found himself in a new part of this wonderful island.

The elegant, light-coloured eurite, in which strata of faintly pink feldspar alternating with light blue-green quartz and mica only made their presence known by a shimmer like that of microscopic hoar-frost, gave all this little bit of landscape a happy aspect, while the endless crevices provided sofas and real armchairs at every step. A strong band of granular, white limestone ran like a girdle straight through the mass of rock, and the fertile gravel, which had been broken down from it by rain and frost, had collected below between moderately high walls of rock. And here, running up to meet him, was a narrow little valley which opened up such an enchanting sight that he stopped in amazement, and sat down on a footstool of rock to enjoy this unexpected and lovely spectacle.

Before him, between the perpendicular walls of rock that were vanishing into the meadow-land, he saw a grassy plot unrolling itself, everywhere shot through with flowers more exquisite and luxuriant than any on the mainland. The blood-red crane's-bill had stepped down from the rocks and sought moisture and warmth here, and the honey-white grass of Parnassus from the damp sedge meadows had met with the blue-yellow cow-wheat of the forest. And the orchids of the south, driven perhaps by the wind from Gotland, that land of vines, had also moved in here: the hyacinth-like spotted orchis, the magnificent military orchis and the stately cephalanthera, a sort of glorified lily-of-the-valley, all of which, in the midst of the most luxuriant green grass, had found their forcing-house between protective walls, in growth-promoting lime and moist sea-air.

In the far background, the wall of rock was hidden by birch and alder which had raised themselves only a modest distance into the air and so avoided sticking their heads into the wind. Planted out here in the middle of the grass were guelder roses, their white snowballs hanging against their vine-like leaves, and leaning against the upright rock as if trained on it grew the contrasting dark-green buckthorn, its shining leaves reminding one faintly of those of the far-famed orange tree, but with more sap, more shades of colour, finer outlines and, as it were, a more sensitive structure.

It was a garden, a bit of inland nature transported here, and when, through a cleft or a dip in the rock, he saw a blue, horizontal stretch of sea, it was by the contrast between them that he first realised the wonder of what he saw.

When he had sat for a while listening to the spring-like song of a chaffinch, interrupted by the croaking and screeching of gulls and guillemots, solitude seemed to be wrapping itself round him like sleep and, as the birds fell silent for a moment and only the gentle sea-breeze soughed in the tops of the birches, unable to reach further down, he unexpectedly heard a cough. It made him jump and look about him, but no trace of a human being was to be seen.

This hollow sound of affliction from a human chest in the midst of silent nature roused him suddenly and unpleasantly and brought a cloud of disagreeable sensations. Was it a solitary being like himself, seeking peace, or a nest-robber? Whichever it was, he wanted to rid himself of anxiety by finding out who was disturbing him. He therefore climbed over the wall of rock by some natural steps formed by clefts in the limestone and now became aware of a third section of the polypoid island. Over a low stone wall, apparently put there to protect the flowery meadow from grazing cattle, he entered a region of conifers growing on gneiss. He passed beneath fir trees, and tramped through bracken, three feet high, which formed the undergrowth beneath the conifers and resembled dwarf palms, but of a fresher green and with more elegant leaves, while at their feet grew wild strawberries, turning red.

When he had climbed out of the ravine, he saw an inlet with rushes, where some abandoned ledger-tackle had been thrown on to the muddy bottom. He stopped to listen and now, on the other side of a rocky knoll, he could hear a voice speaking. It rang out high-pitched and gentle, like a child's voice, but then sank somewhat so that he thought it must belong to a youth who had dared to sail so far afield. But the words seemed so unaggressive, so attractive, winning and inviting, that he would have been surprised to hear a boy expressing himself in such a civilised manner. The vocabulary was not large, the speech was that of the most ordinary cultured conversation. It was completely lacking in concrete, colourful expressions, and whenever any definite information was given it was incorrect. The voice mentioned the foliage of the trees, but failed to name the species, it called black-backs gulls, the chaffinch a bird, gneiss granite, rushes reeds.

Of course a young man might talk at such length, with so much assurance and insistence on being heard that he would not allow himself to be interrupted by the gently droning older person's voice that now and then murmured an objection or a piece of information. But now the youthful voice laughed, an unmotivated laugh, to judge by the conversation, a laugh in order to hear a beautiful voice, or to show white teeth. A laugh unprovoked by an amusing incident, a string of ringing notes without other meaning than that of jealously diverting attention from some reality that tried to intervene. A call to attention, a siren's call! This was without doubt a young woman.

He could not resist climbing the last hill after first adjusting his necktie and his hat, and now he saw beneath him a scene every detail of which remained forever in his memory. On a grassy patch of dry land, under a group of ancient whitebeam trees, round a drill napkin on which stood a marble butter-dish in the midst of other provisions for a picnic, sat an elderly lady with beautiful grey hair and a well-fitting gown, and beside her a local fisherman in his shirtsleeves, holding a sandwich in his hand. Standing opposite them was a young woman with a full glass of beer in her hand. She was holding it out to the embarrassed sailor with a mocking curtsy, and the vestiges of her recent laugh on her lips.

Borg was instantly captivated by the young woman's appearance, and though his reason immediately whispered to him that she was flirting with the lad, he felt irresistibly drawn to her dark, olive-coloured complexion, her black eyes, and her stately figure. She was by no means the first woman who had instantly fascinated him, but she belonged to the class of women who never failed to attract him. He could not blame solitude and lack of alternatives for his sudden choice as he had experienced the same thing when seeking for a necktie of a particular colour and, after having gone gloomily from shop to shop, without the sensations of pleasure that what he sought would have brought, he had suddenly stopped in front of a shop window where the right one lay and had instantly felt relief as he thought to himself: there it is!

After wondering for a moment whether to advance and introduce himself or to turn back, he made a movement that betrayed him. The girl, who saw him first, instantly lowered her arm and surveyed this unexpected apparition with the expression of a frightened child. This immediately gave the intruder courage to step forward and give the company an explanation.

Raising his hat, he advanced to greet them.

V

Half an hour later the inspector was seated in the little party's sailing-boat with his own yawl in tow. He had already established his position as guide to the two ladies who, for reasons of health, had found themselves accommodation for the summer on Österskär, and were therefore to be his neighbours. The conversation meandered agreeably between the three new acquaintances with that headlong eagerness which manifests itself when those who have met for the first time compete to show off their accomplishments, and their good sides. The person who made the least effort was the old lady who had introduced herself as the mother of the young beauty. She seemed to have achieved complete serenity and resignation and to have rubbed off all her corners. Living on her memories, she regarded with partial indifference everything going on around her, and expected nothing from outside. Prepared as she was to accept everything good or bad that life had to offer, she captivated by her equable and gentle disposition.

Contact had already been established between the young man and the young woman. She seemed to enjoy receiving and he, who for so long had been waiting to give, felt his powers increase now that the surplus he had been accumulating for ages was allowed an outlet. And for half an hour he gave with both hands all that he had gathered in the way of information that might interest those who were about to enter, for a time, surroundings of which they knew nothing. He described all the assets and all the defects of the island, painted a picture of life there which sounded as tempting as, for the moment, it seemed likely to be, now that he was no longer alone. And the young woman, who had never seen the island, gained her first impression of it from his description. She saw the red cottage, in which she and her mother would live, as the pretty and attractive place he wanted her to see it as, so that she would feel at home there and want to stay. And while he was talking it seemed to him that he got something good and strong in return, and that from the lips she held half-open – not as if she was swallowing what he held out to her, but as if speaking themselves – he heard new thoughts and new points of view. And when her two large trustful eyes looked up at him with surprise and admiration he believed that everything he said was true and, as his self-respect increased, he felt new powers quickening in him, and his old powers growing in strength and endurance. And when they landed, and he helped the ladies out of the boat and carried their heavy baggage ashore, he felt so truly grateful that he involuntarily spoke his heartfelt thanks, as for a kind deed performed in time of need.

The young girl responded to his civility with a 'don't mention it', but as if what she had given from her abundance was nothing compared to what she still had in reserve.

When the inspector had conducted the ladies to their new abode, which turned out to be Öman's cottage, the young girl, who was still under the influence of Borg's exciting descriptions, poured forth her delight. The outside of the dilapidated house was unusually picturesque, for it had not a single straight line. Gales, salt water, frost and rain had distorted the contours of all its main features, and now that the mortar in the chimney had come away, this looked like a lump of tufa. They were even more pleasantly surprised by the interior, which was really homely, old-fashioned and comfortable. Its two rooms lay one on either side of the entrance, with the kitchen between them. The main room was spacious. It had dusky-brown wallpaper which, from smoke and age, had acquired a benevolent shade of brown against which all colours looked well. The low ceiling, which left no vacant space above it that you could people with your fancies, revealed the beams that supported the loft. Two small windows with dingy old panes six inches square afforded a view of the sea and the harbour, and the great expanse of light from without was pleasantly reduced by white net curtains which concealed you from the view of those outside, but did not keep out the daylight. They hung like bright summer clouds over yellow balsam and geraniums in mugs of English faience decorated with pictures of Queen Victoria and Lord Nelson in yellow and green. The furniture consisted of a large, white folding-table, a Gustavian bed[1] with several layers of bulging eiderdowns, a rib-backed settee painted white, a grandfather clock made in Mora[2] and a chest-of-drawers in birch with a mirror in a frame of alder-root, both enveloped in a bridal veil and loaded with porcelain objects. On the chest-of-drawers there was a stuffed parrot under a glass dome and on the walls were some coloured lithographs of Old Testament subjects, two of which had been hung over the bed with intentions apparently less than admirable. One represented Samson and Delilah, very shamelessly portrayed, and the other Joseph and Potiphar's wife. In one corner an open fireplace for cooking occupied a good deal of room, and would have seemed horrific if the black chasm had not been concealed behind a white curtain, running on a draw-tape.

All was homely comfort, idyll, cleanliness.

The other room was like the first, but had two beds, a wash-stand and rag-rugs whose variegated colours were an album of memories from grandfather's singlet to grandmother's jacket, from mother's cotton dress to father's pilot's uniform. The girls' red garters were there too, the conscripts' yellow breeches, the summer visitor's blue bathing-drawers, duffle and corduroy, cotton and baize, wool and hessian, from every fashion and every wardrobe, poor man's and rich man's alike.

In this room stood a large, white sideboard with painted door-panels, portraying marvellous little landscapes framed by trailing ivy of mosaic bronze: cornflower-blue bays, banks of reeds, sailing boats, unknown varieties of trees from paradise or the Carboniferous era, turbulent seas where the waves were as straight as the furrows in a potato field, a lighthouse like a pillar on a rock of doorsteps. It was all as naive as a child's simple conception of rich nature's infinite variety of form and colour, which only a highly trained eye can discern.

But all this old-fashioned simplicity was the very ingredient needed for the cure of wearied brains looking for a resting-place in the past. The worn-out clockwork could be left unwound for a time, so that the tense springs could relax and regain their spent strength. Association with the lower classes does not stimulate competition in the struggle for the morsels of power. On the contrary, they themselves, quite involuntarily, remind those above them daily and hourly of the position it has cost them so much to win. Irritation is reduced and the power-hungry lulled with the thought that there are stages which they have already put behind them.

The inspector had already prepared the minds of the strangers to see and feel in this way, and the two women never tired of expressing their satisfaction with their new abode. They were so occupied with investigating the premises that they did not notice that their companion had withdrawn in order to leave them undisturbed.

. . .

On the afternoon of that Sunday the inspector sat by his window and watched the two ladies busying themselves in their cottage. As he followed their supple, irregular movements with his eyes it seemed to him that he was listening to music. The same modulation that a series of notes sounded in chords produce on the eardrum, thence to be transmitted to the nervous system, were now gentle vibrations set in motion through the eye which, resounding through the white strings stretched from the cranium to the sounding-board of the thorax, made the very foundations of his soul quiver. A feeling of general well-being streamed through him when he saw the undulations of these female hands as they unpacked small articles from their bags and placed them on tables and chairs, saw the elastic rise and fall of hips and shoulders which a coarser gaze would not have observed. And when the young woman walked through the room there were no straight lines, no corners, no edges when she turned, and no angles when she bent down.

He was so completely captivated by what he saw that for a while the commotion out in the loft, the creaking of the steps up to it, the sound of latches being raised, escaped his notice.

What was engrossing him was his contemplation of the young lady whose exterior seemed to him perfect, except in one respect, and this defect he was trying to accustom his eyes not to see. Her chin was in fact several sizes too big and suggested a lower jaw that was quite unnecessarily developed for a being who no longer had to seize, hold and tear uncooked meat. When he saw it in profile he was able to construct the physiognomy of the witch she might become when, as an old woman, her teeth had fallen out, her lips had receded to form an obtuse angle, and her nose had sunk towards her protruding chin. But he must overcome this reminder of the beast of prey, so he pursued her face with his eyes, drew it again in his imagination, forced himself when looking at it to see it as a whole.

But now, from down in the yard he heard footsteps and shouts and, in wild excitement, Öman's wife and a group of women appeared bearing down to the drying sheds in triumph the net they had re-taken.

Feeling that this was an insult to his authority he flung on his hat, went down to the customs officer, and demanded his help as a servant of the Crown and therefore obliged to lend a hand.

The customs officer was sitting at the coffee-table and, as usual when Vestman was out fishing, had his arm round his sister-in-law's waist. When the inspector entered, he removed his arm and, in his fear of being exposed, showed a greater willingness to oblige than he would otherwise have done. After putting on his braided cap he went out and, suddenly feeling the need to be an upright man, he stormed towards the cluster of women and seized the net.

'You damnable old hags. Don't you know that it's penal servitude for those who break the Crown's lock and seal?'

The women answered with a chorus of invectives heaped on both the inspector and the customs officer, the upshot of which was that they did not care a damn for the Crown's lock and seal, and that both gentlemen deserved to be locked up in Långholmen,[3] the sooner the better.

At this the customs officer fired up, and shouted to a coast-guard to fetch the sheriff.

On hearing the word 'sheriff' people began to gather, and came creeping out of holes and corners like ants when you rake their heap.

They immediately seemed ready to take sides with the women, and threatening words were uttered. The inspector decided that he must now intervene personally if he was not to shelter under the protection of a subordinate. He therefore advanced towards the mob and asked what they wanted.

When this failed to produce an answer he turned to the women and addressed them in a polite but determined tone of voice.

'As I told you before, Parliament – that is your own elected representatives – has decided that, for the sake of your children and your descendants, fishing must be protected by forbidding the use of gear that ruins it without bringing you any advantages. You have had three years to wear out the old nets, but you have continued to make new ones that do not comply with the law. Consequently I have been obliged, on behalf of the Crown, to confiscate the gear which contravenes the law. Nevertheless, and in defiance of the law now in force, you have broken the Crown's lock and seal, for which you may have to pay with penal servitude. All the same I am prepared to temper justice with mercy if you will submit and obey. I therefore ask you for the last time: will you hand over the nets of you own accord?'

To this the women replied with more shouting and a further shower of abuse.

'Very well,' concluded the inspector. 'As I am not a policeman and you outnumber us, I must ask the customs officer to send for the sheriff and his assistants, and at the same time send off an application to the Governor of the Province for a warrant for the arrest of goodwife Öman.'

When he had uttered the last word he felt two soft, warm hands grasping his right hand, saw two large, child-like eyes looking into his, and heard a voice speaking with the accents of a mother pleading for her child's life:

'In heaven's name have mercy on a poor unhappy woman and do her no injury,' begged the young girl who, on hearing the uproar, had come out of the cottage.

The inspector would like to have freed himself and turn away from those large eyes, whose expression he could not endure. But he felt his hand being still more firmly held, being pressed against a soft bosom, heard words uttered in melting tones and, completely conquered, he whispered to the young beauty: 'Release me, and I will let the matter drop.'

The girl let go her hold, and the inspector, who in a split second had formed his plan, took the customs officer by the arm and led him up to the customs house, as if he was intending to give him some orders. When they reached the door the inspector said briefly and decisively, as if he had just arrived at a new decision:

'I shall communicate personally with the Governor by letter. Thanks for your help all the same.'

He thereupon retired to his room.

When he was alone and had collected his thoughts he had to admit that his last action had been dictated by low motives. His sexual impulse had so far got the upper hand that he had allowed himself to be duped into acting against the law. There could be no question of compassion for people who were comparatively well off. They owned houses and fishing grounds, boats and gear to the value of many hundreds of crowns. They owned seal-rookeries and bird-rocks, and moreover paid taxes on capital and a couple of small places that they rented out. The false idea that he had been defeated by a woman had no hold on him. He was perfectly conscious, on this point as on all others, that he had fallen to his own impulses, his own desire to win something from this woman. But *vis-à-vis* the inhabitants his authority was at an end, his reputation tarnished, and from now on there would not be an old hag or a young lad who did not think themselves his superiors. This was of no great importance, for to possess or not to possess power over these miserable creatures was a matter of indifference to him. What seemed to him worse was that this woman, to whom he felt he must bind himself if he was to be happy, would feel, right from the beginning, that she had won a victory over him and thus the equilibrium of their relationship in a future union would be upset.

Of course, he had had many fancies for and relationships

with women before, but he was so convinced of the superiority of man over that intermediate form between man and child which is called 'woman', that he had been unable to conceal his conviction for long and consequently his affairs had been of short duration. He wanted to be loved by a woman who would look up to him as the stronger; he wanted to be the adored, not the adorer; he wanted to be the stock on to which the weak shoot must be grafted. But he had been born in a period of spiritual pestilence when womankind was ravaged by epidemic megalomania, caused by degenerate, sickly men and political nonentities who needed masses of new voters. He had therefore been forced to remain alone. He well knew that in love man must give, must let himself be duped, and that the only way to approach a woman was on all fours. And sometimes he had crawled, and as long as he did so all had gone well. But when he had finally straightened up, it had all come to an end, always with a lot of false accusations that he had feigned submissiveness, that he had never loved and so forth.

Moreover, as one who enjoyed the highest intellectual pleasures, who knew himself to be an exception among human beings, he had never felt a lively desire for the lower emotions, never wished to be the host for a parasite, never longed to feed competitors. His strong ego had revolted against being the means by which a woman could reproduce her kind, a role he had seen assumed by nearly all his contemporaries.

But now he just as much as they was back in the same predicament: should he assimilate a woman by letting himself be assimilated by her? He could not dissemble, or allow himself to express outwardly what he did not feel. But he possessed a great ability to adapt himself to the people he was with, to enter into other people's thoughts and feelings, for in others he found earlier stages that he himself had passed. Thus he only needed to recall memories and experiences, to give way, and to reduce his eagerness to press forward. And he had always enjoyed the company of women as a form of rest and distraction, just as – and for the same reason – being in the company of children can be a rejuvenating and refreshing diversion if it does not last too long, and degenerate into effort.

He had now felt growing within him a determination to possess this woman. But though he was a scientist, and knew that man is a mammal, he was fully aware that human love, like everything else, had developed and absorbed elements of a higher, spiritual nature without discarding the sensuality on which it was based. He knew precisely how much he would have to eliminate of the unhealthy sanctimony smuggled in as a result of the Christian reaction to the purely animal. He did not believe in the prudishness which denied the existence of what could not be shown, any more than he admitted copulation to be the sole object of the marital state. He desired an intimate and perfect union of body and soul, in which he, as the stronger acid, would neutralise the passive base. It would not, as in chemistry, create a new, indifferent body, but on the contrary would leave a surplus of free acid, which would always give the union its character and would lie ready to be used against any attempt by the substratum to free itself. For human love was not a chemical compound, but a psychic and organic one which resembled the chemical in some respects, but was not the same. Thus he was not expecting any augmentation of his ego, nor any addition to his strength, but only an increase in his zest for life. Instead of seeking a support he was offering himself as one, in order to experience his own vigour and feel the pleasure of meting out his strength, of strewing his soul with full hands, without thereby growing weaker or suffering need.

With these thoughts in his mind he again let his gaze stray through the window and immediately found what he was seeking. The young girl was standing in her porch, having her hand shaken by women and men, patting children on the head, and seemingly overwhelmed by the emotions that so much public approbation evokes.

What extraordinary sympathy for criminals, thought the inspector. What love for the feeble-minded. And how well they understand each other's impulses, which they boast are emotions and which they believe to be greater than clear, fully developed thoughts.

The whole scene was such a tissue of absurdities that no sense could be made of it, mirroring as it did all that was chaotic in the first feeble efforts of these brains and marrows to use their reason.

There stood the woman who had fooled him into breaking the law being worshipped like an angel. And if indeed this law-breaking was the beautiful, noble act they thought it, he should have received their thanks for letting mercy temper justice. But the mob thought otherwise. They knew that the motive behind his action was not goodwill towards them, but perhaps tender feeling for a young girl, gallantry, or the hope of winning her. Yes, but in that case, the motive behind her behaviour might be to win the approval of the mob, to be liked, popular, to have her hand shaken. And as for the mob, they were playing the part performed by the onlookers in a ballroom, the strollers on the streets or in the market-squares. She had fooled him into acting badly by physical contact – innocent maybe, calculated possibly, probably half and half – and for this she was worshipped.

But now he must win her; consequently he must stuff all his reflections about their relationship into his pocket. For he had instantly realised that through her he could transmit his ideas and his plans down to the mob. By this means he could move the masses, oblige them to accept his benefactions, make them his vassals. Then he would sit like a god, smiling at their folly in thinking that they had created their good fortune themselves, when in fact they were big with his thoughts, his plans, eating the draff from his magnificent brew, while the strong malt liquor itself would never pass their lips. For what did he care whether these barren islands supported a half-starving, unnecessary population or not? What compassion could he entertain for his natural enemies, who represented the inert lump that had lain so suffocatingly on his life, hindered his growth – enemies who, themselves lacking any vestige of compassion for others, persecuted their benefactor with the hatred of wild beasts, though his only revenge had been new benefactions.

How greatly he would enjoy sitting unnoticed, being regarded as a fool, though in fact he was directing their destinies, while they believed they had subdued him, cut him off from his contacts and bound his hands. He would strike these fools blind, distort their vision so that they would imagine they were his superiors and he their servant.

While these thoughts were gathering in him and developing into a firm decision there came a knock at the door, and in response to the inspector's 'come in', the customs officer appeared with an invitation from the ladies to take tea with them.

The inspector sent his thanks and promised to come.

After he had smartened himself up and thought over what he would say or not say, he went down.

In the porch he met Miss Maria who seized his hands with exaggerated warmth and pressing them declared emotionally: 'Thank you for what you did for that poor woman. It was noble, it was great!'

'No, dear lady, it was neither,' answered the inspector quickly, 'it was a bad deed on my part which I regret, and which was prompted solely by a desire to be polite to you.'

'You malign yourself by your everlasting politeness, and I should appreciate a little frankness a good deal more,' replied the young lady, just as her mother arrived on the scene.

'Ah! What a good child you are,' exclaimed her mother with unshakeable conviction, and invited the inspector into the main room where tea was already served.

Instead of involving himself more deeply in unfathomable questions he entered the house. He saw at one glance that the simple furnishings of the fisherman's cottage had been criss-crossed with odds and ends from the threadbare luxury of a town house. There were yellowing alabaster vases on the chest-of-drawers, photographs among the flowers in the window, an easy chair, upholstered in flowered cretonne with brass-headed nails, in the corner by the fireplace, and a few books on a sofa table round a moderator lamp.

Everything was neatly arranged with anxious, mathematical precision, yet at the same time awry and askew instead of straight as intended. The tea-service of old Dresden china with gilded edges and a cherry-red monogram was cracked here and there, and the teapot lid was riveted. After he had examined the portrait of the deceased paterfamilias, but without daring to enquire what profession he had followed, he saw that he had been a civil servant and realised that these people were the genteel poor (*pauvres honteux*).

At first the conversation glided round all the external objects that caught the eye, passed on to the events of the day, and thus to the inhabitants. The inspector soon gathered that the ladies were interested in the affairs of others and lived in a state of morbid concern for the welfare of the lower classes. He had noticed that his frankness had offended the ladies and, as it was not his intention to hurt them by pressing his opinions, he lay to and let himself drift. Now and then he protested inwardly and would have liked to hazard a comment, or a bit of information, but immediately soft hands seemed to be laid on his lips and rounded arms twined about his neck, so that his words were stifled. And for that matter their opinions were so rooted, everything so finalised, all questions settled, that they only smiled kindly with gentle commiseration when they read in him a hint of doubt about their axioms. But then the conversation sheered over to the spiritual condition of the inhabitants, and here the inspector was entirely with them. He described with heat the vulgarity, drunkenness and fights of that morning, deplored the lack of enlightenment, and finally told of scenes that betrayed a state of complete paganism. He spoke of how fishermen made offerings on votive stones, loaded their guns with the lead from church windows, talked of Thor's goats when it thundered and of Odin's wild hunt when the grey-geese came in the spring, and of how the people of the interior of the islands let the magpies destroy the chickens as they did not dare to tear down their nests for fear of unknown avengers.

'Yes,' put in the old lady, whom a label on one of the bags still standing under a table showed to be the widow of a senior official of the Crown Lands Judiciary Board.[4] 'Yes, it's not their fault. If they were not so far from a church, things would be very different.'

The inspector's thoughts had not travelled in this direction, but he instantly saw what an ally a great power like this would be. Developing the seed of thought sown in him that morning by the sight of the religious service held on board the man-of-war he burst out with genuine enthusiasm:

'Why of course, we can get a mission-house quite cheaply. What if I were to write to the Mission Board?'

The ladies embraced the idea with the greatest enthusiasm, undertook to write to the Church Authorities themselves, and also to various other societies. They proposed a fair, but reminded themselves that there was no dancing public on the island.

The inspector removed all their difficulties by offering to advance the money and see to it that a building was obtained. It could be bought pre-fabricated from a factory – all the ladies needed to do was secure a lay preacher. But he added that, in this instance, and for a start, they should preferably choose one of the fiercer variety who would be able to cope with the populace and set in motion an evangelist movement of the greatest severity; half-measures would be out of place here.

The ladies raised some slight objections and recommended a more loving approach, but the inspector pointed out that fear was the foundation upon which the first stage of education must be built. After that love could be introduced.

A great common interest welded these souls together as they warmed themselves red-hot by the blaze of their great love. They talked themselves into a state in which they overflowed with compassion for all created things. They pressed each other's hands, and parted blessing and congratulating each other that fate had brought together three human beings who would work in harmony for the benefit of mankind.

When the inspector got outside he shook himself, as if he wanted to rid himself of dust. He felt as he had done when visiting a mill: a certain pleasure in seeing everything coated in a soft, semi-white, mealy tone which tuned iron, wood, linen and glass in one key; the same subdued sensation of sensual pleasure as when touching locks, handrails and sacks powdered with slippery flour-dust, but at the same time a difficulty in breathing, a need to cough, to take out his handkerchief.

All the same it had been a pleasant evening. The imperceptible warmth that radiated from the mother had helped his shrunken thoughts to expand; the atmosphere of ardour and child-likeness about the young woman had rejuvenated him. The innocent faith in what, during his youth, had been the naive idealism of the day: the belief that you could raise up what was low, protect what was stunted, sick and weak – all that he now knew was the very opposite of what would promote the felicity and improvement of mankind, and which he hated by instinct, as he saw how all that was strong, every expression of originality was persecuted by the unfortunate. And now he was going to make a pact with these things against himself, work for his own destruction, drag himself down to a lower level, feign sympathy for his hereditary foe, supply a fighting-fund for his opponent. Thoughts of the pleasure these trials of strength would bring intoxicated him, and he directed his steps shorewards in order to seek for himself again in solitude. And now, in the still warmth of the summer night, as he strolled on the sand where he recognised his footprints of the preceding days, where he knew every stone and where this or that plant grew, he noticed that everything had assumed a different aspect, taken on a new form, made entirely other impressions than they had when he strolled there the day before. A change had taken place, something new had intervened. He could no longer summon up that feeling of great solitariness, and of confronting nature and humanity quite alone. For someone stood beside him, behind him, his isolation was broken and he was soldered to petty, everyday life. Threads had been spun about his soul, consideration for others bound his thoughts, and the cowardly fear of holding other views than those held by his friends was digging its claws into him. He did not dare to build his happiness on treacherous ground, for when he had built as far as the roof-ridge, all might collapse at once, and then his fall would be greater, his pain the deeper. Yet that was what must happen if he wanted to possess her, and that he did with all the rock-shattering strength of his mature years. Raise her up to his level? How could he do that? He could not turn her from a woman into a man, could not free her from the irrepressible impulses which her sex had implanted in her. He could not give her his own upbringing which had extended over thirty years, nor bestow on her the development he had undergone, the experiences, the knowledge that he had struggled to acquire. Then he would have to sink to her level, but the thought of thus sinking was a torment to him as being the greatest imaginable evil, like drowning, going to the bottom, beginning all over again, which for that matter was impossible. All that remained was to make himself into a dual personality, to cleave himself in two, create a being that she could reach and comprehend, he could then act the part of a deceived lover, learn to admire her inferiority, accustom himself to the role she wanted him to play, and then, in silence, live the other half of his life in secret for himself, sleep with one eye and keep the other open.

He had climbed the island without noticing it. And now he saw lights down in the fishing-village, heard wild shouts, shouts of rejoicing over the defeat of their enemy, who had wanted to lift their children and grandchildren out of poverty, had wanted to spare them work and give them new enjoyments. And instantly there awakened in him once again a desire to see these savages tamed, to see these worshippers of Thor kneel to the White Christ,[5] the giants defeated by the bright Aesir.[6] The barbarians must pass through Christianity as through purgatory and learn respect for the power of the spirit and the muscularly weak. The survivors of the migration period must experience the Middle Ages before they could emerge into the renaissance of thought and the revolution of action.

The chapel should stand here, on the highest ridge of the rock, and its little spire stick up above the look-out and the flag-pole, and hail those far out at sea like a reminder that . . . He paused here for reflection and a smile passed over his pale face as he bent down to pick up four splinters of gneiss. He laid these out in a rectangle from east to west after he had paced out thirty steps in length and twenty in breadth.

What a splendid landmark for seafarers, he thought, as he descended the rock and went home to bed.

VI

The inspector had stayed indoors for two days in order to work, and when on the morning of the third day he went out to take a walk along the shore, he accidentally met the widow lady. She looked worried, and when the inspector asked after her daughter he was told she was unwell.

'Perhaps for lack of entertainment?' he said at random.

'Yes, what can she do in this isolated place?' asked her anxious mother.

'The young lady must take a boat, go out fishing and sailing, and get some exercise,' he prescribed without thinking much about what he was saying.

'Of course,' rejoined the mother. 'But my poor Maria can't go out alone.'

As this left him only one possible answer he said:

'If the ladies can put up with my company I shall be most willing to oblige.'

The mother thought he was all too kind and accepted his offer, saying she would immediately instruct Maria to put on outdoor clothing.

The inspector went down to the harbour to get the boat ready, and on his way he began to drag his feet, as if he was going down a hill and his weight was pushing him down more quickly than he wished. It went against the grain to feel that, before he had had time to collect himself, he had been driven into action by a force outside himself, and now he wanted to resist but could not do so. It was too late, so he allowed himself to drift, aware that even if he did he would always be able to control the rudder and decide the course.

He had hoisted the foresail on his Blekinge boat,[1] put the rudder in place and made the painter loose and ready to cast off, when the young lady and her mother appeared on the shore. The girl was wearing an ultramarine-blue costume with white trimmings and a blue woollen tam-o'-shanter which suited her admirably and gave her a dashing, boyish air, utterly remote from the angelic aspect she had exhibited two days before.

After the inspector had greeted her and enquired after her health, he held out his hand to help the ladies on board. The girl accepted his outstretched hand and jumped lightly into the boat where he seated her in the stern by the tiller. But when the same hand was held out to her mother the latter explained that she could not accompany them as she had to cook the dinner. The inspector, upon whom surprises had been sprung so violently, again felt an inclination to resist the gentle pressure that was taking him in a direction he had not chosen, but he was held back by the fear of appearing discourteous. After making short work of expressing his regret that he must forgo the old lady's pleasant company, he released the painter, ordered Miss Maria to shift the tiller, put the mainsheet in her hand and hoisted sail.

'But I can't sail,' cried the girl. 'I've never held a tiller.'

'There's nothing to it. Only do as I tell you, and you'll be able to sail at once,' answered the inspector, seating himself opposite the girl and helping her with the manoeuvre.

A gentle breeze was blowing and the boat glided out of the harbour close-hauled.

The inspector held the foresheet and, to start with, instructed the beautiful navigator. He took hold of her wrist now and then, and pressed the tiller against the wind until they were out in the open, had gained speed, and were on the track which would take them straight out to the skerries.

The responsibility, the exertion, the feeling that she could control the boat which encompassed their two lives, awakened dormant power in her weak female body, and her eyes, which followed the position of the sail attentively, glowed with courage and confidence when she saw how the boat responded to the least pressure from her hand. If she made a mistake he corrected it with a friendly word, talked her into continuing by praising her vigilance, and removed difficulties by explaining the whole procedure as something self-evident.

She shone with happiness and began to talk of the past, of her thirty-four years, and of how she had believed that life and the courage to live was over. She said she felt young once more and that she had always dreamed of a life of action, above all of manly action, of being allowed to devote her energies to mankind, to others. She knew that as a woman she was a pariah.

The inspector listened to it all as well-known secrets, formulas for the absurd struggle to make equal what nature had purposely made as unequal as possible in order to spare mankind trouble. But he saw that it would be useless to answer, and he stuck to his role of grateful listener, and let her pour out her sick fancies which the fresh wind would blow away. So, instead of taking a knife and cutting away the tangled knots with which her muddled thinking presented him, he quite simply preferred not to see them, to bundle them away, and by collecting the impressions he had purposely induced in her, rewind the old tangles and use them as bobbins which would carry the new threads spun from his rich distaff.

He hastily improvised a plan whereby, using the visual material provided by the skerries, he would, without her noticing it, lead her in a few hours by means of living pictures through sensations that she would believe to come from the outside world. In this way he would slip the net of his soul over hers, tune her strings in harmony with his instrument. He indicated by a movement of his head that the boat should fall off and, after he had eased the sheet a bit, the boat dropped land and splashed its way through the inlet to the open sea. The wide horizon, the sea of light where not a trace of any object could be seen, cast a brightness over the beautiful face. Her small features seemed to grow larger, almost invisible wrinkles were smoothed away, the whole expression was that of a person freed from daily cares and petty thoughts. To her eyes, which could survey such a large part of the earth at a glance, everything seemed to be on a grand scale, so that her little person swelled, felt her relative power and, as the long rollers of the sea gently raised and lowered the boat in their powerful rhythm, he saw that rapture was mixed with a grain of fear that sought to damp it down.

The inspector, who observed that this splendid spectacle had not failed in its effect, now decided to put a text under the soft music of this surge of emotion, thus to lead her dawning thoughts out on to the great highway – his wish being to loosen the shells of the swelling seeds so that the sprouts could spring forth.

'It looks like a planet!' he improvised. 'And earth, so commonplace, so dull, so crumbling, has become a heavenly body. Don't you feel that we are already partaking of heaven now that we have made an end of the contrasts, the false contrasts between heaven and earth, which are one, just as the parts of the whole are one? Don't you see how you grow instead of shrink when you outwit the wind and force it to take you to the right, when it wants to take you to the left? Don't you feel what great power there is in you when you ride a wave which wants to press you down to the depths with its weight of thousands of pounds? The being whom we believe created the wings of the birds and required fifty thousand years to make a creature that flies out of one that crawls, was less intelligent than the being who first put a canvas on a pole and instantly discovered navigation.

'Is it then surprising that man created God in his own image, inferring from his own ingenuity a being even more ingenious?'

The girl, who had listened attentively to his outburst, kept her eyes firmly fixed on his face, as if turning her own to a fire for warmth. The unusual words she had heard seemed to have completely captivated her mind and to be working like yeast. Benumbed and lulled by his soft, persuasive tones she accepted without reflection the new view he gave her of the monotonous landscape – which for her had formerly lacked life – and of the origins and meaning of existence. Without recognising that her own religious belief was being buried before it was destroyed, she accepted the new and piled it on top of the old.

'You talk as I have heard no one talk before,' she said dreamily. 'Talk some more.'

He remained silent and by another gesture directed the boat on a new course.

They drew near the ghastly volcanic formation of Svartbådan. The gleaming black diorite with the deathly white navigation mark called 'The White Mare'[2] looked even more strikingly gloomy in the sunshine, which was vainly trying to bring into harmony the glaring extremes of black and white.

A cloud passed over the girl's face. Her features shrank, her eyebrows moved up and down, as if they wanted to drop and hide the oppressive picture. An imperceptible movement of the tiller indicated that she wanted to keep away from the island, but he gave the boat a forward direction and the compressed power of the wind drove it into the gully between the black cliffs where the sighing waves sucked it on.

Silence fell on the boat, and the inspector, not wanting to guess at the dark memories that were awakened in his companion, contented himself with pointing to the bleached skeleton of a long-tailed duck, left lying on the black rock.

The wind took the sails again, filled them and carried the boat out to open water.

They passed the skerry with the solitary rowan and the wagtail, and approached Svärdsholmen, where he had first seen her. They landed there and he led her by the same route he had followed on that Sunday morning, allowed her to experience the same impressions he had himself received, led her down to the flowery meadow, and showed her through the wild apple trees, the place where he had first caught sight of her.

This put her into an exuberant mood for, surely, if he remembered all these trifling matters, it must mean that he was in love. She laughed when he told her that the first he'd heard of her was a cough and, in a fit of playfulness, she told him to go down to the same spot and talk, and she would guess who was speaking.

He obeyed, jumped down from the ledge of rock, stood behind the whitebeam trees and imitated the bellowing of a bull.

'Why, how beautifully he can sing,' bantered the girl. 'That must surely be a Hottentot actor.'

The inspector found her childishness agreeable. He had not played with children for many years and continued in his role. Advancing on to the greensward, with his coat turned inside out, and his lorgnette hanging from one ear, he improvised a savage dance, accompanied by a song he had heard Hottentots singing in the Jardin d'Acclimatation.

The girl seemed both surprised and amused. 'Do you know?' she said. 'I like you better now that I see you can be a human being for a moment and stop looking like a philosopher.'

'Is a Hottentot more of a human being in your eyes than a philosopher?" let slip the inspector. But at once regretting having made her self-conscious, he broke off a branch from the whitebeam tree and, twisting it into a wreath, handed it to the girl, whose face had darkened as she realised that she had said something extremely foolish and given herself away.

'Now you shall wreathe the sacrificial beast! Miss Maria,' said the inspector, evading the issue. 'I wish there were a hundred of me so that I could go to the slaughter for you like a hecatomb.'

He fell on his knees and received the wreath from the pacified beauty, whereupon he began to run towards the shore with the girl after him.

Down by its sandy edge they stopped.

'Shall we play ducks and drakes?' she suggested.

'Certainly,' he responded, picking out a flat stone.

They threw stones into the water for a while until they were warm.

'Shall we bathe?' cried the girl suddenly, as if she had been brooding for some time on an idea which now had to burst out.

The inspector did not know how to take this. Was it a joke or seriously meant, with reservations – such as a tacit understanding that they should keep some of their clothing on, or that one party should retire to a distance.

'You bathe and I'll go elsewhere for a time,' was the answer that seemed best to him.

'Won't you bathe too?' asked the girl.

'No, I've no clothes with me,' answered the inspector, 'and what's more I don't bathe in cold water.'

'Hahahaha!' A cold, unpleasantly jeering laugh rang from the girl's larynx.

'You're frightened of cold water,' mocked the girl. 'And perhaps you can't swim?'

'The brutality of cold water is too much for my sensitive nerves. But if you have a cold bathe here, I'll go over to the northern point and have a warm one.'

The girl had already kicked off her boots and, with a glance of disdain and wounded vanity, she said:

'You won't be able to see me from there, will you?'

'Not unless you swim out too far,' replied the inspector, and moved off.

When he reached the northern steeps of the island he sought out a dip in the rocks sheltered from the northerly winds by a wall of rock about fifty feet high.

The black hornblende-gneiss, rendered as glossy as agate by the surge of the waves, undulated in slight, dainty ridges that resembled the muscles of the human body and slipped under the hollows of a bare foot like a feather bed. Not a puff of wind reached this place. The sun had blazed for six hours upon the smooth, dark rocks so that the air in here was heated to several degrees above body temperature and the stones almost burnt the soles of his feet. He had gone down to the boat to fetch an axe, and with this he now chopped off the driest of the heather and lyme-grass and made a flaming bonfire on the rocks while he undressed. The bonfire rapidly died down and then, having swept the surface as you do a bakestone, he threw crystal-clear sea-water over the hot stones with the bailer and allowed the steam to swirl round his naked body. He then sat down on one of the easy-chairs the sea had sculptured out of the lumps of rock, pulled his rug round him, curled himself up with his knees under his chin, shut his eyes and seemed to fall asleep. But he was not sleeping, only using these means to 'wind himself up', as he called it, and let his brain rest for a few moments so that it might recover its vigour. For he found it an effort to adapt himself when he had to associate with the muddled thinking of others. His thought-processes suffered from contact with other people and became as restless and as unreliable as the needle of a compass when in contact with iron. And every time he wanted to think clearly about something or to reach a decision, he induced a state of harmonious numbness in his soul by taking a hot bath and thus reduced his consciousness to a doze by thinking of nothing for a few moments. In this state all the material he had acquired by observation seemed to be thrown into the melting-pot, and when he roused himself to consciousness and switched off the fire the alloy welled forth.

After he had sat for a while and the sun had warmed him thoroughly he suddenly got up, as wide awake as after a whole night's sleep. His thoughts were working again and he looked happy, as if he had solved a problem.

She is thirty-four, he thought. I had forgotten that under the influence of her youthful beauty. Hence this chaos of past stages she has behind her, these bits and pieces of roles that she has successively played in life, the masses of shifting reflexes from men whom she has tried to win by adapting herself to them. She must recently have been bankrupted by some love-affair. The man who had held all these ragged bits of a soul together had dropped her, the sack had burst open, and now everything was lying about like a rag-and-bone man's junk. She had exhibited samples of the romanticism of the parsonage of 1850, along with belchings of philanthropy from the beginning of the century, fanatical faith from the fashionable streams of *The Voice of the Dove* and *The Pietist*,[3] cynicisms from George Sand and the hermaphrodite period. He was too wise to waste time trying to find the bottom of this sieve through which so many soups had passed, or to seek the answer to a riddle that was no riddle. All that remained was to select from the heap of bones those which could be made into a skeleton. He would then supply it with living flesh and breathe his spirit into it. But of this she must be unaware, otherwise she would not allow it. She must never see that she was receiving from him, for that would only arouse hatred and opposition. He would grow underground like the rootstock, and graft her on to himself so that she would shoot up, be visible to the world, and bear the flower that mankind could admire.

Now he heard the gulls screaming and realised that she must have swum out. He therefore dressed himself hurriedly and after collecting his belongings he took out of the boat's hold a little picnic and laid it out on the moss under a pine with a short trunk which looked like a stone-pine.

There were only a few dishes but everything was costly and choice and served on the remains of a collection of china he had once begun to make. The butter, yellow as egg-yolk, gleamed in a box made of serpentine with a screw-top that stood in a fragment of Henry II[4] faience filled with ice. The biscuits lay in a filigree dish of Marieberg,[5] and the sardines on a saucer of mottled blue Nevers.[6] Fear of the ever-increasing banality in art, industry and daily life had driven their owner out on the modern search for the unusual. The horrible triviality and hatred for originality displayed by his contemporaries had driven him, as it had others, to over-refinement in an effort to preserve his personality from being ground down by the great avalanche of boulders. His finely developed senses were not looking for commonplace beauty of form and colour which ages so rapidly. He wanted to see history, mementoes of world events in the things that surrounded him. Thus this scrap of Henry II faience, its creamy-white pipeclay encrusted with red, black and yellow, awakened memories of the beautiful Loire district with its Renaissance castles, while its bookbinder's style of ornamentation put him in mind of the châtelaine Hélène de Genlis[7] and her librarian who, with the help of a potter, had introduced into printing a style that was purely personal, but nevertheless took colour from the age of chivalry – an age when the beauty of life was revered and handicraft was subordinate to learning and art, as if it recognised the advantage of giving precedence to what was spiritual.

When he had finished he surveyed his work, and it seemed to him that he had introduced a bit of civilisation into this semi-arctic wilderness. Sardines from Brittany, chestnuts from Andalusia, caviare from the Volga, cheese from Gruyère in the Alps, sausage from Thuringen, biscuits from Great Britain and oranges from Asia Minor. In addition there was from Tuscany a bottle of Chianti enveloped in basket-work, to be drunk from goblets with Frederick I's[8] monogram in gold.

The whole effect was haphazard, with nothing of the collector or museum about it, and the touches of colour here and there were like flowers pressed between the leaves of a guide-book, instead of in a herbarium.

He now heard the girl's voice calling hello from the bathing place and he responded. Soon afterwards she emerged from the bushes erect, brisk, radiating health and zest for life. When she saw the picnic he had laid out she raised her cap and bowed jestingly, but was impressed against her will by the elegance of the entertainment.

'Why, what a magician you are,' she said. 'Allow me to make my bow.'

'Not for such a trifle,' answered the inspector.

'You mean that you are capable of more. But that business of controlling nature that you were babbling about recently, that would be too much for you,' objected the girl in her mother-knows-best tone of voice.

'Young lady, I did not express myself so categorically. I simply reminded you that we have partially learnt to subjugate the forces of nature which we ourselves in part obey – observe the important little words "in part" – and that we have it in our power to change both the character of a landscape, and the entire intellectual life of its inhabitants.'

'Good! Produce an Italian landscape with marble villas and stone-pines out of this horrible *paysage* of grey stone.'

'I am certainly no conjurer, but it you command me, I promise you that on your birthday, three weeks from now, I will transform this unspoiled bit of nature, the like of which you will search for in vain in Europe, into the parched, treeless, cauliflower-patch landscape you admire.'

'Done! We'll bet on it. In three weeks then; and if I lose?'

'I shall win – shan't I?'

'We'll see about that!'

'Yes, we'll see. But meanwhile will you do my work for me?'

'Your work! What is that? To lie on a sofa and smoke cigarettes?'

'Yes, if you can do my work from a sofa as I can, by all means do so. But you can't and I'll now tell you why, and the meaning of my presence here on this island. Take a glass of wine with your sausage first.'

He poured out a glass of the dark-red Chianti and handed it to the girl, who emptied it at one gulp.

'You know,' began the inspector, 'that my official business at this fishing-village is to teach the inhabitants to fish.'

'That must be nice for you who boast that you have never held a fishing-rod.'

'Don't interrupt me. In any case I'm not going to teach them to fish with a rod. You see, it's like this: these dunces, conservative like the rest of the mob . . .'

'What kind of language is that?' the girl interjected again.

'Plain language. However, as a result of ignorance and conservatism these aborigines are undermining their position as fish-eating mammals and this gives the State leave to put them under a guardian. The Baltic herring – God bless it – which represents the chief source of nourishment for these autochthones is threatening to run dry This certainly does not worry me, for it is a matter of complete indifference for the world in general if this superflous race of ichthyophagi increases or diminishes by a few hundreds more or less. But the Ministry of Agriculture and Fisheries wishes them to survive, so I must prevent them from fishing away their meagre living. Do you admit that this is logical?'

'It is inhuman, but you are made of the stuff of hangmen.'

'For that reason, on my own responsibility, and without demanding to receive the Order of Vasa,[9] or any thanks, I have hit on a new source of sustenance which can replace the old one for, even if the Baltic herring shoals again in thirty years' time when the population of the archipelago has emigrated, this branch of the industry is threatened by a competitor who has risen up more deadly than ever after his hundred years' rest. Did you know that the herring will come back to Bohuslän[10] this autumn?'

'No, I've had no letters from it for ages.'

'All the same it will. Consequently we must stop fishing herring and fish salmon instead.'

'Salmon! In deep water?'

'Yes, it must be there, though I haven't seen it yet. You've got to find it.'

'But what if it isn't there?'

'I'm telling you, aren't I, that it is there. You shall catch the first one. Then the salmon-fishing season will open.'

'But how do you know there is salmon when you haven't seen it?' objected the girl.

'By a large number of investigations which are too extensive to be dealt with conversationally, some of them carried out at sea . . .'

'Only once!'

'Thanks to my unusual intelligence I work with the speed of twenty men, partly on my sofa, but mostly with books. But enough of this. Will you join me in subverting the population first with salmon, and later with the Mission-Board chapel that you have forgotten?'

'You are a demon, a devil,' cried the girl, half-joking, half in earnest.

The inspector, whose sceptical attitude was the result of a whim, now saw that it was most effective, and decided to adhere to the role.

'You surely don't believe in God?' asked the girl, with an expression which suggested that she would despise him forever if he assented.

'No, I don't.'

'And you want to be an Ansgar[11] and introduce Christianity into the island?'

'And salmon. Yes, I want to be a demonic Ansgar. But will you also lay the salmon lines and thus be blessed by the Parliamentary Auditor?'

'Yes, I will work for these people in whom I believe. I shall devote my feeble efforts to the oppressed, and I shall show you that you are a blasé effete scoffer. No, in fact you are not. You make yourself out to be worse than you are, for you are really a good child. I saw that on Sunday . . .'

She uttered the words 'good child' seemingly having calculated for certain that he would rise to the bait and place himself under her like a child, good or bad. But he had already tasted the pleasure of playing the superior and more interesting demon, so he continued with this more grateful task. Of course he knew from experience that the easiest way of ingratiating oneself with a woman was to let her play the mother, with all a mother's freedom for intimacies. But this was such a threadbare game, and might so easily lead to ineradicable bullying on her part. Better to give her the more grateful role of a female redeemer, which did not imply absolute superiority, but only gave her the Madonna's task of intermediary, thus putting her in the position of arbiter between two equally strong powers.

But the transition was not easy to find, and in a fit of boredom with the whole game, which was nevertheless essential if he wanted to reach his desired objective, he pretended that he must go to see if the boat was properly moored, as the wind was getting up.

When he reached the shore he heaved a sigh, as if he had been making an effort beyond his strength. He unbuttoned his waistcoat which felt like an iron corselet, cooled his head, and cast a longing glance upon the open water. Now he would have given much to be alone, to shake off the chaff that had fallen upon his soul during his contact with a lower intelligence. At that moment he hated her, wanted to be quit of her, to possess himself again, but it was too late! The spider's web had fastened on his face, soft as silk, sticky, invisible and impossible to remove. At the same time when he turned, and saw her peeling a chestnut with her long fingers and sharp teeth and was reminded of a mandrill he had seen in a menagerie, he was seized by infinite compassion, a whiff of the melancholy that the fortunate experience when they encounter the unfortunate. He thought then of her delight at seeing him as a Hottentot, grew angry again, restrained himself and, with all the self-control of a man of the world, went towards her and, in order to be the first to speak the palliative word, reminded her that they must embark as the wind was increasing. Meanwhile, she had noticed the expression of weariness and abstraction that had remained on his face, and with an astuteness that for the moment totally cooled his feeling, she replied:

'You are tired of my company. Let us go.' But when he did

not reply with a compliment she resumed with an emotion which it was difficult to assess as genuine or assumed:

'Forgive me for being horrid. But I've become like that, and I'm ungrateful. That's how it is!'

She dried her eyes, and with the habitual care of a housewife, began to gather up the dirty dishes.

And now, as she stooped over the remains and the greasy plates with a napkin tied round her waist as an apron, and carried the china down to the beach to rinse it, he hurried forward to relieve her of her burden, driven by an irresistible desire to avoid seeing her in the guise of a servant. It caused him a pang to be waited upon by one whom he wanted to raise high above himself while at the same time she would look up to him as the person who had given her power over him.

During the mock-struggle that ensued over who should serve the other, the girl dropped the china. She gave a cry but, after surveying the broken pieces, her face cleared.

'What luck that it was all old! Goodness how scared I was.'

He immediately suppressed his niggling regrets at his loss by aligning himself with her as the person struck by misfortune. And, happy to bring to a boisterous end the conflicting emotions that were tearing him apart, he threw ducks and drakes into the bay with the fragments and rounded off the critical situation with a joke:

'Well, Miss Maria, now we shan't have to wash up.'

Whereupon he offered her his hand to help her into the boat which was already tugging at the painter in the increasing surge of the waves.

VII

On a summer morning of cloudless sunshine the inspector sat with his pupil in the wooden pavilion he had caused to be erected on the highest ridge of the island, close beside the newly laid stone foundations of the chapel. Down in the harbour a schooner was unloading the previously prepared parts of the building, which were then carried up to their destination and assembled by the foreman and his labourers. Consequently there had been an unusual amount of life on the island for some time, and a number of skirmishes between the fisher-folk and the urban workers had already taken place. The former had been subjected to bullying by the latter, and this had led to a number of reconciliation parties, with more drunkenness, fighting and attacks on decency and property. For a moment the inspector and the widow lady had come to regret that they had undertaken to civilise the population, since the results of their first steps appeared to be so lamentable. Moreover, disturbances at night, singing, shouting and complaints had interfered with any kind of work, and with the rest of those who had come there solely for peace and quiet. The inspector, who had forfeited all esteem because of his one failure to assert his authority, had been unable to restore the peace; Miss Maria, on the other hand, had been more successful and, by a brisk manner and occasional kindly word, had known how to quell the storm. As she refused to attribute this to her beauty and her charming ways she had given herself credit for more strength and understanding than she possessed, and had so entered into her part of a person with unusual mental ability that even now, in the position of a pupil with her teacher, she received his learned words as if they were well-known facts, and with remarks that were more sarcastic than sagacious, and seemed to be correcting and exposing rather than absorbing.

Her mother, who was sitting beside them embroidering an altar-cloth for the pulpit of the chapel, seemed now and then to be astonished by her daughter's penetrating understanding, when suddenly the latter, with a foolish question, had rendered her master speechless.

'You see, Miss Maria,' lectured the inspector, still deluding himself with the hope that he could educate her, 'the untrained eye has a tendency to see everything simply, the untrained ear to hear simply. You see about you only grey granite; the painter and the poet do the same. That is why they paint and describe so monotonously, and why they find the archipelago so dull. Nevertheless, look at the geological map of the region and then cast your eye over the landscape. We are sitting in the region of red gneiss. Look at this splinter that you call "granite", what a richly varied fusion it is of black mica, white quartz, and rosy-red feldspar.'

He had taken his sample from the piled-up stones that the men laying the foundations had blasted from the rock and put together to form the foot of the building.

'As you see, here is another. This is what is called eurite. See its delicate changes of colour from salmon-red inside to flint-blue. And here is white marble, or primaeval limestone.'

'Is there marble here?' asked the girl who, at the thought of this luxurious stone had brightened up.

'Yes, there is marble, though on the surface it looks grey without being grey. Also, if you examine them more carefully, you will see what an infinite richness of colour there is in these lichen. What a scale of the most delicate colours, from the Indian-ink black of the ramaline lichen through the ash-grey of the crottle, the leather-brown of the ground liverwort, the Scheele's green of the parmelia lichen, the spotted copper-green of the lungwort, to the egg-yellow of the wall-moss.

'And then look more carefully at the skerries, lit up now by sunshine and you will notice that the rocky islets have different colours, and that the inhabitants, who are used to observing things, have named them after these colours, which they knew without being aware of it. Don't you see that Black Rock is blacker than the others because it consists of hornblende, and that Red Rock is red because it is made of red gneiss, while the White Skerries are eurite, washed clean? Is it not more to know why than just to know? And is it not less to see nothing but an even greyness, like the artists, who paint all the islands with a blend of black and white? Listen now to the "roaring" of the waves, as the poets summarily call this symphony of sound. Shut your eyes for a moment and you will hear better while I analyse this harmony in single notes. You will first hear a roar, such as one hears in an engine-room or a big city. That is the great masses of water beating on themselves. Next you hear a hissing sound and that is the lighter, lesser units of water being whipped to scum. After that comes a scraping, like that of a knife against a grindstone. That is the wave grating against the sand, and then a rattling like someone emptying a cartload of gravel, and that is the waves tearing up the small stones. This is followed by a dull thud such as you hear when you hit your ear with a cupped hand. That is the wave pressing the air ahead of it into a cavity. Finally comes a rumbling as of distant thunder, and that is the great blocks of rock being rolled about on the stony bottom.'

'Yes, but you are spoiling nature for yourself,' cried the girl.

'It puts me on intimate terms with nature. It soothes me to know that I have thereby freed myself from the poet's half-concealed dread of the unknown, which is nothing more than a recollection from the savage's poetic age, when man sought for explanations, but could not readily find them and, in his need, resorted to stories of mermaids and giants. But now we must come back to the fishing which has got to be revived. We'll leave the salmon for the moment and first devise new ways of catching the Baltic herring. In two months the great fishing season will open and, if I am not wrong in my calculations, it will be a failure this autumn.'

'How can you foretell such a thing from your sofa?' asked the girl with more sarcasm than sagacity.

'I can foretell it on the grounds that I have seen – from my sofa – how this spring the drift-ice has scraped the bottom clean of kelp and other algae in which the herring spawn. I can foretell it on the scientific grounds that the small crustaceans – no matter what sort – upon which the herrings live, no longer inhabit the shallows now that the kelp has been scraped away. What can we do? To begin with we can try fishing in deep water. If the fish will not come to me I must go to the fish. We must therefore try with drift-nets, that float behind a drifter. It's simple.'

'It's splendid!' exclaimed Miss Maria.

'It's old,' objected the inspector, 'and it's not my invention. But now, like wise people, we must also think of our retreat for, even if we do catch herring, we may not get a price for it, as the West Coast is also catching herring. We must have something else in reserve.'

'And that is the salmon.'

'Yes, the salmon, which must be here though I have not seen it.'

'We got as far as that just now. This time I want to hear how you can be so certain.'

'I'll make short work of it and, in a few words, tell you the reason for my certainty. Like other birds of passage the salmon migrates.'

'Is the salmon a bird?'

'Certainly, a real bird of passage. He is found off the rivers of Norrland, has been found a couple of times in nets in the northern archipelago, is fished off Gotland and the whole way south, so he must pass this way. It will be your business to find him with a drifting long-line. Would you like to be my assistant, and have the pleasure of a fee?'

The last words were intentionally brisk, but did not fail to take effect.

'Mama, I'm going to earn money,' cried Miss Maria in a bantering tone, which was intended to conceal her real delight. But then added: 'What do you intend to do?'

'I shall lie on my sofa and I shall spoil nature for you.'

'What is that you're going to do?' asked the mother, who thought she had not heard aright.

'I'm going to make an Italian landscape for Miss Maria,' answered the inspector. 'And now, ladies, I'll leave you while I sketch it out.'

'What a strange person,' said the mother when the inspector had departed.

'An unusual person at least, and I shall never believe he's quite sane. All the same he seems to be a man of high principle, and on the whole well-meaning. What do you think of him?'

'Give me my wool, child,' answered the old lady.

'No, but say something, say whether you like him or not,' reiterated the girl.

Her mother only replied with a half-sorrowful, half-resigned expression which seemed to say: 'I don't really know.'

. . .

Meanwhile the inspector had gone down to the harbour and taken his boat to row out to the skerries. Summer warmth had prevailed out here for a month, so that the air was hot. But drift-ice was still coming from the north, where an unusually severe winter on the coast had resulted in the formation of bottom-ice, which, drifting south, had so chilled the water that the lower layers of air were denser than those above. Consequently refraction had distorted the contours of the skerries and, during the last few days, had produced the most magnificent mirages. These spectacles had given rise to lengthy disputes between the inspector and the ladies, and the fisher-folk had been called in as arbiters, they being more competent to judge as they had witnessed these natural phenomena since childhood. On one morning, when refraction had increased the height of the pink-gneiss skerries, and the different densities of the air had made them look like the steep, stratified cliffs of Normandy, Miss Maria had maintained that they really were these limestone cliffs which, by a still unexplained natural law, were now being reflected up here in the Baltic. At the same time the white surf of the waves among the stones of the shore had been enlarged and multiplied by refraction, so that it looked as if a flotilla of Normandy fishing-boats was beating up under the cliffs. The inspector tried, but in vain, to give the only correct explanation, and thereby eliminate the supernatural, especially as the populace wanted to see in the phenomenon prophecies of forthcoming misfortunes and this belief in an unlucky future might paralyse their will to act. Thus he found himself in the position of having first to appear as a magician in order to gain a hearing, while intending later to remove the magic element by telling them how he had achieved his wizardry.

He therefore asked the credulous if they would believe that they were seeing a reflection of Italy if they saw an Italian landscape, and when the answer was yes, he determined to combine the useful with the entertaining. By making a few minor alterations he would produce the promised southern landscape for Miss Maria's birthday, so that when the next mirage occurred this, seen through the colossal magnifying-glass provided by the varying density of the layers of air, would appear on the horizon greatly enlarged.

Sitting in his boat he studied Svärdholm with his diopter, the lenses of which he had considerably strengthened. The first thing would be to produce the most characteristic feature of the formation, i.e. to make the stratified rocks stand out, and this, to some extent, nature had already done. In addition he needed a stone-pine, a cypress, a marble palace and a terrace with espalier oranges.

After he had observed and drawn the contours of the skerry his plan was laid, and he soon landed from his boat, into which he had stowed an iron crowbar, a ship's-scraper, a roll of zinc wire, a bucket of yellow ochre and a large tar-brush, together with an axe, a saw, nails and a supply of dynamite cartridges.

When he had landed and unpacked his equipment he felt like a Robinson Crusoe having a set-to with nature, but keener and more confident of victory, since he had with him all the aids of civilisation. After he had erected a plane-table on a tripod, and placed a sight-rule upon it, he set to work.

From the ridge of rock, whose steep layers were so fortunately reminiscent of the stratified sedimentary rocks of the south, all he had to do was to scrape away the lichen, when there was any, leaving a few horizontal lines darker than the strata. It was not hard work as the ship's-scraper travelled over the smooth surface like a retouching-brush over a scene-painter's large canvas.

Sometimes he felt disgusted with himself for wasting his time and energy on childishness, but physical exertion drove the blood to his head and small things looked large. He felt like a Titan[1] storming creation, correcting its originator's blunders, twisting the earth's axis so that the south turned a few degrees northwards. When he had put streaks on the surface of the rock for a few metres – all that was necessary, as it would be made to look many times larger by the layers of air – he set to work to make a stone-pine. On the crest of the ridge stood a group of medium-high pine trees, which together normally appeared in a mirage like the edge of a forest. It was merely a question of felling half a dozen of them in order to isolate the best one, which would then be silhouetted against the sky.

Sawing off those that were superflous took half an hour. The remaining one was a slender tree whose growth was concentrated in its crown simply because the others had stood so close to it that no branches had been able to develop on the trunk. But now, in order to bring out the characteristic umbrella shape with its ribs, he had to thin out the crown with his axe. It was soon done, but when he viewed his creation with his diopter, he saw that the shape was still not perfect but that he would have to train some of the top branches upwards with his zinc wire, and the lower branches somewhat downwards and outwards. When he had finished the stone-pine he drank a glass of wine and looked round for material for the cypresses. This soon presented itself in the form of a couple of conical junipers. It was only a question of choosing those that stood out against the sky and trimming them with his axe and knife. But as they were still too light in colour he took a bucket of water in which he had dissolved some lamp-black and sprinkled them with it to make them the right graveyard colour.

When he regarded the results of his handiwork he grew horribly uneasy and remembered the gloomy story of the girl who trampled on the loaf of bread,[2] and when the white gulls emitted fearful screeches over his head he thought of the two black ravens who came from the sky to fetch souls to hell.[3]

After he had sat for a while and the blood had returned to his head he smiled at his handiwork and his childish fears. If nature had not gone to work quite as rapidly when originating the various species, it was not from lack of will, but only from lack of ability.

It was now a question of the marble palace, but as everything had developed from it and he had worked out the whole plan at home on his sofa, this part of his task was not much more difficult than the rest.

The limestone layer was perfectly vertical and ready to form a façade, certainly one of only a few square metres, but no more was necessary. All he needed to do was to loosen the slabs of eurite which were already crumbling from the limestone as a result of weathering. At first the crowbar proved sufficient, but at the base he had to insert a dynamite cartridge in the crack.

When the report came and the splinters rained down he experienced something of the poet's longing to hurl the ammunition wagons of the standing armies into a volcano, and rid mankind of the tribulations of existence and the troubles of development.

But now the slabs of marble were revealed, and the crystals of the granulated limestone were sparkling like loaf sugar in the sunshine. With his paint pot he then picked out a rusticated socle, and drew two small square windows. On the rocky ledge above he drove in two poles and bound a third across them so that the whole formed a pergola. After this all he had to do was to lift up the fathom-long runners of the bearberry and plait them round the poles. His vines were now in place, hanging down in festoons.

Finally he touched up the whole area with a tin of hydrochloric acid diluted with an equal part of water and thus he obtained a gleaming shade of white among the green grass. This produced an effect of bellis, or galanthus, so characteristic of the Roman Campagna[4] in its 'second spring', which occurs in October after the end of the grape harvest.

And now his work was at an end.

But it had lasted until evening. In order that the marvel should produce the required effect it remained to foretell when it would take place, preferably the exact day. He knew that great heat was prevailing in southern Europe, and consequently that it would not be long before there was a northerly wind. It had been in the east for some time because the barometer pressure over the North Sea was low. According to reports the drift-ice lay off Arholma,[5] and as soon as the wind veered some degrees north the drift-ice would have to follow the channel that runs west of the Åland Islands where the Gulf of Bothnia empties into the Baltic. If he could only get a north wind one evening he was sure it would last for a couple of days. A north wind was always accompanied by a clear atmosphere, so he would be able to forecast the appearance of the phenomenon at least one day in advance. If he could get thus far, it would be a minor matter to foretell the hour, for mirages only appear a few hours after sunrise, usually between ten and twelve o'clock.

When he entered his room he locked the door in order to be able to get on with his work, his great work, which he had planned ten years ago and intended to finish by the time he was fifty. This objective kept him alive, but he carried it about with him as his secret. He rejoiced in the thought of possessing himself for a few hours. In the weeks that had passed since the ladies arrived he had been occupied every evening in keeping them company, and what should have been a relaxation and a pleasure had become a duty and a labour. He loved the young girl and wanted to live with her in marriage, in a perfect union, where leisure moments of confidences and rest were improvised. But this half-and-half state of affairs, in which he had to present himself at stated times and converse, whether he was in the mood for it or not, tormented him like an official duty. She had fastened on to him and never tired of taking from him, particularly as he was able to be forever new and entertaining. But he, who never received anything from her, found in the long run that he needed to renew himself. Yet when he drew back she became uneasy and nervous, and plagued him by asking whether she was being too importunate, to which, as a well-brought-up man, he could not answer yes.

He now opened his manuscript cupboard in which his cartons of notes were ranged. These were spontaneous thoughts on his observations, written on small slips and pasted on half-sheets of paper as in a herbarium. It amused him to rearrange these time after time according to new principles, in order to discover if actual phenomena could be arranged in as many ways as the brain desired, or if they could only be arranged on the principles of classification ordained by nature, if indeed nature had been bound by any fixed law. This occupation awakened in him the feeling that he was the true regulator of chaos, who separated light from darkness, and that chaos would only cease with the arrival of the discriminating organ of consciousness, since light and darkness were not as yet separated. This thought intoxicated him. He felt his ego expand, his brain-cells increase, break through their shells, multiply and form new types of ideas which would one day go forth as thoughts. These would fall into other brain-pans like yeast and, if not before his death then after it, would cause millions to become the forcing-beds for the seeds of his thoughts.

There came a knock at the door and, in an agitated voice like that of a man disturbed at a clandestine meeting, he asked who was there.

It was a message from the ladies asking if the inspector would come down.

He replied by saying that unless his presence was required for some urgent reason, he had not time that evening as he had to work.

After this there was silence for a time. As he thought he knew for certain what would follow he abandoned his interrupted work, and put away his manuscripts. He had just finished doing this when he heard the footsteps of the widow lady on the stairs. Instead of waiting for her knock he opened the door and greeted her with a question: 'Miss Maria is ill, isn't she?'

The mother recoiled, but soon recovered herself and asked the 'doctor' to come down and look at her as it was impossible to get a physician.

The inspector was not a medical man, but he had read through the elements of pathology and therapeutics, and had observed himself and all the sick people who had come within his orbit. He had also philosophised over the nature of diseases and their remedies, and finally drawn up a system of therapy which he used on himself. After he had heard that the girl was suffering from convulsions he promised to come in half an hour, bringing with him medicines.

In fact it had not been difficult for him to guess the nature of her complaint. There had been no mention of illness in the first message. It must therefore have occurred between the two messages and been a result of his refusal to come. That is to say, it was a psychological ailment which he easily recognised, and which went under the still indeterminate name of 'hysteria'. A little pressure on the will, a thwarted plan, would be immediately followed by general depression, during which the soul tried to assign the pain to some part of the body without being able to localise it. In pharmacodynamics he had often seen beside the name of a remedy and its effect, a cautionary note stating 'in a way as yet not understood', or 'action not completely known'. From this he had come to the conclusion by observation and speculation that, because of the unity of spirit and matter, a remedy might have both a chemical and psychical effect simultaneously. A more recent medical theory had eliminated the medical remedies, that is to say the material foundations, and adopted either hypnotism – a purely psychic remedy – or the commonplace and often harmful mechanical method of diet and physical exercise. He saw these exaggerated methods as necessary and beneficial transitory stages, irrespective of the fact that they had claimed their victims, as in the case of a nervous person who had been further irritated by cold water instead of being soothed by warm baths, or a weak subject who had been worn out by strenuous walks in raw air.

He believed he had discovered that the old remedies could be used to produce what is popularly known as 'material for object lessons', as they could rouse and alter moods. And just as a certain group of astringents could really effect a contraction of the stomach, so these could induce a concentration of the dispersed powers of the soul, something the debilitated drinker is aware of when in the morning he winds up his run-down mechanism with bitters.

This woman felt physically ill without actually being so. He therefore prepared a series of medicines, the first of which would produce real bodily discomfort, whereupon the patient would be obliged to discard her spiritual ailment and assign her illness to some part of her body. To this end he took from his medicine-chest the most disgusting of all drugs, asafoetida – the best thing for inducing a state of general indisposition – and measured out such a large dose of it that it would bring on real convulsions. Then her whole body and her senses of smell and taste would rise up in revolt against this foreign substance, and all the functions of her spirit would be directed toward eliminating it. Thus her imaginary sufferings would be forgotten and all that remained would be to bring about, step by step, transitions from one disgusting sensation through a progression of weaker ones to final relief from the last stage by means of a rising scale of cooling, palliating, mellowing and soothing remedies. These would restore a complete sense of well-being as after trials and dangers now past, which are sweet to remember.

After having attired himself in a cashmere jacket and knotted a cream-coloured neckcloth, faintly striped with amethyst, he put on his bracelet – the first time he had done so since the arrival of the ladies. Why he did all this he could not say, but he did it under the influence of a self-induced mood picked up from the sick-bed he was about to visit. When he looked at himself in the glass without observing his face, he noticed that his appearance struck a mildly sympathetic but unusual note, which would draw attention to himself without agitating a nervous person.

He then collected his properties like a conjurer who is going to perform in public, and set off for the sick-bed.

When he had been led into the room he saw the girl lying on a sofa attired in a Persian dressing-gown, and with her hair hanging down her back. Her eyes were unnaturally large and she stared disdainfully at the intruder. For a few moments the inspector felt embarrassed, but only temporarily, after which he advanced and took her hand.

'How are you, Miss Maria?' he asked kindly.

Her glance became keener, as if she wanted to see through him, but she did not answer.

He pulled out his watch to take her pulse, and said: 'You have a temperature.'

This was a lie, but he had to win her confidence, as that was part of the cure.

The expression on the girl's face changed immediately.

'I should just think so. I feel as if I were on fire.'

She had been allowed to complain. Her antagonism towards the intruder had evaporated, and contact had been made.

'If you promise to obey my instructions I will cure you,' the inspector went on as he put his hand on her forehead.

At the word 'obey' he felt the patient start, as if she had no intention of obeying, but at that moment the bracelet fell down from beneath his cuff, and the opposition of the hypochondriac ceased.

'Do what you like with me,' she said submissively, her eyes fixed on the gold bracelet which fascinated her, and aroused in her fears of the unknown.

'I am not a physician by profession as you know, but I have studied the art, and I know what is necessary in the present circumstances. Here is a drug which is very unpleasant to take, but which is infallible. I'm no mystery-monger, and I shall tell you what I'm letting you in for. This is a resinous gum (asafoetida), prepared from a perennial herb that grows in Arabia Petraea.'[6]

At the word 'Arabia' the girl became very attentive, for it probably awakened the thoughts of perfumes which could not smother Lady Macbeth's stinking crime.

She therefore took the spoon and sniffed its contents, but immediately threw back her head crying:

'I can't!'

He put his arm firmly but kindly round her neck, held out the spoon, and coaxed:

'Come now, show me that you are a good child.' Whereupon he poured the drug into her and met with no resistance.

She fell back on to the sofa cushions, her body writhing from the pain of the repulsive sensations produced by the garlic-smelling drug, her face full of dread, as if all that was disgusting in this world were heaped upon her. In a pleading voice she begged for water to relieve her nausea.

This she was not allowed, but was made to lie down and surrender herself unconditionally to the unpleasant effects of the medicine.

When he saw that she was disintegrating with loathing he took out drug number two.

'Now, Miss Maria, your desert journey in Arabia Petraea is over. You shall climb the Alps, and drink the mountain air, concentrated in the bitter root of the brave gentian, golden as the sun,' said the inspector, in an encouraging, resolute voice.

The girl accepted the bitter drug passively, but fell back as if someone had plunged a knife into her.

However, she very soon sat up, as if her scattered strength had been jerked together and her energy restored. The violent medicine had eliminated the disgusting taste of the previous one, but its acerbity had irritated the membrane of the stomach and quickened her pulse.

'Now we will smother the fire with blankets,' the inspector continued. 'And we will go to the sea-shores of Brittany, and gather balsam from the mellow Carrageen alga.[7] Can't you feel how softly and protectively the mucilage spreads over the irritated walls of your stomach, and can't you smell the salts of the sea?'

A quiet peace spread over the patient's agitated face and, as her physician now believed that she was strong enough to listen to what he said, he began to reminisce about the coast of Brittany, about sailing in the Atlantic, about his life with the fishermen of Quimper and about hunting sea-birds in Sarzeau.

She followed what he was saying but still seemed rather exhausted, so he broke off and gave her what he called a 'symphony', which reproduced in words the classical meadow rue, known as a wine spice by the bridal parties of the Middle Ages, the heavenly angelica, the homely smelling spearmint, adding a little touch of the blessed thistle[8] to keep up her spirits, and a drop of juniper oil to remind her of the forest.

He massaged her as it were with moods, jerked her from her sickly thoughts by letting her journey in imagination from place to place, travel through the Old and New Worlds, have visions of all manner of scenery, all races of men and all climates. When she seemed to tire he gave her a spoonful of lemon juice with a little sugar which cooled and soothed her after the frightful half-hour through which she had passed. She accepted this simple form of refreshment as a great pleasure, and it induced her to smile.

'Turn to the wall now and pretend to sleep for five minutes,' directed the inspector, 'while I go out and talk to your mother.'

The inspector felt that his strength was waning, and that he must get out into the fresh air to recover. And he only needed to glance at the dusky night sky, the steel-blue sea, close his eyes and think of nothing, to feel his disordered brain straightening out again to continue on its painful growth forwards, after having been wound backwards for a stretch.

But as he stood half-asleep with his arms folded on his chest he heard a thought humming in one ear: a child of thirty-four!

And so he awoke, and returned to the cottage.

Miss Maria was sitting on the sofa with her long hair falling coquettishly round her, but otherwise looking completely well and cheerful.

The inspector now took from his basket a bottle of Syracuse and a packet of cigarettes.

'Now you must pretend to be well,' he said, 'and that we have met after a long journey. Then we will drink a glass of sweet Sicilian wine and smoke a cigarette, for that is part of the cure.'

The girl seemed to be trying to suppress some secret suffering, but drank, with her eyes fixed on his bracelet all the time.

'You are looking at my bracelet,' said the inspector, breaking the silence.

'No, I'm not,' contradicted the girl.

'It was given to me by a woman, who is of course dead, since I have not given it back.'

'Have you loved anyone, you?' asked the girl with great scepticism.

'Yes, but with my eyes open. As it is considered praiseworthy to use one's reason, why should one abandon it when intending to take one of the most important steps of one's life?'

'Oh indeed, so you think love should be calculating?'

'Strongly, unbelievably calculating when it is a case of releasing one of the most primitive impulses.'

'Impulses?'

'Yes, impulses.'

'You don't believe in love?'

'You present me with questions to which there are no answers. Believe in love in general? What do you mean by that? There are many kinds of love which are as opposite as black and white. I can't believe in both at once, all at once.'

'And the highest sort?'

'The intellectual, on three floors like the English house. On the top the study, under it the bedroom, and on the ground-floor the kitchen.'

'How practical! But love, great love is not calculating. What I picture to myself as the highest love is a storm, a thunderclap, a waterfall.'

'Like a crude, uncontrollable natural force? That is how it manifests itself among the animals and the lower forms of human beings.'

'Lower? Are not all human beings alike?'

'Why yes! All human beings are as like as two berries; youths and old men, men and women, Hottentots and Frenchmen. Of course they are alike. Only look at the two of us. Exactly the same, only my beard to distinguish us. Forgive me, dear lady. I can see that you've recovered, and I will leave you. Sleep well.'

He had risen and picked up his hat, but the next moment the girl was standing beside him, with both his hands clutched between hers, and with the expression on her face that had first captivated him she begged: 'No, stay!'

He imagined that what he experienced under her burning gaze and from the pressure of her hands must be something like what a young girl feels when attacked by a fiery seducer. He became confused, and there arose in him a feeling of insulted modesty and wounded masculinity. He disengaged his hands, drew back, and said in a calm voice, sharp with an assumed coldness:

'Control yourself.'

'Stay, or I shall come to you in your room,' was the girl's impassioned answer, which seemed to signify a threat against which there was no appeal.

'In that case I shall lock my door.'

'What are you? A man?' came her ringing challenge, with a hard laugh.

'Yes, and in such high measure that I must be both the chooser and the attacker. I don't like being seduced.'

Whereupon he departed and heard behind him the noise of a human body falling to the ground and striking against furniture.

When he got outside he was about to turn back. As a result of his mental exertions he was in a weak condition, which made him very susceptible to the sufferings of others. But when he had been alone for some seconds and had had time to collect himself, his strength returned, and he felt determined to break off a relationship which threatened to encroach upon the whole of his intellectual life. He would cut adrift from this affair with a woman who had clearly shown that she only desired his body while spitting on his soul, the very thing he wanted to pour into this lifeless image of flesh. She rejoiced in the sound of his voice, but his thoughts she would not receive unless they could be of direct use. He had often caught her regarding the contours of his figure and sometimes, absent-mindedly, she had seized hold of his upper arm, whose swelling muscles bulged under the soft cloth. He now remembered the many times she had challenged him, about bathing, about sailing, about ascending the look-out – to which he never went as it upset his nervous system to stand on a height without sufficient support. And now this evening, after seeing this eruption of uncontrolled hysteria, he realised with dread that this woman was not a civilised being who could individualise her love upon a particular person, but that for her his role was merely the general one of the indispensable sexual opposite.

He had wandered down to the shore to cool himself, but the night was warm. The sea had come to a standstill, the north-west sky was a pale-melon colour, while across the water in the east, the night lay at rest. The rocks by the shore were still warm, and he sat down on one of the many easy-chairs that the frost had blasted and the waves worn smooth.

The recent happenings receded from him and now, in a calm frame of mind, he saw matters in a new light. This was what his dream had always been, that he would awaken such love in a woman that she would come begging, grovelling to him saying: 'I love you, condescend to love me.' That was nature's way; the weaker approached the stronger in a humble spirit and not the reverse. The opposite was still the case with those who lived on vestiges of superstitious conceptions of the mystical superiority of women, even though research had shown that the mystical was only disorder, and the superiority a poetical anthology of the concentrated demands of male appetites.

Now she had come in the way he had dreamed she would. This woman, emancipated from prejudice by a new era, had exposed the whole depths of her glowing nature, and he had drawn back. Why? Perhaps the dictates of usage and habit still ruled him. For there was nothing immodest about her outburst, not a trace of the whore who offers herself for sale, not an indecorous gesture or an impertinent glance. She loved him in her way. What more could he ask? And with a love like that he could safely form an attachment, for perhaps not many men could boast of lighting such a flame. But he felt no pride in having won her, for he knew his own value. Rather he experienced a sense of crushing responsibility, of which he wanted to rid himself. Consequently he must depart.

Sitting there he began in his mind to pack up his belongings. He took the things from his desk and saw the empty green cloth; he removed the lamp that had spread light in the evenings and glittering colour by day. Emptiness again. He denuded the walls of their pictures and hangings, and the dismal white mathematical figures reappeared. He lifted down the books from their shelves and horrible desolation leered at him – monotony, nakedness, poverty!

Then came weariness from his bodily exertions; travel nerves with their paralysing effects; fear of the unknown, into which he would now be thrown; regrets for the habitual, and for her company. He saw the young girl in all her childishness and her majestic beauty; heard her lament, saw her pale cheeks, which another would make rosy again in the course of time.

Thus he endured all the miseries of parting for a whole fifteen minutes, which seemed to him as long as hours, when suddenly, in the half-light of the summer night, he saw the figure of a woman on the hill-top, silhouetted against the bright sky. The heavenly contours he knew so well assumed nobler proportions against the clouds now pale yellow which could equally well mean the end of sunset or the beginning of sunrise. She seemed to have come from the customs house, and to be seeking someone or something. Bare-headed, her hair still hanging over her shoulders and casting her head this way and that as she searched, she seemed suddenly to have found what she was looking for and, with hurried steps, rushed down to the shore where the object of her search was sitting, immovable, without the power to flee, without the will to make his presence known. When she reached him she sank down, laid her head on his knee, and speaking wildly, timidly, beseechingly, as if annihilated by shame, she sobbed out:

'Don't leave me. Despise me but have mercy. Love me, love me, or I will go to a place from which I shall never return.'

Now there awoke in him all his manhood's tremendous longing for love. But when he saw this woman at his feet he was also stirred by man's hereditary chivalry, which makes him want to see his mate as a queen, not as a slave, and he rose, lifted her up and, putting his arm round her waist, he pressed her to him.

'By my side, Maria, not at my feet,' he said. 'You love me because you know I love you and now you are mine for life. And you will never escape me alive, my love, for our whole long life. And now I will set you on my throne, and I will give you power over me and mine, my name, my possessions, my honour and my deeds. But if you forget that it is I who gave you the power, and if you misuse it or hand it over to another I will cast you down as I would a tyrant, and so deep that you will never see the sunshine again. But you can't, for you love me, don't you? You love me?'

He seated her in his rock-chair, knelt down and laid his head in her lap.

'I lay my head on your knees,' he continued. 'But don't cut my hair as I sleep on your breast.[9] Let me raise you up, but don't drag me down. Become better than I am for you can when I guard you from contact with the filth and misery of the world, which I must face. Ennoble yourself with the great qualities that I lack, and together we shall become a perfect whole.'

His feelings had begun to take on the cool colour of thought, and he seemed to want to quench her exaltation. But she interrupted him by laying her glowing cheek against his, and when he did not respond to her caress, she pressed a burning kiss on his mouth.

'You child,' she said. 'Do you not dare to kiss me when there is no one to see?'

Then he sprang up, seized her neck and kissed her throat many times, until she released herself with a laugh and stood erect before him.

'You are a real little savage,' she scolded.

'The savage is there, beware,' he answered, putting his arm round her waist, and walking forwards with her on the warm sand that whispered about their feet.

Now that the air had cooled and the dew was falling, the lighthouse began to flash in the distance. Out from the reef the call of the seals sounded like the cries of the shipwrecked.

They walked on for an hour or more, and they talked about their first meeting, and now and then about their secret thoughts. They talked about the future, about the coming winter, about foreign travel, and in time they reached the point where a cross had been erected on a cairn in memory of those drowned in a shipwreck.

Suddenly they caught a glimpse of two shadows that sneaked away and disappeared.

'That was Vestman and his sister-in-law,' said Borg. 'Shame! If I were her husband I should drown her.'

'Not him?' the girl burst out, more sharply than she intended.

'He is not married,' answered Borg curtly. 'That is the difference.'

Silence fell, unpleasantly, so that they began to search for topics of conversation. And meanwhile their thoughts, no longer spellbound, began to whisper, and he already yearned for the enchantment, the intoxication that blinded, that changed grey to rosy red, that built pedestals, that painted golden rims on cracked porcelain.

At the rock wall they turned to make their way back. The wind that had slept began to blow against them, and in his depressed state the awakened lover could feel that it blew cold. It was the north wind that he had expected and which he greeted as a deliverer. For in the second during which the girl's contradiction on a vital matter had caused something in him to snap – and he had realised that, unless he abandoned resistance and surrendered completely, her personality could only be soldered to his, not fused – he seized the opportunity to rise again, without trampling on her.

'Why do the people hate me?' he asked abruptly.

'Because you are their superior,' the girl let slip without realising the confession she had made.

'I don't believe that,' he answered, 'for they have not wits enough to appreciate my superiority.'

'Their hatred may have distorted their vision.'

'Excellently answered. But if they were to behold a miracle their eyes might be opened.'

'Perhaps, if the miracle awoke fear.'

'Well then, they shall have a miracle. Tomorrow, at ten o'clock, it will happen.'

'What?'

'What I promised you.'

The girl looked at his face with amazement, as if she did not believe what he said. Then she objected with a laugh:

'But what if it's cloudy?'

'It won't be,' answered the inspector with assurance. 'Meanwhile, as we have got as far as talking about the weather, we might as well think what your lady mother is going to say about this.'

'She won't interfere,' the girl answered promptly.

'Surprising if a mother does not attach importance to what kind of man it is that her daughter is going to bind herself to, and whose name she is going to bear. Can she be indifferent?'

'Goodnight, now,' interrupted Miss Maria, and held up her mouth for a kiss. 'Early tomorrow you will pay us a visit, won't you?'

'I certainly shall,' he answered. 'Be sure of that, be quite sure.'

And she departed.

But he remained standing where he was, watching her slender figure rise against the now sulphur-yellow clouds as she climbed the hill. When she had reached the top she turned and threw him a kiss, and then she seemed to sink behind the slope until he saw only her head and her long hair fluttering in the north wind.

VIII

Next morning, when the inspector sat with his fiancée at the coffee-table, after having been received without any ado as a son-in-law, he again became aware of complicated emotions. He felt great peace at having been accepted into a small circle bound together by common interests and absolute trust, but simultaneously a fear that he might have to surrender himself when faced with considerateness in the many forms to which sympathy and relationship give rise. The previous evening had rushed upon him in the mixture of small and great that life offers. The whole of his love-story, which he had imagined with open eyes, had taken place all the same with his eyes deliberately blindfolded. He had closed them to the girl's pretended or fancied illness, closed them so tightly that he had deceived himself into taking her seriously. Had he not done so, but instead said from the first 'get up and be well, you are only imagining your illness', she would have hated him for the rest of her life, and his goal was to win her love. Now he had won that love, perhaps because she thought she had tricked him. That is to say, her love bore a direct relationship to his gullibility, and when, in the morning, he asked himself over and over again 'Do you believe in your Maria?' his intelligence, having had a full night's sleep, translated it into 'Am I sure that I can outwit her?' No, there could be no love with open eyes: to win a woman with frankness was impossible. To approach her with head held high and with unambiguous words would be to push her away. He had begun with lies, and he would have to keep up the pretence. Meanwhile, as the conversation went forward, frolicking between trifles and effusions of emotion, there was no time for brooding. The pleasure of being in a home with two women made everything so smooth and easy that he resigned himself to the joy of being the cherished child, the little one, a son to his mother-in-law. He did not even notice how the daughter, who had already grown beyond her mother's control, and was calling her '*du*', and treating her like her child, by a slight turning of the tables had gradually begun to talk down to him, who called by the name of 'mother-in-law' the woman she did not treat as her equal.[1] But this reversal of the order of nature amused him, and he always had before him the example of the giant who let the child pull three straws from his beard, but only three. As they were thus sitting chatting over their coffee they heard the murmur of voices from the people down by the shore.

From the window they could see that the inhabitants had collected by the harbour. Sometimes they stood quite still, shading their eyes with their hands, and sometimes they rocked from foot to foot, as if the ground beneath them was on fire, or as if their uneasiness made it impossible for them to stand still.

'It must be the miracle,' cried the girl, and rushed out, followed by her mother and her fiancé.

When they got outside the house the women stopped as if struck by fear: they saw swimming on the surface of the sea, in the middle of a clear sunny morning, a colossal moon, deathly white, rising over a churchyard of black cypresses.

The inspector, who had not calculated what the effect would be from this viewpoint, and who did not grasp the hang of the matter swiftly enough, turned deathly pale himself from shock. He had never expected an otherwise law-abiding nature to produce such a monstrous phenomenon. The women seemed turned to stone and unable to move, so he hurried past them down to the shore where the populace was assembled. In a moment he had solved the riddle. The marble palace he had intended had unintentionally become enclosed on one side by a curving wall of projecting rock, and on the other by the crown of a pine tree. Thus the sheet of chalk appeared to be circular, while the windows, which were altogether too faintly painted, looked like the map on the face of the moon.

The populace, who had been warned by the inspector that

the miracle would occur at a stated time, regarded him with frightened but respectful eyes as he approached, and contrary to custom some of the men raised their hats and caps.

'Well, what have you to say to my mirage?' he said jestingly.

No one answered, but the senior pilot, who was the bravest, pointed to the north-western expanse of sky, where the real moon, in its first quarter, hung palely.

The miracle was thus overwhelming, and the strong impression produced by the two moons was too deep to be obliterated by an explanation. And when the inspector tried to give one, no one listened to his opening words, but all stood stock-still, bewitched, infatuated as it were with their own terror at the inexplicable, and he gave up all attempts to shake their belief. He had wanted to give them a sign to show that neither he nor nature could break laws, but all the same chance had transformed him into a magician.

When he turned round he found his fiancée in an ecstatic state, held back by her mother. But on his approach she wrenched herself free, and falling on her knees cried with half-mad gestures and words that she seemed to have borrowed from some spiritualist circle:

'Mighty spirit, we fear you, take away our fear so that we may love you.'

Matters had already taken a questionable turn and the inspector summoned up all his art to explain the involuntary miracle, but in vain. The pleasure of being bewitched, the paralysing effects of fear, and behind these the lurking pride that made her unwilling to admit hallucination, had taken such complete possession of the young girl's mind that no remonstrances or protestations were of any avail.

By now the attention of the crowd on the shore had been attracted by Miss Maria's shrieks and gestures to her and away from the spectacle out at sea. And when they saw the young girl on her knees before the white-clad man, with his deep, dark eyes, standing bare-headed on the hillside, some recollection of the Bible story of the young man who worked miracles must have come into their minds. They hastily crowded together and began to whisper and, prompted by the senior pilot, one of the women hurried into her cottage nearby, and came out with a three-year-old child, who had a festering sore on his cheek. Ability to produce mirages must be accompanied by a supernatural knowledge of how to cure illnesses.

The inspector now found assigned to him a role that began to torment him beyond measure, and when he saw fishermen, pilots and customs officers abandoning their labours, carpenters and joiners interrupting their work on the chapel to listen to his words, as to those of a prophet, he grew afraid – as if faced by a natural force that he had summoned up, but could not restrain. The moment had come when he must speak firmly, clearly and disengage.

'Good people,' he began, but then came the silent reflection: how should he begin, what words should he use, when every word would require an explanation, and this again presupposed knowledge that was lacking. During the few seconds in which he contemplated the gulf that lay between these people and himself he heard footsteps approaching and turned round to see a man who looked like an old sailor on leave.

The man raised his round felt hat and for a moment looked rather taken aback. But on coming nearer he drew himself up and seemed just about to speak, when the inspector relieved him of his embarrassment by asking:

'Are you perhaps the preacher from the Home Mission whom we are expecting?'

'The same,' replied the newcomer.

'Won't you say a few words to these people who are in a state of turmoil due to a natural phenomenon, which they don't want to have explained and of which, at the moment, I cannot give them any interpretation,' said the inspector, eagerly grasping this way of escaping from a false situation.

The preacher immediately declared himself willing, stroked his long goatee, and took a Bible from his pocket.

When the people saw the black book a tremor passed through them and some of the men bared their heads.

The preacher leafed through the book for some minutes, paused, cleared his throat, and began to read.

'And I beheld when he had opened the sixth seal, and lo, there was a great earthquake; and the sun became black as sack-cloth of hair, and the moon became as blood. And the stars of heaven fell unto the earth, even as a fig tree casteth her untimely figs when she is shaken of a mighty wind. And the heaven departed as a scroll when it is rolled together; and every mountain and island were moved out of their places. And the kings of the earth, and the great men, and the rich men, and the chief captains, and the mighty men, and every bondman, and every freeman, hid themselves in the dens and in the rocks of the mountains. And said to the mountains and rocks: "Fall on us, and hide us from the face of Him that sitteth on the throne, and from the wrath of the Lamb. For the great day of his wrath is come; and who shall be able to stand?"'[2]

The inspector, who had seen immediately what an alarming turn things were taking, had dragged his fiancée half by force from this dangerous neighbourhood, and taken her down to the shore where, by getting her into the right position, he would be able to show her that it was not the moon fallen from the heavens, but simply the Italian landscape he had promised to arrange for her birthday.

But it was too late. The girl had already seen the original form of the vision with her inner eye, and the preacher's inflamed interpretation had etched in the initial illusion. Borg had played with the spirits of nature, he had conjured up an enemy to help him, as he thought, and now everything had gone the enemy's way and he was alone.

As Maria still stood fascinated by the preacher on the rock he tried turning to her mother and whispered:

'Help us out of this. Come with us to the island and see that it is a trifle, a birthday joke.'

'I cannot judge in such a matter,' answered the old lady, 'and will not judge. But I think you should get married soon.'

This was a piece of advice – sober, prosaic advice – but coming from the old woman who was herself a mother it sounded wise, all the more so as it appealed to his own keen mind, though he found her way of looking at things rather simple. But after the hint she had given him, he walked straight up to the girl, put his arm round her waist, looked into her eyes with a smile she must understand, and kissed her on the lips.

This instantly seemed to set the girl free of the wizard on the rock. She unresistingly hung on her friend's arm and, almost dancing, accompanied him to her mother's cottage.

'Thank you,' she whispered, her eyes meeting his. 'Thank you for . . . how shall I say it?'

'Freeing you from the mountain troll,' put in Borg.

'Yes, from the troll!'

And she turned round to look at the danger she had survived.

'Don't look back,' her fiancé warned her, and drew her in through the door, while snatches of the flow of words from the sermoniser on the mount drifted down to him on the wind.

IX

One morning eight days later when the inspector awoke after a good night's sleep, his first clear thought was that he must get away from the island, go anywhere to be alone, to collect himself, to rediscover himself. Of course the arrival of the preacher had had the intended effect in one direction: 'to intimidate the mob'. Disturbances and brutalities had ceased, but on the other hand the inspector had not derived any pleasure from this newly won peace, as his fiancée's exalted state of mind had meant that he could never let her out of his sight. Consequently he had kept her company, had literally tended her from morning till night and, during their endless discussions on religious matters, had attempted to preserve her from the preacher's seductive talk. Everything that he had fought his way through in his youth he now had to go over again. And as new counter-evidence had been discovered, he had to revise the whole of his defence. He improvised psychological explanations of God, faith, miracles, eternity and prayer, and imagined to himself that the girl understood them. But when, after three days, he realised that she was back at the same point and that this was a question of feeling, beyond the reach of reason, he threw up the sponge and tried by rousing her erotically to introduce a new focus for her emotions, and thus drive out the old one. But he soon had to give up, as talking about their life together only made the girl still more excited, and he was quick to observe that there were secret bridges between religious and sensual ecstasy. From a love for Christ she sprang lightly over the broad drawbridge of love for your neighbour to love for the man himself. From abstemiousness she tripped over the plank of privation to its neighbour, mortification. A little tiff could produce the unpleasant emotion of guilt, which had to be resolved by the pleasurable sensation of reconciliation.

Of necessity he had first to tear down these bridges, bring her face to face with naked lust, arouse her desire for earthly things, which he painted in glowing colours. But when, having succeeded, he withdrew at the last moment, the chill of miscalculation came over her, and when he then tried to ennoble her emotions by leading them on to thoughts of offspring and family, she shrank back, and declared emphatically that she would not have any children. She was even capable of employing a manner of speech very popular among a certain set of women: she would not become the womb he lacked or bear his heirs who she would have to bring into the world for him with danger. Then he felt that nature had erected something between them but he still did not know what. He consoled himself by imagining that this was the butterfly's fear of laying eggs and dying, the suspicion of the flower that its beauty would fade if it set seed.

But these eight days had worn him out. The fine wheels of his brain had begun to jerk on their bearings, and the springs in the machinery had become slack.

On a day following over-exertion of this kind, when he wanted to work for a couple of hours his brain would be full of rubbish. Little words recurred in his ears, almost audibly; gestures and facial expressions she had used during their conversations loomed up; suggestions, ways in which he should have answered then or then or then sprang to his mind, while the memory of an apt reply that he had produced gave him momentary pleasure. In a word, his head was full of trifles. He realised that he was trying to reduce chaos to order, that he had chatted with a schoolboy instead of exchanging ideas with a mature woman, that he had given off masses of energy without getting anything in return, that he had put a dry sponge into his soul, and that the sponge had swelled up while he had become dry.

He was sick of it all, tired, and longing to get away for a time, since flee for ever he could not.

When he looked out of his window at five o'clock that morning all he could see was a thick mist that hung motionless, in spite of a light southerly wind. But instead of being frightened off he was tempted by this bright, translucent darkness that would conceal him, cut him off from the small fragment of land to which he felt bound.

The barometer and the weather-cock told him that there would be sunshine later in the day. He therefore got into his boat without much preparation, only taking with him a chart and a compass on which he never intended to rely, as he could hear the sounding-buoy some miles out at sea in the very direction he wanted to take in order to go ashore.

He immediately hoisted sail and was soon in the middle of the mist. Here, where his eyes were set free from all impressions of colour and shape, his first feeling was the pleasure of isolation from the constantly changing outer world. It was as if he were surrounded by his own atmosphere, floating forwards alone as if on some other celestial body in a medium that was not air but vapour, more agreeable and more refreshing to inhale than the dehydrating air, with its unnecessary seventy per cent of nitrogen, which had been left behind without obvious purpose when the material of the earth was sorted from the chaos of gases.

The mist was not dark or smoke-coloured, but bright, like newly melted silver, a sieve for the sunlight. It enveloped his tired self like warmth-giving, healing wadding, and protected him from jolts and pressure. For a while he revelled in this conscious repose of his senses, free of sound, of colour, of smell, and he felt that his tortured head was being cooled by knowing that it was safe from contact with others. He was sure of not being questioned, of not needing to answer or talk. His apparatus stood still for a moment, since all its leads had been cut, and then he began to think again, clearly, collectedly, about all his experiences. But what he had recently gone through was so inferior, and so petty, that he had to let the stagnant water of these last days run away before fresh water could run in.

In the distance, at intervals of several minutes, he heard the call of the sounding-buoy and, guided by it, he steered a course straight into the mist.

Then again there was silence and only the splash of the boat and the ripples in the stern gave him a sense of forward movement. Suddenly, from the heart of the mist came the scream of a black-backed gull, and simultaneously he thought he heard from astern the lapping and swishing of a moving boat, but when he hallooed to ward off danger he received no answer and only became aware of the sound of rushing water from a boat that was bearing away.

After sailing on for a while he noticed to windward the top of a mast with mainsail and foresail, but nothing could be seen of the hull or the steersman, for they were hidden by the high wall of the swell.

In other circumstances this incident would not have disturbed his thoughts, but now it made an impression as being something he could not for the moment explain. This inspired fear, from which only a step led to thoughts of persecution. His newly aroused suspicion rapidly gained momentum when, immediately afterwards, he saw the ghost boat shoot past him to leeward looking like something painted on the mist. He still could see nothing of the steersman as the latter was hidden by the rectangular spritsail.

He called again, but instead of an answer the boat fell away enough for him to see that the transom was empty. Then the vision disappeared into the all-devouring mist.

Accustomed as he was to rid himself of fear of the unknown, he immediately mustered up suggestions for an explanation. But the question of why the steersman was hiding himself brought him to a halt, for he had no doubt that there must be a steersman in a sailing-boat that was not drifting. Why did he want to avoid being seen? Usually people wanted to remain invisible if they were out on unlawful business, if they wanted to be alone or to frighten someone. It seemed probable that the unknown sailor was not seeking solitude as he was keeping the same course. And if he wanted to frighten a fearless man not prone to superstition he could have found a better way of doing it. Meanwhile Borg kept on his course down to the buoy, always obstinately pursued by the ghost boat to leewards, though at a distance that made it look like condensed mist. When he got further out to where the wind had freshened, the mist seemed to thin, and the sunlight it had silvered lay like a long bar of silver bullion on the crests of the waves. As the wind increased, the call of the buoy grew louder and where the mist had parted, he steered right into clear sunlight and ran at full speed towards the buoy. There it lay rocking on the waves, vermilion-red, damp and shining like an extracted lung, with its great black wind-pipe pointing aslant up into the air. And when a wave next compressed the air, it raised a cry as if the sea were howling for the sun. As its bottom cable ran out it rattled, and then when the wave receded and sucked back the air, a roar arose from the depths that might have come from the giant trunk of a mastodon.

It was the first tremendous impression he had received after a month of twaddle and pettiness.

He admired the genius of man that had so belled that sly wolf the sea, and thus compelled it to warn its defenceless victims itself. He envied this solitary being, who could lie chained to a rock on the sea-bed in the midst of an ocean, and roar in competition with the wind and the waves, day and night, so that it could be heard for miles around, be the first to wish the stranger welcome to its land, and have power to groan out its suffering and be heard.

He passed the vision swiftly and dimness once again enveloped the boat which fell away as he made for the skerry where he intended to rest. For half an hour he kept to the same tack until he heard the thud of the breakers on the shore, then he bore away to leeward and soon ran into a bay where he could land.

This was the outermost skerry of the approach channel and consisted of a couple of acres of red gneiss, bare of any vegetation except for patches of lichen in places where the drift-ice had not scraped the rocks quite clean. Only common gulls and herring-gulls sought a resting place here, and these now squawked in alarm as the inspector moored his boat and climbed to the crown of the skerry. Wrapping himself in his rug he sat down in a well-polished crevice that provided him with a comfortable easy-chair. Here, free from witnesses or listeners he delivered over the reins to his thoughts, made confession to himself, ransacked his innermost being and heard his own voice from within. After only two months of rubbing up against other people he had lost the best part of himself by obeying the law of adaptation. He had accustomed himself to agreeing in order to avoid controversy, had practised yielding to prevent a breach, and had developed into a characterless, pliable society man. A head full of trifles and the necessity of having to express himself in an abbreviated and simplified vocabulary had made him feel that the scale of his speech had lost its semi-tones, that his thoughts had been side-tracked on to old worn-out rails which led back to where they had taken on ballast. Slack, out-of-date sophisms about respecting other people's beliefs, and saying that everyone is made happy by his own rubbish, had crept back into him. Out of sheer politeness he had exhibited himself as a magician and finally brought upon himself a dangerous competitor, who threatened at any moment to detach from him the only human soul he wanted to unite with his.

A smile crossed his face as he remembered how he had tricked these people who thought they were tricking him. But the word 'asses' involuntarily uttered half-aloud, made him spring to his feet, alarmed at the thought that someone might have overheard him. After that he continued to think in silence. They believed that they had captured his soul, but he had captured them. They had imagined that he was doing their work for them, not knowing that he was using them to exercise his soul, and to feel the joy of power.

But these thoughts that he had previously not dared to acknowledge as his now declared themselves to be the children of his soul – big, healthy children who he accepted as his. And what had he done except the things they had wanted to do but not been able? And this young woman believed that she had tuned a barrel-organ for herself, never suspecting that she was destined to be the sounding-board for his soul . . .

Suddenly he sprang up, cutting short the course of these dangerous thoughts, for he had clearly heard footsteps on the slabs of rock behind the mist. And though he immediately guessed that this must be an aural illusion, produced by solitude and the fear of being taken unawares, he directed his steps down to his boat. But when he found it in good order he determined to walk round the skerry in search of that other person, for a person there must be, as some other human being had landed here. He clambered over the stones along the shore and soon found, behind the next point on the leeside, a sailing-boat with the same spritsail rigging he had noticed out at sea. It was also clear that the man sailing it must be on the skerry, and the inspector began a razzia in the mist, always keeping in the neighbourhood of the boats so that he could cut off any retreat. Later, after he had called several times but received no answer, he finally realised that he would have to leave the boats if he wanted to catch the mysterious being. He therefore went down to them and removed the tillers, thus making flight impossible. Then he again entered the mist. He heard footsteps ahead of him, followed them by ear, but soon heard the sound from a quite different direction. Tired by the hunt, and annoyed by the futility of his exertions, he decided – since he did not want to wait for the mist to disperse – to bring the performance to a sudden end.

In the loudest voice he could muster he called out: 'If there is anyone there, answer, for I am now going to shoot.'

'Oh, Lord Jesus, don't shoot,' was the answer from within the mist.

The inspector thought he had heard that voice before, but very long ago, perhaps in his youth. And when he neared the place where the unknown man was standing, and saw his silhouette outlined in grey against greyness, old memories of this human contour awoke in him. The knock-knees, the arms that were much too long, and the crooked left shoulder had counterparts in a forgotten picture stored in his memory of a schoolmate in the third class of his elementary school. But when he saw the itinerant preacher's American beard advancing out of the mist the pictures did not match, and he saw only the man on the rock, who had applied the Revelations of John to his mirage. With a raised cap and a frightened expression on his face the preacher now approached the inspector. The latter did not feel at all sure of this furtive pursuer, though in fact he carried no firearms, and in order to conceal his uncertainty he adopted a sharp tone of voice as he asked:

'Why have you hidden yourself from me?'

'I haven't hidden myself, the mist has done that,' answered the preacher softly and cringingly.

'But why were you not sitting at the tiller in the boat?'

'I didn't know one was obliged to sit on the transom, so I sat on the leeside, to get the boat to ride the waves. I had a sheet attached to the tiller as we usually do up in Roslagen.'[1]

The answers were acceptable, but did not answer the question why he had followed the inspector out here. The latter now felt that there would have to be a hand-to-hand fight between their souls, for it was not by accident that they had met.

'What are you looking for out here?' asked the inspector, taking up the broken thread.

'I don't know how to put it, but I sometimes think that I have, as it were, a need to be alone with myself.'

This answer produced something of an echo from the questioner and, reading the expression of understanding in his face, the preacher added:

'For you see, when I seek myself in reflection and in prayer and find myself, I also find my God.'

A naive confession lay in these words, but the inspector did not want to translate the involuntary heresy and draw the conclusion: I myself am God or, God is in me, because he was seized by a certain feeling of respect for this man who could be alone with a fiction, and thus in a sense alone.

But as he regarded the preacher's face which, except for his upper lip, was overgrown by a long brown beard – the sort worn by sailors and itinerant preachers, probably because they want to express themselves in words and yet look like apostles – the inspector thought he could detect another face behind it and, plagued by the work his memory was unconsciously undertaking, he asked bluntly:

'Haven't we seen each other before in our lives?'

'Yes, that we have,' answered the preacher. 'And you, sir, perhaps without knowing it, interfered so profoundly in my life, that one might say that you decided its course.'

'You don't say so! Tell me about it for I remember nothing,' begged the inspector, sitting down on the slab of rock and inviting the other to be seated.

'Yes, it must be twenty-five years since we were together in the third form . . .'

'What were you called then?' interrupted the inspector.

'I was called Olsson, nicknamed Ox-Olle, because my father was a farmer, and I wore home-woven clothing.'

'Olsson? Wait a minute, you were better at figures than all of us, weren't you?'

'Yes, I was. But then the day of the Head Master's fiftieth birthday arrived. We had decorated the school with leaves and flowers, and when lessons were over someone suggested that our class should gather bunches of flowers, and take them to the Head Master's wife and daughter. I remember that you thought this unnecessary, as the Head Master's womenfolk had nothing to do with the school, but often interfered with its business in a tiresome way. However, you joined us and I went too. But when I mounted the steps of the house I suppose you caught sight of my home-woven garments and noticed that I had the prettiest bouquet, for you burst out: 'Is Saul also among the prophets?'[2]

'I had quite forgotten that,' said the inspector curtly.

'But I shall never forget it,' protested the preacher in a trembling voice. 'It was thrown in my face that I was the mangy sheep, the outsider, whose homage could never be taken seriously by a woman of good station. In order to earn money rapidly and to learn fine manners and cultivated speech, I left school and devoted myself to trade. But I never got a better position. My appearance, my speech, my manners, were against me. Therefore I began to walk alone, and in solitude I found growing in me powers the existence of which I had never guessed. I had previously thought of becoming a parson, but now it was too late. Solitude inspired me with a fear of human beings, and my fear of them made me utterly alone, so much alone that I came to find my only companionship in God, and in our Lord Jesus Christ, the saviour of the unfortunate, the mangy and the stigmatised. I have you to thank for that.'

The last words were spoken with such bitterness that the inspector thought it wisest to bring everything out into the open by exclaiming:

'So you've gone about hating me for twenty-five years?'

'Boundlessly! But not any longer, now I've left revenge to God.'

'Indeed, so your God is the kind who takes revenge! Do you believe that you are his chosen instrument, or do you think he will cause his electric sparks to rain down on me, or does he intend to blow my boat over, or give me smallpox?'

'The ways of the Lord are past knowing, but the way of the unrighteous is apparent to all.'

'Do you think that a boy's careless talk is so unrighteous that God will persecute him for a lifetime? I wonder if that vengeful God isn't in your own heart where you said just now that you arrange to meet him?'

Ensnared by his own words the preacher could no longer control himself.

'Blaspheme if you will. Now I know who you are! But the apple does not fall far from the tree. Now I understand all the devil's tricks. You build the Lord a house to be a brothel, an offering to a harlot! You play the magician and the sorcerer to make the people fall down and worship the apostate. But thus saith the Lord: "Blessed are they that wash their robes, that they may have the right to come to the tree of life, and may enter in by the gates into the city. Without are the dogs, and the sorcerers, and the fornicators, and the murderers, and the idolaters, and everyone that loveth and maketh a lie!"'[3]

He flung out these last words, for which he had no need to seek in any other place than on his own lips, with incredible dexterity and exaltation, and then, as if fearing a crushing answer which would weaken their impact, he turned his back and went down to his boat.

. . .

Meanwhile the mist had lifted, and the pure blue sea lay spread out, soothing and liberating.

The inspector remained sitting for a while in his rocky chair pondering on the subjection of the soul to the same laws that govern the physical powers. The wind whipped up a wave down near Estonia, this wave pursued another, which transmitted the movement to the Swedish coast and shifted a little pebble that was supporting a block of stone. Then, after a generation, came the consequences. The boulder collapsed, and the now unprotected cliff was undermined still further.

Twenty-five years ago his brain had thrown out what was to him a meaningless word. That word had penetrated an ear and set a brain in such violent motion that it was still vibrating after changing the direction of a whole human life. And who knew whether this innervation, reinforced by contact and friction, might not once more discharge with increased force, bring other contrary forces into action, and produce tremors and ruin in other people's lives.

Now, when the preacher's boat shot forwards round the point, and held course for Österskär, the inspector had such a decided feeling that in it sat an enemy who was marching upon his positions, that he rose to go back to his boat, sail home, and put himself in a state of defence.

. . .

Once in his boat, and soothed by the gentle rocking of the waves, he felt a strong desire to spend a few more hours of complete solitude at sea, and let the recent disturbing impressions blow away.

Why should he fear this man's influence on his fiancée? If she sank to the level of the uneducated she would in any case show herself to be an impossible person for a lifelong union. All the same it annoyed him that this fear was there. It reminded him of the behaviour of those men who live in fear of losing something, and are stamped with the ridiculous word 'jealous'. Did this feeling of an inability to retain reveal a weakness in him? Or was it not rather a weakness in her in not being able to hold on when the balloon was rising, leaving behind the sheet-anchor of religion and casting away the ballast sacks of feeling? No doubt this was the more likely, despite the fact that such weakness had obtained a certain prescriptive right from those who had nothing to lose.

He had now tacked about and lay to the south-east of the island, a side from which he had not before studied his prison.

On the top of the hill was the skeleton of the unfinished chapel with its scaffolding, but though the morning was far advanced he could see no workers. Nor could he see any boats out fishing. A great peace seemed to reign over the whole island, and there were no people visible by the customs house, or the pilots' look-out. He set the boat on a new course, intending to sail around the island. But when he got to the outer side the waves were so much higher that he gained little by tacking and it took him a whole hour before he could run with the wind behind him into harbour. He could now see the cottage where the females were living and, just as he shot past the harbour-point, he noticed that all the inhabitants of the island had collected round the house, on the porch of which the bare-headed preacher was holding forth.

Fully aware that a battle was imminent he landed, took down the sail, and went up to his room.

Through the open window he now heard a psalm being sung.

He would have liked to sit down and work, but the thought that he might be interrupted prevented him from even starting.

A painful half-hour passed during which he realised more clearly than ever that he no longer possessed himself, no longer had control over a square metre where he could shut himself in and thus avoid contact with other souls which, like mussels that fasten on the hide of a whale, would finally hinder his progress by their weight.

After a few knocks the door was opened and Miss Maria stood before him with a new expression on her face resembling hurt reproach and supercilious compassion.

She came too with the feeling that she had the opinion of the masses behind her, and was consequently in a strong position faced by this solitary man.

He let her speak first in order to have a point of departure.

'Where have you been?' she began, trying not to sound too arrogant.

'I've been out sailing.'

'And not invited me to go with you?'

'I didn't know that you would insist on that.'

'Yes you did, but of course you wanted to be alone with your dark thoughts.'

'Perhaps.'

'Certainly! Don't you think I've noticed. Don't you think I can see that you are getting tired of me.'

'I haven't got tired of you. I've shepherded you day in and day out. But this one early morning, when you are usually asleep, I took the liberty of sailing for a couple of hours. You've got tired of fishing, for I haven't seen you at sea once.'

'There is no fishing now, as you well know,' answered Miss Maria, convinced that she was speaking the truth.

'No, so I see!' rejoined the inspector, intending to approach the mine itself and risk an explosion. 'I see that people have abandoned their work in order to listen to sermons . . .'

Everything was now set for an outburst.

'Wasn't it you who wanted to have a church out here?'

'Yes, on Sundays. Six days shalt thou labour, but go to church on the seventh. Nowadays no one here works on any day, but on all of them there is preaching. And instead of supplying themselves and their families with a decent income here on earth, they are all running races for something as uncertain as heaven. Even the men at work on the chapel have left it, and I'm expecting any moment to hear that poverty has broken out, so we ought to be considering charity . . .'

'That's just what I wanted to talk about!' interrupted Miss Maria, glad to have avoided bringing the matter up, while disregarding the fact that the inspector had already exhausted it.

'I have not come here to practise charity, but to teach the people to live without it.'

'You are at bottom a heartless person though you make yourself out to be otherwise.'

'And you want to show off your great heart at my expense, without being willing to sacrifice one metre of the pleats in your dress.'

'I hate you! I hate you!' the girl burst out with a horrible expression on her face. 'I know you for what you are. I know everything, everything!'

'Well then, why don't you leave me?' asked the inspector in a cold, steely voice.

'I will leave you! I will!' cried the girl, approaching the door, but not going.

The inspector, who was sitting at his desk, picked up a pen and began to write, in order to avoid the temptation of resuming a conversation that was at an end, since everything had been said.

As if in a dream he heard someone sobbing, heard a door being shut, the sound of steps on the landing, the creaking of the stairs.

When he awoke and read from the piece of paper over which his pen had flown, he saw that he had written the word 'Pandora' a great many times, from which he concluded that a considerable time had elapsed since the performance ended.

But then he was struck by the word and was curious about its meaning, which he had forgotten during the course of the years. Having a faint memory that it belonged to mythology, he picked up a concise reference book from the table and read:

> Pandora, the Eve of antiquity, the earth's first woman. Sent down to Man by the Gods as a revenge, because Prometheus had stolen fire. With her came all the miseries that have since peopled the earth. Presented by poetry in the guise of a virtue which is a blinding evil, a creation designed for treachery and taking by surprise.

This was mythology like the story of Eve who had been the cause of man's ejection from Paradise. But since the story had been proved true, age after age, and he himself had experienced how the presence of a woman on this little patch of earth out in the ocean had already brought dusk where he had tried to spread light, a thought must certainly have lain behind the imagery of the Hellenic and Jewish poets.

That she hated him he knew and admitted, for had she not made common cause with the crowd down there? But he did not doubt her love either, even if this love was only the attraction of the dandelion to the sun, from which it wanted to borrow rays for a poor imitation of the golden disk. But there was something base there too, as there is in the debased, something evil that wanted to inflict harm, an unjustifiable struggle for power, whereas what mattered to him was a victory over unreason. To tell her this would mean breaking off their relationship, since this depended on his subjection, or at least on recognition of her superiority. But to recognise that would be to build a life on an obligatory lie, which would grow and flourish and possibly smother any chance of an honest life together. The deepest reason for the relative misery of all marriages lay in the fact that the man entered into a union with what was sometimes an insidious lie, and was often enough the prey to a hallucination, as he fabricated an image of himself in the being whom he wanted to assimilate. Mill was befooled by this visual illusion, 'second sight',[4] to such an extent that he believed he had got all his clever ideas from the stupid woman whom he had educated to be his companion.[5]

From time immemorial the price of love has been that men have kept silent about what woman is, and on their silence the centuries have built a chaos of lies, with which science has not dared to interfere, which the most courageous statesmen have not dared to touch, and which has made theologians deny their Paul in the matter of women in the churches.[6]

But his love had only just begun. It had fired up when he saw her appealing eyes, saw her looking up to him. And this love had fled when she came to him with the triumphant smile of folly, after having trampled down what he had wanted to create for her own good and that of others. 'Over!' he said to himself as he got up to close the door. Over were his youthful hopes of finding the woman he sought. 'The woman who was born wise enough to recognise the inferiority of her sex to the other.'

Now and then he had certainly met one or two who admitted the fact, but who in the end had made reservations about the reasons for the situation, had blamed non-existent oppression and promised themselves that with greater freedom they would overtake men, and after that the battle had been joined.

He was not going to wear out his intelligence in an unequal battle with midges which he could not hit with his stick, they were too small and too numerous. Consequently his vain search for what did not exist must be over for ever. He would devote all his energies to his work, lay aside kith and kin, family, home and sex, and leave the procreation of the race to other 'reproductive animals'.

The sensation of being free put his soul at rest; it seemed to him that a pawl had been released in his brain which began to function without regard for others. The thought that he need no longer make himself externally attractive caused him to lay aside a certain collar that had inconvenienced him, but which his fiancée had declared was chic. He combed his hair in a more comfortable way, and noticed how this soothed his nerves, as there had been constant strife about the style of coiffure his fiancée preferred. His tobacco-pipe, that he loved like an old friend but which he had been forced to discard, was taken out again. His dressing-gown and moccasins, which he had not dared to use for a long time, put him in mind of more airy surroundings in which he could breathe freely and think with ease.

And now, freed at last from the obligation to adapt himself, he noticed for the first time under what tyranny, even in details, he had been living. He could be in his room without the fear of being disturbed by knocks on the door, and could abandon himself to his thoughts without feeling false.

He had not enjoyed his newly won freedom for long before there came a knock on his door. His body jerked as if some moorings were still attached to him, and when he heard the old lady's voice the depressing thought struck him like a blow from a club that this was not the end, and that he must begin all over again.

At first he thought of letting the door remain closed, but then feelings of courtesy and a fear of being considered cowardly drove him to open it. And when he saw the old lady's wise, friendly eyes, as she entered with a kind smile and a roguish shake of her head, it seemed to him that his performance during the past half-hour had only been a dream from which he had now awakened, glad that it was over.

'Have we been having yet another tiff?' began the old woman, disguising the unpleasantness of the remark with the familiar 'we'. 'You children must get married before you break with one another. Believe the word of an old woman, and don't imagine you can test each other's hearts while you are engaged, for the longer you are engaged, the worse it will get.'

'But then it will be too late to break it off. And when one had already discovered such great differences in temperament and opinions, well . . .'

'Opinions! What are you talking about. Indeed, you haven't different opinions, but the girl was having a dull time while you were away, that's why she ran after the preacher. And as for temperament, that comes and goes according to the state of your nerves. And you, Axel, knowledgeable as you are, should know what women are like.'

At first he wanted to kiss her hand, so delighted was he to meet with a woman who knew her own sex. But then he reflected that he had heard this sort of talk about women every time a woman had wanted to win him over, and that it was more a matter of flattery than an admission for, if taken seriously, it was always withdrawn with interest. He therefore confined himself to saying:

'We will wait and see, Mother dear. I can't marry out here, but let us get back to town in the autumn . . . provided that Maria shows more sympathy for my work and my way of looking at the world and living my life.'

'Axel, you are so dreadfully deep, it's not surprising that a poor girl can't always keep up with you.'

'Yes, yes, but if she can't follow me upwards I certainly can't follow her downwards. But she seems determined that I shall, so determined that today it struck me that disguised hatred lay behind it.'

'Hatred? That is only love, my friend! Come down with me and say something friendly, and she will be all right again.'

'Never, after the words we exchanged today! For either those words meant something, and in that case we are enemies, or they meant nothing, and then one partner at least must be incalculable.'

'Yes, she is incalculable, but Axel, you must know that a woman is a child until she becomes a mother. Come along, my friend, and play with the child, otherwise she will choose other playthings, which might be more dangerous.'

'Yes, but dearest, I can't play all day without getting tired.

Nor do I believe that Maria is particularly pleased with being treated like an infant.'

'Oh yes she is, if it isn't made obvious. Alas, what a child you are in these matters, Axel.'

Once again a civility which, from someone not a mother-in-law, would have been an insult. And when she then took his hand to lead him out, he felt that all his will to resist was gone. By leaving his argument unanswered she had removed the question from the discussion; she had blown on the tangle, not unravelled it; she had caressed his doubts to rest, swept away his anxiety, and with her feminine atmosphere and motherly manner she had got him to relinquish his desire for personal freedom.

She was still chattering when, after changing his coat, he followed her obediently, and almost with a feeling of pleasure, down the stairs to continue the game and assume his shackles again.

But when he got down to the porch he met the preacher who handed him a letter with the Ministry of Agriculture and Fisheries' label.

The inspector broke the seal at once and stuffed the letter into his pocket, and, glad to have been given something – a subject of conversation, a lightning conductor – he hastened to communicate the contents to the old lady who was waiting.

'We are going to have a visitor,' he said. 'The government is sending me a young man who wants to learn to fish.'

'But how nice for you to have some male company, Axel,' said the old lady with genuine sympathy.

And the inspector walked buoyantly to meet his waiting fiancée, aware that with a piece of news to offer, he would be able to skip over what would be the most disagreeable of explanations.

X

Some days later, the inspector had been out sailing alone in order to lay out salmon lines in secret and, having failed to turn up for dinner, was coming up from the harbour when he heard the sound of chattering and laughter coming from outside the women's cottage. With no intention of listening, he advanced in that direction and when he got to the western gable-end, he saw through the two windows of the large room, which were in the angle formed by the corner, that the two ladies were eating dinner out-of-doors, and had a male guest at their table. He took a step forwards, and caught sight of Miss Maria's flashing eyes as she picked up a glass of wine and handed it across the table to their guest, of whom all he could see was a pair of broad shoulders. He suddenly recalled that he had seen this gesture and this expression in the girl's eyes before, and he remembered the first time he had seen her out on the skerry, offering the sailor a glass of beer, and how he had thought: she is flirting with a servant! Now it surprised him that he had never seen this expression in her eyes when she looked at him. Did her glances only reflect his? Or did she always conceal her innermost thoughts from the man who was to be her victim?

He regarded her for a while, and the longer he did so the more unfamiliar became the expression on her face, so unfamiliar that he grew frightened, as you do if you discover that you have been deceived by the person nearest to you. 'If you see so much when you are yourself unseen, what will you not hear?' he thought, and stopped behind the corner of the cottage.

The mother now rose and went into the kitchen, leaving the two young people alone.

They immediately lowered their voices, and Miss Maria's expression became sensual as she listened to the words the stranger spoke with such warmth.

'Of all vices, jealousy is the dirtiest. Love gives no right to possession . . .'

'Thank you for those words! A thousand thanks!' said Miss Maria and raised her glass, while her eyes grew damp with half-shed tears. 'You are a real man though you are young, for you believe in woman.'

'I believe in woman as the most heavenly thing in Creation, the best and the truest,' the young man went on with increasing fervour. 'And I believe in her because I believe in God.'

'You believe in God?' rejoined Miss Maria. 'That shows that you are also intelligent, for only the foolish deny the Creator!'

The inspector thought he had heard enough and, as he also wanted to see how good at dissimulation his chosen partner for life might be, he stepped forward quickly, after having readjusted all his facial muscles, and assumed a radiant expression as if delighted to see again the girl he longed for.

The girl retained on her face her delight and enthusiasm, and received her fiancé's embrace with the same passion she had shown for the recent declaration of belief in woman. She returned it with a kiss that was more ardent than ever before.

She then playfully introduced the assistant, Mr Blom, who had arrived early that morning and had won all hearts on the island, as he was a fisherman without equal.

'And we were just talking about the herring in Bohuslän when you came and disturbed us,' she concluded.

The inspector allowed the lie, the dangerous word 'disturbed' and the provocative 'all hearts' to run off his back, and extended his hand to a gigantic young man of something over twenty who, lacking the ability to dissimulate, held out his hand with a guilty expression and stammered out a few unintelligible words.

At that moment the mother came out, greeted her son-in-law, and began to arrange the table.

Conversation was soon under way, and Miss Maria, probably feeling that she had support, began to make jokes about her fiancé's apparel.

'That veil you know, that's expensive,' she teased. 'You ought only to have your parasol when you sit at the helm.'

'All in good time, all in good time,' answered the inspector, concealing the disagreeable impression made on him by this display before a subordinate and a stranger.

His assistant, who already felt himself superior to his considerate senior, but who, at the same time, could not help feeling uncomfortable at the cruel treatment the latter was receiving, was seized by a tactless feeling of compassion and, touching with his long fingers the veil the inspector was wearing on his hat he said:

'Yes, but it's very practical,' and then added in the flirtatious manner he had adopted from the beginning: 'And if Miss Maria took the same care of her beautiful complexion . . .'

'As you do of your beautiful hands!' the girl let slip, as she touched the hand that rested on the table crumbling bread, thus quickly reverting to the mood which her fiancé guessed must have prevailed all morning.

Feeling absurd, as you do when you have to eat alone in the company of those who have already eaten, Borg had to summon up all his nervous energy to suppress the distress he felt when listening to their conversation. They are already praising each other's bodily parts in my presence, he thought with disgust. But he realised immediately that he would be lost if he showed the least sign of displeasure at their improper behaviour, as that displeasure would immediately be branded as the dirty vice about which he had just heard them talking.

'My assistant really has an unusually beautiful hand which bears witness to his intelligence,' he said as, with the air of a connoisseur, he studied the object of his fiancée's admiration.

'You can't talk of intelligent hands,' she burst out, with a laugh that sounded a bit tipsy.

'That's why I used the more correct expression "bears witness to intelligence . . ."'

'Oh you philosopher!' jeered the girl with a laugh. 'You're in such a dream that you can't see that we've eaten up all the radishes.'

'I'm glad that the traveller has enjoyed them, and I'm pleased to see that you have anticipated me in looking after his comfort,' said the inspector lightly. 'Permit me to wish you welcome, Mr Blom, and to hope that your stay here in our solitude will be a pleasant one. And now I will leave you in Miss Maria's charge. She can give you all the introductory information about fishing, while I go up and rest. Farewell, my dove,' he said, turning to the girl. 'Look after the young man and lead him along the right path. Goodnight, Mother dear,' addressing himself to the widow lady, whose hand he kissed.

His departure had come quite unexpectedly, but the good reason given for it, and its urbane tone which left not a hint of adverse feeling behind it, had saved him from protests and, at the same time, let him have the last word, an advantage which they had not intended to grant him.

. . .

Back in his room he had hardly had time to do more than wonder at the fact that the 'fear of loss' had been able to inspire him with such an unbelievable ability to dissimulate, to suppress disagreeable sensations and to make himself hard, before he lay down on his sofa, pulled a rug over his head, and fell into a dreamless sleep. When he awoke after a couple of hours he rose, having come to the decision which he knew he would cling to for life: he must rid himself of this woman.

But she could only be gnawed out of his soul by the same means as those which, by force of habit, she had employed to eat her way in. The vacant space he would leave must be filled by another, the man whose soul seemed to have set her on fire at their first meeting.

He got no further before there came a knock on the door. It was the preacher, who entered with many apologies and, in some confusion, tried to squeeze out of himself what he had to impart.

'Have you noticed, sir,' he began, 'that the people here are, as it were, far from conscientious?'

'I noticed that immediately,' answered the inspector. 'What has happened now?'

'Well you see, sir, the men working on the chapel say that some planks are missing, so that there are not enough left to finish it.'

'That does not surprise me, but what can I do about it?'

'Yes, but you see, sir, you were there and provided what was required.'

'That is so. But I regret it now that I have seen how your sermons have taken people from their work, and indirectly turned them into thieves.'

'You cannot say they did so "directly" . . .'

'No, that's why I said "indirectly". But if you want money, go to someone else. Just tell me one thing: who is the new assistant here?'

'Well, they do say he's been a naval cadet, and now he's going to teach fishing, as his father is rich, or so they say.'

The inspector had sat down by the window when the conversation started, and was now watching Miss Maria and his assistant playing at throwing the discus. He had observed that her dress rose up in front every time she leant back to hit the other's ball.[1] He now saw his assistant bend down playfully as her dress flew up, indicating by his gesture and expression that he had caught sight of something.

'Now listen,' he resumed. 'I've long thought that if people had a shop here, it would be to their economic advantage. Then they would not need to row to the town to do their shopping. The shopkeeper might possibly let them have goods on credit too, in return for the right to dispose of their fish. What do you say to that, Mr Olsson?'

The preacher stroked his long beard, while his face reflected a mass of varying desires and alternating views.

The inspector now saw through the window that his assistant had climbed the look-out post and was hanging on by his arms, while Miss Maria stood below, clapping her hands.

'But tell me, Mr Olsson, if we could set up a shop here could it do anything but good?'

'Yes, but the local council would never allow it, unless we could get a shopkeeper whom they could trust, I mean someone . . .'

'We'll engage a godly man, and let some of the profits go to the chapel fund. In that way we shall get both the local council and the Church Authorities on our side.'

Now the preacher's face cleared.

'Yes, done in that way it would be all right.'

'Well, think it over, and try to find a suitable person, who won't fleece the people or wrong the Church. Think it over at leisure. Now to something else. I think I've detected that morals on the island are pretty low. Have you seen or suspected, Mr Olsson, that things don't hang together as they should down at the Vestmans?'

'Hm! Yes they do say, of course, that something is up, but one doesn't know. And I don't think one should meddle with it.'

'Say you so? But I wonder if we should not take steps in time, before they give themselves away. Things like that usually end badly out here.'

But the preacher seemed to have no inclination to interfere, either because he didn't think it was important, or because he didn't want to offend the populace. Moreover, his sickly appearance suggested that his thoughts were about his own sufferings. Now he abruptly changed course, and came out with his real errand.

'It's like this, sir, I was going to ask you if you had anything that you could give me, for I think I've picked up the ague out here in this damp place.'

'The ague? Let me see.'

On the impulse of the moment, and without forgetting for an instant that this was an enemy who had challenged him, the inspector took his pulse, looked at his tongue and the whites of his eyes, and was ready with his diagnosis.

'Is the food bad at the Ömans's?'

'Why yes, it is miserable,' answered the preacher.

'You are suffering from the ague that comes of malnutrition. You shall have food from my table. You've probably forsworn strong drink too?'

'Yes, that's to say I drink beer, of course.'

'Well, to begin with, here's a preparation that contains quinine. Take it three times a day, and when it's finished let me know.'

He then handed the preacher a bottle of alcohol laced with quinine, took his hand and said:

'You mustn't hate me, Mr Olsson, for we share many important interests, though we work in different ways. If I can be of any help to you I'm at your service whenever you wish.'

The simple device of showing a little apparent goodwill was enough to throw dust in the eyes of this artless man, who thought he had found a friend. He held out his hand and, with sincere emotion, stammered out:

'You once did me wrong, but God has turned it to good. And now I thank you for everything, and ask you not to forget what you said about the shop and the local council.'

'That I won't,' said the inspector, raising his hand in a gesture of dismissal.

After collecting himself for a few minutes he went outside to look for his assistant, whom he found engaged in a fencing match with Miss Maria. He was doing his best to make her wrist and upper arm supple enough for him to bend them into an elegant posture of defence.

After a compliment, and an apology for disturbing them, he explained that he must talk to Blom about the problem of his official residence.

'There is no room vacant on the whole island except the attic-room above the ladies,' he said, audaciously suggesting that he had been trying his hardest to find another.

'But that won't do!' cried Miss Maria.

'What's that you're saying?' objected the inspector. 'What makes it impossible? That's the only room to be had, unless Mr Blom takes mine. In which case I should have to live in the same house as the ladies, and that would certainly not do.'

As there was no other choice the matter was settled, and the assistant's luggage was carried up.

'But now to serious matters,' continued the inspector, after things had calmed down. 'The herring has arrived, and in eight days the fishing will begin. Consequently Mr Blom must go out with the nets immediately, preferably tonight, while this wind lasts, and try out drag-net fishing, which he understands.'

'May I go too?' begged Miss Maria, imitating the squeaky voice of a child.

'Of course you may, my angel,' answered the inspector, 'so long as Mr Blom does not object. But you must excuse me if I leave you alone now, I shall have to write reports all night. You must be out by one o'clock. You can take the coffee-pot with you.'

'Oh, what fun, what fun!' rejoiced the girl, who seemed to have grown ten years younger.

'Now I'll go and see that the boat and the drift-nets are ready for you. Mind you go to bed early this evening, so that you don't oversleep.'

With that he departed, amazed at the incredible certainty with which he imposed his will now that he had abandoned an impossible defence and gone over to the attack.

For the first time he entered the cottage of that great fisherman, the hostile Öman.

He noticed the prevailing chill and dislike immediately, but he asked questions and gave orders with such assurance that they fell in with everything. He inserted a few friendly questions about the children, promised that better times for the island were coming soon, took all the risks upon himself, threw in a word about the shop, urged people to have barrels of salt in readiness, and said that if they had no money for purchases they would be able to get goods on credit. He left the house everyone's friend and had to promise that he would soon send down some strong medicine for the old man, who had caught a chill.

Then he went down to the boat-houses, selected a number of drag-nets with good floats and strong cord, inspected the best boat and requisitioned the services of two capable boys.

When he had finished making these preparations the bell for supper was rung from the ladies' cottage.

At the supper-table he conversed with the mother while the young people, as he now called them, devoured each other with their eyes, bickered and nudged as if their bodies were being irresistibly drawn to each other.

'Are you going to leave those two alone in that state?' the mother whispered to him when he said goodnight before going back to his room.

'Why not? If I seem displeased I shall appear ridiculous, and if I don't seem displeased . . .'

'You'll be even more ridiculous!'

'Meaning: I'm bound to lose. So it doesn't matter what attitude I adopt. Goodnight, Mother.'

XI

It rained for eight days after the first attempt with the drift-net, the only result of which had been a little scene between the engaged couple. The inspector, who had intentionally misled the young people, well knowing that there were no fish to be caught, went down to the shore to meet them on their return and had thereupon been called an idiot by his fiancée, who was quite worn out by being up all night. Her remark had provoked a sly grin from the boatmen, and the assistant, who feared a storm, had intervened with a joke. At the dinner-table the jeering about the new method of fishing had assumed greater proportions and the inspector had pretended to be so deeply humiliated that Mr Blom thought it necessary to defend him several times in an extremely wounding manner.

Since then, rainy days had kept the party indoors, and intense intimacy had developed among those living in the ladies' cottage, where the assistant had introduced the practice of reading aloud from the works of the Swedish poets. The inspector had listened at first, but had later withdrawn, explaining that Swedish poetry was written for confirmation candidates and ladies, and that he would wait until there was a poet who wrote for men. By a unanimous vote he was declared 'unpoetical', which pleased him, as it released him from any obligation to attend the séances.

The rainy weather had even halted work on the chapel, and the workers sat in the cottages, inviting people to drink spirits with what coffee they could get.

The preacher, who could no longer collect people out-of-doors, passed the first few days in the cottage kitchens, offering to read from the Bible. But he was received with indifference and quarrelled with the workers, many of whom were free-thinkers. He had then retreated to his room, declared that he was ill, and sent someone to the inspector for quinine as his bottle was empty. Then suddenly he disappeared, and was said to have gone by steamer to the town.

But on the previous evening, he had returned to the island, accompanied by a male individual whom he called his brother, and who brought with him a boatload of various wares, mostly beer. These were unpacked in a boat-house, at the open door of which a plank served as a counter, the local council having given permission for the opening of a shop.

During the last few days the fishing population from islands nearer the mainland had begun to gather. Boat-houses were opened in which whole families were housed, cottages were filled with relations and friends, and the entire island hummed with life, in glaring contrast to its usual seclusion.

As the island and its fishing-grounds belonged to individuals living on the mainland, every boat paid a fixed fee, which was collected on the spot by a bailiff. The inspector had immediately got on to a bad footing with this man because he would insist on talking about fishing with drift-nets, which would mean abandoning the shallows and thereby bring an end to the fees. But he knew how to turn these apparently unfavourable circumstances to his advantage. As a result of opposing what was new the bailiff was driven to make propaganda for what was old by means of alcohol, thus, unintentionally, he would create the dark background against which the effectiveness of fishing with drift-nets would look even more magnificent. Borg was quite certain of victory. He had taken samples of the water at all hours of the day, and had dragged, bobbed and searched the depths with his marine telescope to find out exactly where the shoals went.

All these details only interested him in so far as they kept his energy in trim for future battles, and restored to him that feeling of power without which no one of exceptional ability can live, as ability can be lost if it is not used.

During the time that had elapsed since the assistant's arrival the daily bullying by the young people had continued, and had gradually accustomed him to playing the part of the inferior – a part he was busily entering into, as he did not want to make the break himself but thought it necessary to cause her to break with him. Between the two young people there was complete understanding on all matters, and he watched the mature woman quickly sinking to the level of the immature man, all of whose half-formed thoughts and improvised ideas were accepted as the height of wisdom. Every effort he made to refute some stupidity came up against their inability to retain the threads of an argument. All their thinking was done under the influence of their desire to possess each other. He had no intention of competing in acrobatic skills, or in songs of praise to the inferior sex, for his aim was to be supplanted and to bring an end once and for all to a bond that was threatening the whole of his future life.

And then there was the state of bigamy in which he was living. On the few occasions that he was alone with his fiancée, all he got from her were reflexes of the other man – the feel of his breath, as it were, on her lips, the sound of his childish utterances echoing from her mouth – all this had ended up by making him loathe a relationship reminiscent of a *ménage à trois*.

Nor were there any limits to the young man's conceit. He was under the false impression that he was above the inspector because he was on a par with Miss Maria, while she produced in him the illusion that she was above the inspector by employing the perfectly correct formula that, if A is bigger than B, and C is as big as A, then C too is bigger than B, but without first finding out whether A is really bigger than B.

He had never believed that he would one day find the secret of youth so openly displayed and being handed to him on a plate as it was here, and how well he recognised himself at a stage he had now put behind him.

Had he too not wept from hunger and lust? Experienced *Weltschmerz* from envy of his seniors, who had already won what he was striving for and were now oppressing him, thus awakening in him a fellow feeling for all those who are small and crushed? This inability to judge your powers because you expect to be able to perform in a single, concentrated action what you might achieve in a whole life-time. All this sentimentality which originates from unsatisfied desires. This overrating of woman while the nursery memories of your mother are still fresh! The flaccid, incomplete thoughts of a brain that is still soft under the pressure of blood-vessels and testicles.

He even recognised those signs of good sense which, in the form of primitive animal cunning and the avoidance of the obvious, are often imagined to be great wisdom, though they are really no more than the fox's simple-minded attempts to be artful, and therefore misleading like the notorious female cunning, priestcraft, or the clever dodges of lawyers.

The young man had even tried to practise thought-reading upon the inspector, thereby revealing that he believed the latter to be concealing some dangerous secrets, as he was so unlike other people. But he had conducted himself so clumsily that the inspector had discovered everything that was being thought or said about him in the ladies' cottage, and instead of giving anything away had so mystified the young man by his answers that the latter had begun to wonder whether his rival was a fool or a demon. By 'demon' he meant a conscious person who, under the pretence of being extremely naive, acts after careful calculation, is always alert, and directs the destinies of others according to his own plans. As 'calculation' – which is a virtue – always had a bad meaning for the young people, who could never calculate the result of an action, his envy took the form common among inferiors, of a passionate desire to drag and trample underfoot.

This was how matters stood when the great day arrived which would decide the whole fate of the fishing population during the coming winter.

The August evening hung like the warmth of a bed over the island. All the rocks and stones remained warm even after sundown, so warm that the dew could not fall on them. Off-shore the sea was spread out smooth and lavender-grey, while beyond it a coppery-red full moon was struggling up, half-hidden for the moment by a brig, which seemed to be sailing on the satellite's *mare serenitatis*. Nearer the shore the buoys of all the nets that had been laid out in rows seemed to lie like flocks of sea-birds rocking on the swell.

While waiting for daybreak before emptying the nets, people had camped on the shore with pots of coffee and bottles of spirits round fires they had lit. In the boat-house, where the shopkeeper was selling beer, the preacher was seated beside his brother helping him to deal with the brisk trade. With a blue apron tied round his waist he seemed to be opening bottles of beer like an experienced old publican.

The inspector, who had gone out to check the set of the current, the temperature and the barometer reading, was now strolling along the sandy shore to rest his mind. Here and there he stumbled on a couple seeking solitude. Their behaviour was so unbelievably naive that he turned his back on them with a grimace of disgust. When he got further out on the headland he climbed over the rocks to find the place where he usually sat when meditating. This was an easy-chair of rock, polished smooth by the waves, and left as warm as a Dutch oven by the burning heat of the sun.

He had been sitting for a while letting himself be lulled half to sleep by the sighing of the swell, when he heard the crunch of sand by the water's edge and later the rustling of dried seaweed. He then saw his assistant and his fiancée come sauntering slowly along with their arms round one another's waists. They paused between the unseen observer and the sheet of moonlight on the water, so that he could see the outline of their figures as clearly as if he had them between the lens and the mirror of a microscope. Now, with the sharp eyes of antipathy he saw her hawk-like profile bending towards the other's great ape-like head with its enormous cheeks, fit only for a trumpeter, and the narrow, conical cranium without a forehead. He noticed now the masses of superfluous flesh on the man's body, whose ignoble outline with its bulging hips put him in mind of a woman or the Farnese Hercules.[1] A masculine ideal from semi-brutish days, when the fist ruled over the cerebrum, as yet not fully developed.

Feeling outraged, as if he had entered into a relationship with a centaur, as if his soul were related by marriage with a lower species, he faced the onset of a crime which, if perpetrated, would falsify all the future generations of his family. It would trick him into offering his one and only life for another man's child, on which he would lavish his finest feelings; then, attached to it, he would drag his humiliation after him like a shackle on his foot, but without any chance of freeing himself from it. Jealousy, 'this dirty vice' – what was it but the fear that the strong, healthy instinct of procreation, with its praiseworthy egoism, might be prevented from perpetuating what was best in the individual? And who lacked this sound passion but the sterile family pimp, the marriage-monger, the weak fool, the *cicisbeo*[2] and the women-worshippers, who believed in platonic love? He was jealous, but when his first anger at the insult had subsided, the uncontrollable desire awoke in him to possess this woman without marrying her. The gauntlet was thrown down, freedom of choice was proclaimed. He was eager to take up the challenge, to break his bonds and step forth as the lover. Victory achieved, he could proceed calmly on his way, conscious that he was not by nature the loser who had been pushed aside in the battle for love. It was no longer a question of honest competition by loyal means, but of an underhand war between burglars. The challenger had chosen the simple implement of a picklock, and the struggle was about theft. With a woman as the prize all scruples had vanished. The beast had awakened, and the savage instincts that hide themselves under the great name of love now raged like elements let loose.

He got up from his rock unobserved, and turned his steps homewards to plan what he called his 'fate'.

XII

At seven o'clock the following morning a stifling silence reigned over the island. The fishing in the shallows had failed for all the reasons the inspector had advanced. The depressed fishermen were sitting in their boats unravelling their drift-nets, now and then picking out a solitary herring, which they threw ashore.

Sinking credit had halted trade at the shop. The preacher had laid aside his blue apron and, with the Book in his hand, had collected around him in one of the cottages a little circle of despairing women. With the incomprehensible but not unusual logic of his class, he told them of how Jesus had fed five thousand men with five loaves and two fishes.[1] This was an approximate parallel as, in the present situation, there were many mouths to feed and few fishes, but how these were to feed so many he was unable to say. As there was no help at hand he had to try to explain why it was that miracles could no longer happen, and he sought for the reason in the general lack of faith. If only they had faith no bigger than a grain of mustard-seed the miracle would be repeated.[2] And they could only obtain faith through prayer.

He therefore urged the congregation to pray. Although none of those present believed in the miracle of the two fishes, of which most of them had never heard as they had not read that story, they followed his example and repeated the Lord's Prayer, which they had learnt fairly well when preparing for confirmation.

When they were half-way through they were suddenly disturbed by a noise from the harbour. Those sitting nearest the window now saw a herring-boat that was just striking its square sail, coming in to the quay. Miss Maria was standing in the prow, her hair flying loose under her blue Scottish cap, while at the helm sat the assistant waving his hat in token of success. The boat was overloaded with nets and among their dark mesh glittered swarms of fish.

'Come here and I'll give you your herring,' cried the girl with the generosity of a victor.

'Just let me weigh them first, then people can have them,' interposed the inspector, who had seen the arrival of the boat from his window and had come down to see the result of all his work.

'What's the point of that?' objected Miss Maria in a decidedly bullying tone.

'It's for my statistics, gracious lady,' answered the inspector, without a trace of annoyance. He knew that the outcome of their fishing was the result of the information he had given them, which was based on the currents, the depths, the temperature of the water, and the conditions of the sea-bed.

'You and your statistics,' jeered Miss Maria, with an expression of the deepest scorn.

'Weigh them yourself then, but let me know afterwards what it was,' said the inspector, breaking off the discussion and retreating to his room.

'He's envious of us,' Miss Maria remarked to the assistant.

'Jealous perhaps?' suggested the assistant.

'Surely he can't be,' rejoined the girl softly as if to herself, thereby revealing the annoyance she had been hiding for several days at her fiancé's incredible indifference in the face of a rival, which she took to be a wounding cocksureness of his own ability to captivate.

The prayer-meeting had broken up, and all the people of the islands were gathered round the newly arrived herring-boat.

'Just see what a capital fellow you are, Miss!' flattered the preacher, thinking to take advantage of the chance to sow what he thought would be a little seed of discord.

'A sitting crow gets nothing at all,' teased the customs officer.

'A man lying on his sofa, he means,' whispered the assistant to Miss Maria.

The girl swelled with pride and dealt out fish by the handful to the people standing on the quay, who never tired of pouring words of praise and benediction upon their guardian angel.

It was not gratitude for blessings received that called forth these beautiful emotions, but a deep need to avoid admitting that they had been wrong in opposing the inspector, at whose methods of fishing they had jeered. It was the reverse side of their hatred for their real benefactor, to whom they were not prepared to bow in gratitude.

When the fish had been taken out of the nets they were found to amount to ten crans and distributed to the poorest people. These were immediately bought up by the shopkeeper and salted down. The money was soon converted into coffee, sugar and beer. It was assumed that they would easily be able to get their own winter herring from the sea now that Miss Maria had told them how to set to work with the new method of drift-net fishing.

. . .

When the inspector got up to his room he found a letter that had been brought by a returning coast-guard. It was an invitation for the inspector and his fiancée to honour with their presence the officers' ball on board the corvette *Loke*, which would anchor off the island at eight o'clock that same evening.

He immediately realised that this was the moment to break off his engagement. He was certainly not going to take another man's mistress with him into society and introduce her as his future wife. He therefore dragged off his engagement ring and put it into the letter to the girl's mother that he had composed the previous evening. In it, using the strongest expressions of despair, he had regretted that his engagement to Miss Maria must come to an end. An older attachment, thoughtlessly formed with a woman who had borne him a child, was now making legal claims upon him which, if they could not force him to marry the plaintiff, had the power to prevent him from marrying anyone else. While not wanting to wound her, he expressed himself ready as a gentleman to assist the undeservedly injured girl, who might also be in straightened circumstances, both in the matter of saving her good name and of providing for her financially.

He considered that this fiction was the only possible way of bringing about a break. It would shield the honour of both parties, most of all the girl's, and must appear indisputable, with no hope of repair, like an unavoidable fate.

When he had sealed the letter he whistled up his orderly and gave him the document, saying it was to be taken down to the widow lady.

He then lit a cigarette and took up a position by the window to observe the effect of his shot. The old lady was standing on the porch, shaking out a bedside-mat, when the man stopped to hand over the letter. She received it with some surprise, which increased when she squeezed the envelope with her left hand to find out what it contained. She then turned and went into the cottage.

A moment later the figure of Miss Maria could be seen moving backwards and forwards behind the curtain in the dining-room. She seemed to be walking to and fro agitatedly, sometimes stopping and gesticulating with her arms, as if she was defending herself against reproaches that were being thrown at her.

This went on for about an hour, after which she appeared on the porch, and threw a vengeful glance at the inspector's window. She then waved to the assistant, who seemed to be coming up from the harbour.

After they had gone into the cottage and been invisible for half an hour, they reappeared and went into the wood-shed. They emerged carrying a trunk and a portmanteau.

So they had made up their minds, and realised that to remain on the island was impossible.

After a while the assistant appeared again, this time bringing with him his own portmanteau, which the inspector recognised by its brass mountings.

So he too was intending to go.

Soon the owners of the cottage and their servants arrived,

and it seemed that the whole place was being turned upside down.

Towards midday, after spending some hours reading, the inspector saw the assistant and Miss Maria come out on to the porch engaged in animated conversation which grew increasingly animated and was accompanied by gestures that suggested an altercation.

They've come a long way, those two, they are already quarrelling, thought the inspector.

. . .

In the afternoon the old lady and the assistant were conveyed by the pilot's boat to an inward-bound steamer. Why Miss Maria remained behind he could not quite understand. Perhaps in the hope of a reunion, perhaps to show her defiance, maybe for some other reason.

Meanwhile, she sat at a window so that she could be seen from the customs house and there she remained, mostly seated, sometimes drumming on the window-pane, sometimes reading a book, and now and then passing her handkerchief over her face.

At 7 p.m. the corvette came into view, steaming up from the Landsort channel, and soon dropped anchor between Norsten and Österskär. When it signalled for a pilot with its steam-whistle, the girl rose to see what was happening. And now, standing on the grass, looking at the handsome vessel that was decked out for a gala, with flags on all its ladders, and a coloured tent over the maindeck, the inspector could see how fascinated she was by this tempting spectacle. She remained standing with her hands held limply behind her back until the wind brought the sound of a festive march and set her feet moving as she stood. Slowly her slender body bent forwards, as if drawn by the sound of the music, and then suddenly her whole person collapsed, her hands covered her face, and she rushed back into the cottage in despair, like a child who has lost a treat upon which it has been counting.

The inspector now dressed for the ball. On his black doctorial tailcoat he hung his six orders in miniature on a chain, and put on his bracelet that he had not worn since the day of his engagement.

When he had completed his toilet and there was still an hour left before the boat was due to fetch him, he decided to pay a farewell visit to Miss Maria, chiefly because he did not want to be suspected of cowardice, but also because he longed to test his power over his emotions. When he arrived at the porch he made a noise to give the girl time to adopt a pose, from which he would be able to decide why she had remained behind and what were her intentions.

He entered after knocking, and found Miss Maria sitting with a piece of needlework, a thing he had never seen in her hands before. Her face expressed contrition, regret and humility, though she was trying hard to look proudly indifferent.

'May I see you, Miss Maria, or shall I go?' began the inspector. Now that she was behaving like a woman, and leaning against him, he felt again the irresistible desire to raise her above himself as a woman, felt it just as strongly as the overwhelming desire to strike her down that he experienced when her demands and manners were masculine. At this moment she appeared to him more beautiful than he had seen her for a long time, so that he gave way to his emotions and, abandoning resistance, opened up.

'I have made you sad, Miss Maria . . .'

When she heard the gentle tone of his voice she immediately drew herself up and bit.

'But you were too cowardly to tell me yourself.'

'Considerate, Miss Maria. I don't find it as easy to slap people in the face as you do. And you can see that I have the courage to show myself, just as you have to receive me.'

This last ambiguous remark was made to find out whether she believed his reasons for the break.

'Did you think I was afraid of you?' she asked, taking a stitch with her needle.

'I did not know how you would take my explanation, even though I thought I could see that it would not cause you inconsolable sorrow.'

There was something about the word 'inconsolable' that

seemed to prick the girl like an allusion to her youthful comforter. But neither of them seemed to want to give themselves away, the one because he did not want to appear jealous, the other because she wanted to find out if he had noticed anything.

The girl, who had been bending over her work, now looked up to read her adversary's face, and noticed, with an astonishment she could not conceal, the many decorations on the lapel of his tailcoat. With childish naughtiness, which was no more than a cloak for envy, she mocked:

'How grand you are!'

'I am going to a ball, you know.'

'The girl's face contracted, contracted so violently that the inspector felt the reflex of her pain and seized her hand just as she burst out crying fearfully. And when he leaned against her she snuggled her head against his chest, and wept so that she shook as if with fever.

'Child, little one,' coaxed the inspector.

'Yes, I am a child. That's why you should have made allowances for me,' sobbed the girl.

'But listen. How far must one make allowances for a child?'

'Endlessly!'

'No, that's something I've never been told. There is a definite point at which self-indulgence approaches criminality.'

'What do you mean?'

And now she was roused.

'I can see that you know what I mean,' answered the inspector, no longer under her spell, as the minute she became hard she also grew ugly.

'So you're jealous!' jeered the girl.

'No, for jealousy is a suspicion that cannot be justified, sometimes it is a safety precaution. But my fears have been shown to be well-founded. So it is not jealousy.'

'And of a boy! A puppy, above whom you stand so much higher,' continued the girl, taking no notice of his explanation.

'All the more humiliating for you!'

'So it was a lie, the whole story,' said the girl, taking evasive action to avoid being hit by the insult.

'From beginning to end. But I did not want to inflict pain on your mother, or shame on you. Do you understand the delicacy of my feelings?'

'Yes, I understand, but I don't understand myself.'

'I could if you told me something of your past life.'

'My past life! What do you mean?'

'So there is a past in your life. That is what I have always suspected.'

'You are taking a liberty by making insinuations.'

'Which, since it no longer concerns me who you are, or what you have been, are . . . But I must bid you goodbye,' cut in the inspector, who had seen a gunner coming up to the cottage to fetch him.

'Don't leave me yet,' begged the girl, catching hold of his hand and gazing into his eyes with the expression of a drowning creature. 'Don't go, for if you do I don't know what I shall do.'

'Why torment ourselves any longer when we must inevitably part?'

'We won't torment ourselves. You will stay with me until the evening, so that we can talk things over before we part. I will tell you all you want to know, and after that you will judge me differently.'

The inspector, who thought that these words told him everything and was now certain that he had escaped the misfortune of being chained to the mistress of one or many, had now made up his mind. He went to the window and dismissed the gunner, saying that he would come later in his own boat.

This done he sat down on the sofa to allow the conversation to get under way.

But now that the girl was freed from her anxiety she collapsed, became taciturn, so that eventually complete silence reigned. They had nothing to say to each other, and the fear of rousing the storm-birds depressed their mood still further, and boredom stared them in the face.

The inspector began to finger the books that were left lying on the divan-table when his eye fell on one which was inscribed with the assistant's signature.

'The story of a young woman, I believe. Have you read it?'[3]

'No, I haven't had time yet. What is special about that book?'

'Well, it's remarkable in a way, as it is written by a woman and is also honest.'

'Really. Then what is it about?'

'It is about free love. A young scholar gets engaged to an emancipated girl. While he is away on an expedition she gives herself to an artist, but later marries her fiancé.'

'Well! What does the authoress say about that?'

'She laughs at it, of course.'

'Shame!' said the girl, and rose to take out a bottle of wine.

'Why so? No rights of possession in love! And the fiancé was a bore, at least in her company, to judge by the description in the book.'

'Now we are becoming boring too,' interrupted Miss Maria as she filled their glasses.

'Then what shall we do to amuse ourselves?' asked her lover, with an insinuating smile that could not be misinterpreted. 'Come and sit down here beside me.'

Instead of being hurt by his brutal tone of voice, and the gesture by which it was accompanied, the girl seemed to look with some admiration on the man whom she had despised for his too respectful behaviour.

Dusk had fallen and the moon that was beginning to wane had laid no more than a yellow-green beam on the floor, silhouetting the shadow cast by the balsam.

Through the open window came the faint sounds of the opening waltz, 'The Queen of the Ball', like a reproach, a greeting from their lost paradise which, all the same, kept alive the hope that all was not over.

Hoping to bind him by the memory of the highest bliss, and after a passionate declaration of love from him, she made the ultimate concession.

XIII

Three days later the inspector stepped ashore on Österskär after having paid a visit to Dalarö. When he learned that the young lady had left and would never return, he felt indescribably relieved, as if the air had suddenly become clearer and purer. Up in his room he lay down by the open window to smoke, and to go over in his mind the alternating sensations of the past few days.

When he had wrenched himself from the girl's arms at midnight, he had seated himself in his boat feeling the satisfaction that comes of performing some pressing duty. It was as if he had for the first time regained his inner balance. His rights had been infringed in a matter in which the law gave him no redress. Consequently he had himself to obtain justice, and he had only acted according to the principles which his opponents had themselves established.

When, after this, he had boarded the corvette and met persons with whom he could communicate in cultivated language, and had discussed learned topics with its doctor, this had at first intoxicated him. It was no longer necessary to degrade his brain by banter, or make himself a semi-idiot in order to be understood. And if he used allusions or shades of meaning he was immediately comprehended. It made him feel that he had lived for three months in a state of barbarism which had by degrees dragged him down into petty quarrels. These had subordinated his intellectual life to the emotional and the vegetative, had elevated the business of reproduction to be the matter of most importance, and tricked him into being a competitor in a match between stallions, out of which he had presumably emerged the victor. Now he understood why the official representatives of the Christian Church, who carried civilisation to the savages of all races, were forbidden to found families, or to bind themselves to woman or child. He realised that there was good sense behind fasting and self-denial for those who wanted to live a higher spiritual life. It was not for the sake of peace that the anchorite sought solitude. It was because just as the single grain of corn that falls by accident on fallow ground could set sixty ears, while the one which jostles in the field among millions on ground that has been manured sets only two, so the individual, struggling for a richer growth than others will only thrive in desert places.

The experiences of three days had confirmed this. When on the corvette or at the bathing-resort he had been dragged about from one circle to another, he had noticed every evening when he went to bed how, during the course of the day, his corners had been polished off, so that like a precious jewel his appearance had been improved, but he had lost carats. His general liking for people and his adaptability had called forth cowardly admissions which he had been tempted to make in such numbers that the improvised ideas produced in public persisted, and cropped up in his mind claiming to be his innermost thoughts. Finally he had tired, and felt on the last day that he had become a false human being who said one thing and thought another. He began to be ashamed of himself, and noticed that the increasing respect he had won in company for his affable manners had lost him all the respect he felt for himself.

If he wanted to avoid sinking further he must isolate himself, and the solitude he had now regained had the same effect on his spirit as a steam-bath, or a swim in the sea which brings freedom from all pressure, from all contact with solid matter. So he decided to remain on the island for the winter.

To this end, and at his own expense, he rented the cottage where the ladies had lived, and began to install himself there that very day. He took one of the big rooms into use as his library and laboratory, and the other as his dining-room and parlour. The attic he furnished as a bedroom.

. . .

When he woke next morning in his new abode after a dreamless sleep, he experienced the pleasure of having a house to himself. In it the suggestions made by other voices were no longer forced upon him, and he was free of all impressions except those he had himself intended. When he had drunk his coffee he sat down in his library, after letting it be known that he would not be at home to visitors until after three o'clock in the afternoon.

Now he took up an old plan for the study of the present ethnography of Europe, which would save him from making fruitless journeys. On printed circular letters under the name of a fictitious firm, he filled in addresses and professional titles, put them into envelopes, and stamped them. He calculated that, in order to get the most complete information about the sizes of skulls and the dimensions of bodies, the desired result would be produced by sending circulars to hatters, coffin-makers, and shirt and stocking manufacturers, requesting information about the sizes most in demand within each country, with a view to the export of these goods by the gross, at a greater profit than usual. In addition, he had sent off another circular letter to both the large and the small booksellers in the capitals and provincial towns of Europe asking for photographs of all kinds of people at a high price, and with cash on delivery, and he had also got in touch with a technician who bought photographs in order to utilise their silver. With these, and the thousands of portraits he had cut out from all the foreign illustrated newspapers, he intended to begin his researches.

By the time he had finished this work it was midday. He went out to eat his lunch, and noticed that a letter had been pushed into the box by the door. The handwriting was familiar, and when he had confirmed that it was from Miss Maria he did not open it, but let it lie beside him on the table while he ate his simple meal in great haste. He knew that the communication could not contain anything pleasant. He had broken his promise to return the next day to say goodbye and, as he now wanted to save himself all unpleasant impressions, he put the letter away in a drawer in his desk, without opening it.

But when he had slept for an hour, and the fever for work and food had subsided, he noticed that his thoughts no longer turned to books, but were drawn towards the drawer. Now he began to pace the floor, to and fro, a prey to a violent and exhausting emotional conflict. It was as if he had part of her soul shut up in that drawer; she was in the room, and the attractive power of her spirit lay stored in the white envelope, on which a red seal shone like a kiss. He saw her sitting there, on this same sofa, heard her whispers, felt her eyes glowing in the dusk, and his flesh again began to burn. How stupid, he thought, to let the highest bliss in life slip through his fingers. As love was a matter of mutual deception, why not let yourself be deceived? Nothing for nothing! And, as perfect happiness did not exist, why not content yourself with imperfect?

He now felt that he should have crawled to her, lied that he was her slave, and acknowledged himself beaten. He could have frightened off his rival, and with her to himself in a complete union it would have been easy to bind her with the bonds of habit and interests. Finally she would not have wanted to take her enjoyment with another.

Then came the fear that this letter might deprive him of his last hope, which was at least better than nothing, and he determined not to read it. He had sat down at his laboratory bench and, almost without thinking what he was doing, he opened an iron retort, stuffed the letter into it, and lit the burner beneath it. After a moment the smoke puffed out of the neck of the retort, and when the smoke ceased he lit the gas with a match. A little yellow-blue flame burnt for some minutes with a whining sound like the squeak of a bat.

The soul of the letter, an alchemist would have said! A mass of paper which, when consumed, became carbon and hydrogen – the same product of combustion as a burning soul in a living body. Carbon and hydrogen. It was all one and the same thing.

The flame flickered, sank, crept into the tube and once more the room was in darkness.

The sky over the sea was again overcast. The waves were running before an easterly wind, thudding on the shore, sighing, spluttering, and the wind was being cut in two by the corner of the cottage, like a wave against a ship's stem. And in the midst of all these sounds of lamentation he heard the buoy shrieking out at sea, rhythmically, like a tragedian reciting with pauses, as if taking a breath, or letting the last word die away before he allowed a new one to come streaming out. It was a solo for Titan with an accompaniment of tempest, a giant organ with the easterly wind tramping the bellows.

The room seemed to him suffocating, and he took his coat and went out into the storm to let the wind blow away his discomfort. Drawn against his will by a lantern in the shop, he steered his course in that direction. As the drift-net fishing had been very productive the shop was much patronised and, hidden by the darkness, he was able to pass close to the fishermen as they conversed without being seen.

'So the assistant pinched his girl from him,' said old Öman, 'and she got a real man instead of that load of . . .'

'Aye, he's not what a man should be,' added the unmarried Vestman. 'Today he wrote near a hundred letters to go with the boat, and what he's busy cooking up in there no mortal man can tell, but I think what I think, I do. And we need to keep our eyes about us with folk like that, who shut themselves up and boil the stuff. We all know that sort.'

'Dammit,' put in the married Vestman. 'Let'm brew his drop himself. It can't turn out any worse for him than it did for old Söderlund, who mashed out on the rocks and lost his still. I don't think we should meddle with it anyhow.'

'Oh, if that was all it was,' resumed Öman, 'of course we'd let 'im get on with it. But you see you, I can't forget that time he wanted to take my net off me, and if I catch 'im by the fin, I'll not let him go before I've got him in the corf.'

'Well, it's a bad man that has no God,' said the preacher. 'For sure it is.'

Though he had no illusions at all about gratitude, the inspector could not avoid feelings of discomfort at finding himself surrounded in this desert by nothing but enemies, and these the most dangerous of the dangerous, who saw in him a fool or a criminal. They believed that he was distilling spirits in order to make a profit of fifty öre a jug. They suspected him of mixing poison for them, and if any misfortune occurred he would get the blame for it. And if they used their illegal nets he would not dare confiscate them without running the risk of some more or less scandalous prosecution, or what was worse, revenge.

They were dangerous company, as mortally dangerous as stupidity itself. He knew that at any moment he wished he could convert them all to friends by inviting them to a jug of spirits and partaking of it himself, but it never for a moment occurred to him to do so. Their hatred left him free; their friendship would have dragged him down into their own mire. Their enmity would only serve to stimulate the current of his power, while their affection would have neutralised it, even if their souls could never make contact with his. There was a certain pleasure in the danger itself, as it kept his mind active and supple, gave him something to react against and practise upon. For that matter the danger among these savages was no greater than it had been up there, in the circles he had recently left, where the power to inflict real damage was greater. Had not the doctor on the corvette regarded him as a sick man when he had said that a way must be found of utilising the enormous quantities of nitrogen gas that were wasted in the manufacture of sulphuric acid, while at the same time expensive Chile saltpetre was imported to compensate for the loss of nitrogen in the soil? And when he had said something about utilising the smoke from chimneys for technical purposes, had not his friends advised him to take a holiday at a bathing-resort and mix with people.

Better far to remain in absolute solitude, and be taken for an idiot by redskins, than be doomed to a civic death by his equals with their authority and jurisdiction, against whom there was no appeal.

After wandering about in the dark for a time he returned to his cottage, lit candles and lamps in his two rooms, opened the doors to the entrance lobby, and thus dispelled the feeling of being shut in.

When he looked at his watch he saw that it was no more than eight o'clock. The long evening and night ahead frightened him. His head was far too tired for work, but not tired enough for sleep. The whistling of the wind round the corners of the cottage, the thunder of the waves and the bellowing of the buoy made him nervous. To rid himself of these suggestive sounds, to which he did not wish to be a slave, he put into his ears his 'sleeping pellets', little steel balls that he had bought in Germany which, when inserted in the ears, prevented the penetration of any noise.

But when he had shut off what is perhaps the greatest channel of communication with the outside world, his imagination began to work at high pressure. A furious curiosity to know what the burnt letter had contained gripped him so irresistibly that he opened the retort and tried to read the ashes. But even the ink had been consumed by the fire, and there was not a trace of writing to be seen. The field was now clear for all kinds of doubts and surmises. At one moment he thought he could conclude from all that had gone before what the contents of the letter had been. At another he rejected this idea when he remembered the girl's illogical way of thinking and acting.

He finally made up his mind to cease worrying about what was incalculable. But his brain was now running wild, fretting independently, grinding and sifting, until he was utterly worn out, yet unable to sleep. And as his thinking organ grew weaker, so his lower passions awoke.

Furious that his soul could not hold out in the struggle with his fragile flesh, he finally undressed, took a dose of potassium bromide, and the wild gallop of his brain immediately stopped. His imagination was extinguished, his consciousness benumbed, and he slept as deeply as if he had died.

XIV

Autumn had advanced, but nothing on the island indicated that summer had flown, for on it there was not a single deciduous tree that could turn yellow. The moisture had made the lichen on the rocks swell up luxuriantly, the ling and the crowberry bushes were putting out new leaves, and the juniper and dwarf pine, those evergreen trees of the north, had been freshened up by the rain and polished free of dust.

The fisherfolk had gone now that their autumn work was over. Silence had fallen again and the shop was shut. The wooden framework of the chapel grew more and more naked as the planks were stripped from it to provide firewood for coffee-making, and wood for carpentry. All that you now saw were the posts, and these resembled a collection of gallows.

The preacher was seldom seen nowadays, for, since becoming a teetotaller, he had misused a wine fortified with quinine and cognac. He already had a buzzing in his ears and palpitations, and slept for most of the time.

The inspector had had to work for a month before he succeeded in healing his soul from the gunshot wound he had sustained during the game he had played with love. By means of potassium bromide and a reduced diet he had cured his desire, and when the misery of his loneliness took hold of him, he made himself a dose of laughing-gas from ammonium nitrate, as he had long ago discovered that alcoholic intoxication was simple-minded, and was followed by dejection and suicidal mania. At first the marvellous nitrous oxide had cheered him and made him laugh, but the sneers of the mob had reduced all his great thoughts and endeavours to nothing, and it was at this nothing that he was laughing. When he found himself down among the mockers who had mocked him, he experienced a need to raise himself above himself again, and he thought of his sorrow and his pain with regret.

But when he had isolated himself completely, and the maid was only allowed to clean and bring him food when he was locked in his attic room, all the memories of the summer began to haunt him. He remembered, without willing it, every word that had been spoken, and the behaviour of the preacher out on the skerry in the mist stood out as something that had been planned. Now that he compared the words the man had uttered about his circumstances and those of his father with what Miss Maria had said about knowing who he was, they took root, grew, and became large. There must be some secret in his life that everyone but he knew. And soon he saw in the behaviour of the preacher a plan to spy on him, supported by those who wanted to persecute him. In his calmer moments he did not believe this, for he knew very well that persecution mania was one of the first symptoms of the weakness that accompanies isolation. Humanity was a huge electric battery of many elements, and the element that was isolated immediately lost its power. The reel wound round with copper wire was paralysed the moment the soft iron rod was removed, and he was on the way to being paralysed now that his iron rod had become tempered steel.

But he was not suffering from that sickly persecution mania that comes from bodily weakness. He had actually been persecuted right from his schooldays as soon as he had revealed himself to be a power, the founder of a new species, that would be able to break away from its family, like the plant that differentiates itself, gets itself a name of its own, perhaps the name of a new family. He had been persecuted instinctively, from below by his inferiors and from above by the mediocre, who later sat like inspectors of weights and measures who decide the yardstick by which greatness should be judged. He had been hated and pecked like the golden bird from the Canary Islands when it escapes from its cage and gets among the siskins in the forest, and these wild birds are annoyed by its far-too-splendid garb.

Nature, in which he had previously sought companionship, was now dead to him, for the human link between them was missing. The sea, which he had worshipped and looked upon as the only magnificent thing in his commonplace country, with its finicking, trivial, summer-cottage scenery, began to seem cramped as his ego expanded. This bluish, turpentine-green ring of grey shut him in like a prison yard, and the monotonous, puny view inflicted the same torture as the punishment cell: lack of impressions. He could not journey away from it all, for he was rooted in this soil, in his small impressions, in his diet, and he could not be dug up by the roots. This was the tragedy of the northerner which finds expression in his longing for the south.

It was then that he began to think out and plan a link with the mainland for this land, this insular country, for the fact that it was attached to the continent by Lapland did not alter matters. First of all a six-hour express train to Hälsingborg[1] with a connection by steam-ferry would make the capital of Denmark the centre of the Nordic countries. Ports at Djurö and Nynäs,[2] made ice-free throughout the year by icebreakers, would keep sea-transport alive all the year round, thus preventing the northerner's winter sleep, so that the nature of the national character – its instability, always ascribed to this six month's cessation of all activity – would be changed. Russian trade with England would go via Stockholm and Gothenburg, and the old plan of Charles XI and Charles XII of directing Persian trade across Russia and Scandinavia would be realised.

Sweden would become a tourist country and foreigners would be tempted to come here. He wanted to change Stockholm into a salt-sea city by shutting off Lake Mälaren at Norrbro and Slussen[3] and at the same time open a system of canals from Strängnäs through Lake Båven out to Trosa Bay.[4] In that way there would be salt-water up to Skeppsbron and Nybroviken, which would change the atmospheric conditions, and with them the people.

He remembered the time when Sweden, by belonging to the great universal Christian Church, had stood in direct communication with Rome, and had consequently been reckoned as part of Europe. And, if it seemed that the great mass of the people could not abandon religion, he wanted to introduce once again the faith of their forefathers, which they had been forced by fire and sword to renounce, and whose martyrs – Hans Brask, Olaus and Johannes Magnus, Nils Dacke and Ture Jönsson[5] – had been so disgracefully besmirched by historians. And Catholicism, our Roman inheritance, the first promoter of the idea of Europeanism, had already spread victoriously round Europe. Bismarck had fallen in the cultural struggle, gone to Canossa,[6] and after he had begun to believe in arbitration without steel cannon, had chosen the Pope to be the arbiter of peace. Denmark had built Catholic cathedrals, and young Danes had already lent their pens to the cause. The Teutonisation of the north, like that of North Germany after the battles of the Huns in 1870,[7] was simply a relapse into barbarism, the result of which had manifested itself in the persecution of everything Latin and hatred of the French. It had found expression in a war of extermination against French literature, in a North German policy for the family, in a Lutheran inquisition and prison for heretics, and in a general fall in the level of intelligence.

Lutheranism was the enemy! Teutonic culture, bourgeois religion in black breeches, sectarian narrow-mindedness, particularism, barriers, imprisonment and spiritual death.

No, Europe must be one again. The way of the people was via Rome, that of the intelligentsia via Paris!

The Swedish farmer should again feel himself to be a citizen of the world. He should emerge from his lower-class position, and once again have a glimpse of that world of beauty the Church had formerly offered him in pictures and music. His divine service should become a true song of praise in the Latin language, a song created by poets and not by the authors of psalmbooks. He would comprehend just enough of it to arouse in him an exalted conception of the thing which, in any case, he could not understand. His High Mass should be conducted by real priests who devoted their lives to religion and the care of souls, instead of to agriculture, dairy-farming, card-playing and office work.[8] Then the farmer's wife would have a spiritual guide to whom, at confession, she could confide her troubles, instead of running to the parsonage kitchen and telling them to the servants.

With the reintroduction of Latin, all the learned men of Europe would be able to read the doctors' dissertations of all the Uppsala students, and every Swedish scholar would feel that he was a member of the great universal body of the intelligentsia under the pontificate of Paris.

He wrote down these and many other thoughts and put them into a drawer, as he knew of no newspaper that would print them, least of all the patriots who 'from envy had no wish to receive suggestions for the improvement of their fatherland'.

He had now received answers to his circulars and the attic room was full of material for his European ethnography. But he had lost interest in the subject, and his spirit had become so seriously depressed that he did not even dare to go out. The sight of another human being aroused such feelings of disgust that he turned back home if he caught a glimpse of anyone. At the same time there grew in him a need to hear his own voice, to unload his over-productive brain by contact with another human being, to feel that he was influencing the life of others, and to have some companionship. For a moment he had thought of getting himself a dog, but to deposit layers of his soul and his feelings in the body of an animal would be to graft vines on thistles, and he had never allowed himself to be duped by the affection of that filthy, sponging animal.

There was only one man to whom he felt drawn, and that was the married customs man Vestman, whose wife lived bigamously, though her husband was unaware of it. This man looked honest, and was quite intelligent. The inspector resumed dealings with him by giving him a salmon-line with hooks attached. At the beginning of the summer he had in fact lent him books and taught him to write from a copy, but since the fishing had speeded up and traffic at sea had increased, their ways had parted.

To persuade the man actually to lay out the salmon-line, the inspector had to avoid telling him that salmon was the objective. If he had, the conservative fisherman would never have agreed to employ what he regarded as absurd and futile tackle. The man was therefore led to believe that it was a question of a new and profitable method of cod-fishing, by which the largest fish could be obtained.

When, after a month of isolation, the inspector rowed out to sea with Vestman, and again heard his own voice, he noticed that from lack of use it had changed timbre and become thinner, so that he thought he heard a stranger speaking. He now intoxicated himself with speech. His brain, which had been externally active only through his hand and his pen, now broke through the sluice-gates of his larynx, and all his thoughts poured out like a waterfall, breeding new thoughts on the way. And when he was able to talk with a human ear for a sounding-board, without being interrupted, and without being questioned, it seemed to him that he had a listener who understood him, and after their first trip together he was convinced that Vestman was the most intelligent person he had met for a long time.

So, on their expeditions, he kept on telling him for eight days about all the wonders of nature. He explained the effect the moon had on the surface of the water, warned him not to believe that what he saw with his eyes was all it 'appeared' to be. He told him, for instance, that the moon was pear-shaped, though it looked like a globe, and that consequently no one could be certain that the earth was spherical . . .

At this Vestman had grimaced, and for the first time had dared to raise an objection.

'Ay, but it do say so in me almanac all the same.'

The inspector saw that he had gone too far and must turn back. But it was too late. An exposition of recent researches on the shape of the earth showing that it was an ellipsoid,[9] with three axes, required some basic knowledge on the part of the listener, and he therefore moved on to another subject. He talked about mirages, and took the opportunity to ask if the Vestmans had visited Svärdholm and seen the havoc he, the inspector, had wrought there.

'Of course we've seen that someone's been mucked things up out there. But no one goes ashore there no more, and we've give up both trawling and sheep-minding,' answered Vestman with complete credibility.

After this confession the inspector retired feeling ashamed of having been a prey to the optical illusion that his listener had understood what he said. He had been talking to a wall, and taken his own echo to be the other's voice.

. . .

Eight days later there was a great commotion on the island, as Vestman had caught a salmon weighing twenty-six pounds. And as he thought himself to be the inventor of that sort of fishing, there was soon a notice in the paper about a new means of livelihood for the archipelago, now that the herring-fishing had begun to decline. The fortunate fisherman, Erik Vestman, had thereby earned himself the respect and gratitude of his fellows, etc . . .

Shortly afterwards a weekly paper of a popular nature printed a slanderous article on Inspectors of Fisheries, who didn't know a thing, but believed that they could teach people everything.

This was followed by a letter to the inspector from the Ministry of Agriculture and Forestry asking for full reports on the fishing being done, in particular the salmon-fishing, to which the inspector replied merely by asking to be discharged.

Devoid of any further interest in the population, and without the slight support that his former official position had given him, he soon became aware that the savages, who believed that he had been 'kicked out', had begun to wage a war of total extermination. They started by casting adrift his boat, which was then driven ashore and broken up, on the pretext that there was no room for it by the landing-stage.

When it next rained he noticed that rain-water was getting into the attic. And after he had complained to Öman some of the other rooms also began to let in the rain, though he was unable to discover a missing tile.

Not long after this someone broke into his cellar at night, and the culprit was said to be an Estonian.

It was quite clear that they wanted to get rid of him, but now it pleased him to defy them. This he did by never making any remarks, and by putting up with everything.

However, now that he was surrounded by real enemies and had to retreat from the community in earnest, the dread of the outlawed man came upon him with redoubled force.

He slept badly at night, despite the fact that he tried to control his dreams by strong suggestions, given just before he fell asleep. But when he awoke he had dreamt that he was a sounding-buoy, cut adrift, floating hither and thither in search of a shore on which to be thrown. In his sleep he had unconsciously sought for support from the bed-board, in order to experience contact with some object, even if an inanimate one. Sometimes he dreamt that he was hovering in the air, and could neither rise nor fall, and when he finally awoke after a fainting fit, his hands were gripping the pillow on which he had laid his head. Then memories of his deceased mother would rise to the surface, and he often awoke after dreaming that he lay like a child at her breast. His soul was obviously in reverse, and the memory of the mother – the source, the link between conscious and unconscious life, the comforter, the mediator – came to the fore. Childhood beliefs in a reunion in another life flared up, and his first suicide plans took the form of an irresistible longing to find his mother again, somewhere, in another world in which he did not believe.

Science could not prevail against a sinking soul which had lost all interest in life. His brain had struggled until it was weary, and his imagination worked out of control.

As Christmas approached he still got up, but he ate little, and took only ether at night. The whole of life disgusted him, and he now laughed at his former exertions. Rain-water had damaged his books and papers; his apparatuses were green with verdigris and rusty.

Care for his own person had faded. His beard had grown long, his hair remained uncombed. It was a long time since he had sent his linen to the wash and he had lost the ability to see dirt.

His clothes had no buttons and the front of his jacket was always soiled by spilt food, since the hands that guided his knife and fork no longer obeyed his will.

If he ever went out the children pulled faces at him, and found nicknames for him.

One morning he had been surrounded by a swarm of children. They had tugged at his coat, and one had thrown a stone that hit him squarely on his chin so that the blood ran. Then he had burst into tears, and begged them not to be nasty to him.

'Oh just be off with you, crazy guy,' shouted a twelve-year-old boy, 'or we'll be having you on the parish.'

At this they all began to throw stones. But then Öman's maidservant came out and seized the boy by the hair. And when she had punished him she went up to their victim and wiped the blood from his face with her apron.

'Poor little fellow,' she said.

And then he leaned against her ample bosom, and said: 'I should like to sleep beside you.'

'For shame,' snapped the girl, pushing him away. 'It's a dirty mind you've got! Fie!'

One evening a few days later, Vestman's maidservant came running down to ask the doctor to come up and attend to the mistress, who was dying. The request came rather unexpectedly to the inspector but, with the clearsightedness which in lucid intervals accompanied his illness, he saw that this was a case of murder, and they required his name and title to replace the medico-legal post-mortem examination. This matter was of no importance to him, but it had a momentarily stimulating effect. Something had happened, and this rare occurence had made an impression, a thing which had long been lacking. He therefore went up to the customs house, and was met by both the brothers, who led him into the sick-room with a civility which seemed highly suspicious. But he said nothing and asked nothing, for he wanted to force the hidden confession into the open by making the man speak first, feeling sure that he would give himself away with his first word.

The child was sitting beside a tallow candle eating a saffron bun, which had not been produced for fun. She was wearing her best clothes, presumably to make her feel that the occasion was a solemn one and she must behave with restraint.

After the inspector had looked round the room, and observed that Vestman's brother had sneaked out, he approached the bed where the woman was lying.

He saw immediately that she was dead, and from the taut

muscles of her face realised that violence had been used. And when he noticed that the hair on the crown of her head had been carefully combed he understood in a flash that the good old method of the nail had been used.

But he wanted the man to speak first, so with half-open mouth and eloquent eyes, as if intending to ask a question, he turned to Vestman. The latter instantly allowed himself to be caught and, trusting to the fact that no great cunning was necessary when talking to a madman, he said:

'Ye can certify that she's finished, can't ye doctor? Then we can bury her right now, for look ye, us poor folk can't afford to fetch a medical man out here.'

This was enough for partial confirmation. But instead of answering, the inspector turned to Vestman who, having brought out his request, was now completely calm, and in a half-whisper asked:

'Where is the hammer?'

At first the man started back two steps as if intending to strangle his adversary. But the inspector disarmed him by casting a glance at the little girl, after which he stood still trembling.

'You don't know where the hammer is, but I know where the nail is,' continued the inspector with unruffled calm. 'You over-wise donkeys who can't think of anything new, but like children playing hide-and-seek, always hide in the same place. I am convinced that driving a nail into the cranium was invented by a nobleman or a priest in the Middle Ages, and has only just got down to the lower classes, who have dug it up to prove how cunning the mob can be. Everything comes from above. Salmon, arsenic, nails, accidental shots, revolutions, freedom for the masses, economic prosperity, folk-songs, country dialects, country-lore and anthropological museums. But they are taken in the first place by stealth, for you, the mob, would steal sooner than receive a gift because you are too mean to say thank you. That's why you put your benefactors in the madhouse, and send your aristocrats to the scaffold. Now put me in the madhouse, and save yourself from prison.'

Back in the cottage he remembered that the pleasure of

speaking out had tempted him into being incautious. Knowing the temper of the people, he realised that in self-defence the murderer might be moved to reduce a dangerous witness to silence. He therefore slept with a revolver in his bed and had bad dreams that woke him.

The following day he stayed indoors, and saw that white sheets were hanging in the windows of the customs house. On the third day the body was carried out and taken away in a boat, and on the fourth day the men returned. After that he no longer slept, and sleeplessness completed the work of destruction. The fear of going mad, of being put in an asylum, coupled with the dread that he might at any time be assassinated, strengthened his determination to leave life of his own free will. But now, as death approached, and the end of a life, of a family, stood forth in all its desolation, it was as if the procreative urge had crept out and was expressing itself in the longing to possess a child. But to take the whole banal course, to seek out a woman, to bind himself to a family, to the earth, to the community, seemed more repellent than ever, and in his weak, shattered condition he thought out a short cut which would bestow on him the joy of procreation, if only for a few hours.

In roundabout ways, against which his sensitivity would have revolted a few months earlier, he obtained, after some delay, the seed of a human being. He had previously constructed an incubator under the microscope, in which a temperature of thirty-six to forty degrees of warmth could be maintained. When fertilisation was taking place he saw the males swarming round the passive females, whom he imagined he could see blushing. And then they pushed, elbowed, and whipped each other in their struggle to give rise to a family, to propagate his talent, to graft his lively, creative spirit on to a strong, wild stock. But it was not the grosser ones with their big, stupid heads and thick tails, but the quickest, most agile, most fiery who first penetrated the membrane, and forced their way to the nucleus.

With his thumb on the screw of the spirit-lamp, and one eye on the thermometer, he watched the unveiling of love's mysteries for a couple of hours. He saw the cells beginning to divide, saw how the distribution of function among the different chromosomes had already taken place. He watched with anxiety for the expansion of the anterior of the medullary canal into the bulb that would form the head. He dreamed that he saw this seat of thought arching beautifully, experienced a second of pride over this, his creation, which had solved the problem of the homunculus,[10] when suddenly a movement of the screw caused the albumen to curdle and the spark of life to die away.

During this time he had lived the life of this other being so intensely that now, when he saw the dull white spot on the glass, it seemed to him that he beheld an eye shattered by death. And, enhanced by his sick mind, the pain of this grew to sorrow, sorrow for his lost child. The bond between the present and the future was severed, and he had no strength to begin all over again.

When he came to himself he felt a strong, warm hand holding his right hand, and he remembered that he had dreamt that he had been a shipwrecked vessel, tossed by the waves between air and water, until he had felt the tug of an anchor-chain and had experienced a feeling of calm, as if contact with dry land had again been made.

Without looking up, and for the sake of being close to a living creature, he pressed the firm hand and imagined that he felt power being transmitted to him through this link between his fragile nervous system and a stronger one.

'How are things with you?' he heard the preacher's voice saying above his head.

'If you were a woman I could live again, for woman is man's roots in the earth,' answered the sick man, using the familiar '*du*' to his old comrade for the first time.

'Thank your luck that you lost that rotten root.'

'Without a root we cannot grow and blossom.'

'But with such a woman, Borg?'

'Such a woman? Do you know what sort she was? I never found out.'

'Well, then all you need to know is that she was not the sort one marries, though she is now engaged, all the same.'

'To him?'

'To him! It was in the paper the day before yesterday.'

After a few moments of silence the preacher got up to go, but the sick man held him back.

'Tell me a fairy-story,' he begged, in a childishly persuasive voice.

'Hm! A fairy-story?'

'Yes, a fairy-story. The one about Tom Thumb, for example. Do please, I beg you.'

The preacher sat down again, and when he saw that the sick man was in earnest, he did as he desired and began the tale.

The inspector listened with close attention, but when the preacher, true to his habit, wanted to draw from it a moral lesson, he was interrupted by the sick man who told him to stick to the text.

'It does one so much good to hear the old fairy-tales,' he said. 'It's like a rest to sink down into one's best memories of the time when one was a little animal, and loved what was useless, absurd and meaningless. Say "Our Father" for me now.'

'You don't believe in "Our Father", do you?'

'No, no more than in fairy-tales, but it does me good, all the same. As death approaches and we turn to the past, we love what is old, and become conservative. Say "Our Father" please. You shall have what I leave, and your IOU back, if you say it.'

The preacher hesitated a moment, then he began to recite.

The sick man listened, first in silence, then his lips followed the sounds and finally uttered them clearly, in the voice of one praying.

When it was over, the preacher said:

'I think it is good to pray.'

'It is like medicine. The old words awaken memories and give us strength, the same strength that they formerly gave to the selfless, who sought for God outside themselves. Do you know what God is? He is the fixed point outside ourselves, desired by Archimedes,[11] with which he would have been able to lift the world. He is the imaginary magnet inside the earth, without which the movements of the magnetic needle would remain unexplained. He is the ether that must be discovered so that the vacuum may be filled. He is the molecule, without which the laws of chemistry would be miracles. Give me a few more hypotheses, above all the fixed point outside myself, for I am quite adrift.'

'Do you want me to tell you about Jesus?' asked the preacher, who believed that the sick man was delirious.

'No, not Jesus, damn him! He is neither a fairy-tale nor a hypothesis. He is the invention of revengeful slaves and wicked women. He is the God of the molluscs as opposed to the vertebrate . . . but wait. I am but a mollusc. Talk about Jesus. Tell me how he mixed with customs officers and whores as I have done. Tell me how the poor of spirit are to people the heavens, since they did not rule on earth. Tell me how he taught dishonest tenants to write false IOUs, taught artisans to loiter, and beggars, idlers and prodigal sons, who owned nothing, to live in fellowship with workers who did.'

'No, you blasphemer! I'm not your fool,' interrupted the preacher, and got to his feet determinedly.

'Don't go, don't go!' cried the sick man. 'Hold my hand and let me hear your voice. Talk to me about what you please. Read, read the Bible. It's all the same to me. *Horror vacui*, fear of empty nothingness. I must be rid of it.'

'You see, you do fear death.'

'Of course I do, like all living creatures who, without a fear of death, would never have lived. But judgement I do not fear, for the master is judged by his work, and I did not create myself.'

But the preacher had gone.

. . .

It was on the day before Christmas Eve when, after a wild night, during which he had thought he heard cannon-fire and the cries of human beings, he went out to wander about on the new-fallen snow. The sky was blue-black, like iron-plate, the waves hurled themselves against the shore, while the sounding buoy cried out in one continuous yell, as if it were calling for help.

And now, out on the reef in the south-east he saw a large

black steamer, whose vermilion bottom shone like a blood-stained, shattered breast. The funnel, with its ring of white, lay broken to one side, and among the masts and the yards hung dark figures, twisted like worm-bait on hooks.

From a rent amidships the waves seemed to be dragging out a mixed cargo of packets, bales, tins and cartons, sinking the heaviest and carrying the lightest ashore.

With the indifference to the fate of the shipwrecked that a man must feel who thinks it a stroke of good fortune to die, he walked along the shore and came out to the headland where the cairn and the cross were raised, and where the waves were foaming more ferociously than anywhere else. Scattered over the green water he saw objects of strange shapes and colours, over which the gulls were circling, screeching angrily, as if cheated of their greedy expectations of prey.

These curious objects came nearer and nearer, and as he studied them he saw that they resembled very small gaily dressed children. Some had fair fringes on their foreheads, others dark. Their cheeks were rosy and white, and their large, wide-open blue eyes stared straight up at the black sky and neither moved nor blinked. But as they came nearer to the shore he noticed that the eyes of some moved, as if they were signalling to him to rescue them, and with the next swell five were thrown up on the shore.

His fixed desire to possess a child was so rooted in his weak brain that it never occurred to him that they were dolls which the belated shipwrecked vessel had been bringing for the Christmas market. He therefore gathered up an armful of these small foundlings bestowed on him by that great mother the sea. With his wet little charges clasped to his breast he hurried back to the cottage to dry them. But he had nothing with which to make a fire, for the people of the island had declared that they had no wood to sell. He himself did not notice the cold, but his little charges must have warmth. He therefore broke up a book-case and made a flaming fire on the large hearth, drew up a sofa, and sat the tiny creatures in a row right in front of the fire. When he realised that they could not get dry unless he undressed them, he began to take off their clothes, but when he saw that they were all girls he left on their little vests.

He then washed their hands and feet with his sponge, combed their hair, dressed them, and left them to sleep.

It was as if visitors had come to the cottage, and he walked about on tip-toe in order not to disturb them.

He had got something to live for, something to take care of, on which to bestow his compassion. And when, after looking at the little sleepers for a while, he noticed that their eyes were open, he thought the light must be bothering them, and drew down the blinds.

As the light in the room began to grow dim he was overcome by an oppressive desire to sleep, which stemmed from hunger, though he was now no longer able to assign the reasons for his sensations to their rightful place, and thus did not know when he was hungry or thirsty. As the sofa was occupied by the little ones he lay down on the floor and slept.

When he awoke the room was dark, but the door had been opened, and a woman was standing on the threshold with a lighted lantern.

'Good God, he's lying on the floor,' he heard Öman's maid-servant exclaim. 'But dear little gentleman, don't you know that today is Christmas Eve?'

He had slept for over twenty-four hours, and into the afternoon of the following day.

Not fully conscious, he got up, but felt that something was missing, for the customs officer had been down and confiscated the flotsam. But he could not remember what it was he missed. He only felt the dreadful emptiness of a great bereavement.

'Now ye must come up to Öman's, and eat Christmas porridge, for see we're all Christians at Christmas-time. Oh my God, what a state of misery!'

And the girl burst into tears.

'To see a fellow critter go to pieces this way. It's enow to make a body weep tears of blood! Come now, do come.'

The half-demented fellow only signed to her that he would follow, but that she must go first.

After she had left him he waited for a while in the cottage. Then he took the lantern she had left and went to the mirror. When he saw his face, which resembled that of a savage, his mind seemed to clear, and his will to tense for a final effort.

Leaving the lantern, he went out.

The wind had veered west and slackened somewhat; the air was clear, and the starry sky glittered. Led by the lights from the cottages he went down to the harbour, slipped into a boat-house, and took out a sail.

Having hoisted it he cast off, took the tiller and, with a following wind, steered straight out to sea.

First he tacked about to look once more on the little fragment of ground which was the scene of his last sufferings. But when he saw a three-branched candlestick in the window of the customs house, where the murderer was paying homage to Jesus – the exonerator, the idol of all criminals and wastrels, by whom all wickedness punished by civil law is excused – he turned about, spat, hauled on the sheet, and set full sail. With his back to the land he steered by the great chart of the stars and took a bearing by a star of the second magnitude between Lyra and Corona in the east. He thought it shone more brightly than all the rest, and when he searched his memory he caught a glimpse of something about a Christmas star, the lodestar to Bethlehem, the place to which the three deposed kings had gone on a pilgrimage to worship, as fallen celebrities, their own insignificance in the smallest of human children, the child who later became the avowed God of all the small . . . No it could not be that. The punishment of the Christian magicians for bringing darkness upon the earth was that not a single point of light had been named after them in the vault of the heavens. Consequently they celebrated the darkest time of the year – how sublimely absurd – by lighting tapers. Now his memory cleared. It was the star Beta in Hercules. Hercules, the Greeks' moral ideal, the God of wisdom and strength, who killed the Lernaean Hydra with a hundred heads, who cleansed the Augean stables, caught the man-eating bulls of Diomedes, tore her girdle from the Queen of the Amazons, brought Cerberus from the underworld, to fall at last because of the stupidity of a woman.[12] She poisoned him from pure love after his fit of madness, during which he served the nymph Omphale for three years . . .[13]

Out towards the one whom at least the heavens had received. The one who had never allowed himself to be whipped or spat in the face without, like a man, hitting and spitting back. Out towards the one who had burnt himself,[14] who could only die from his own strong hand, without begging for grace from the chalice. Out to Heracles[15] who had bred Prometheus, the bringer of light, himself the son of a god and a human mother,[16] though the barbarians later misrepresented him as a virgin boy, whose birth was celebrated by milk-drinking shepherds and braying asses.

He steered his course out towards the new Christmas star, out over the sea, the mother of all, in whose womb the first spark of life was lit, the inexhaustible well of fertility and love, life's source, and life's enemy.

Notes

Chapter I

1. Österskär. The Swedish word *skär* means a rock sticking up above the surface of the sea. It is applied indiscriminately to large and small rocks. Where the context indicates a larger or inhabited rock I have translated it 'island'; in the case of smaller rocks 'skerry'. Huvudskär, called Österskär in *By the Open Sea*, is the largest island of the most easterly group of islands and skerries in the Stockholm archipelago. Strindberg visited it in 1881, eight years before he wrote this book, and has described it thus in *Svenska Folket*:

Right out at sea, off the north-eastern point of Södertörn, lies Huvudskär. It is a rocky island without a tree, now a customs and pilot station, but primarily a harbour for the most important Baltic-herring fishery in the Stockholm archipelago.

2. Strindberg is probably thinking of the Uroborus, the dragon or serpent that bites its own tail and which in ancient alchemy was the symbol of the eternal cycle of birth and death, as well as of latent power. This is the function of the bracelet in *By the Open Sea*. It is only brought into prominence when Borg is about to perform some extraordinary feat.

3. Dalarö. A small fishing-centre and seaside-resort on a peninsula about forty-three kilometres south of Stockholm. Today it has both bus and boat transport, in Strindberg's day probably only boat. In *By the Open Sea* when people talk of going to the mainland it is Dalarö they mean.

4. Tom Thumb is the pigmy or dwarf who outwits the giant.

Chapter III

1. Strindberg uses 'it' for fish, birds etc. that he dislikes and 'he' or 'she' for those he likes.

2. The Hall of the Nobility (*Riddarhussalen*). The large hall in the House of the Nobility (*Riddarhuset*), in which the nobility met for deliberations or festive occasions from 1657 to 1866 when their political power was annulled.

3. Parliamentary representation in Sweden before 1866 was divided into Four Estates (Nobility, Clergy, Burghers and Farmers i.e. free peasant proprietors). By 'a fourth part', Strindberg means the Estate of the Nobility. The Estates met and deliberated separately when a parliament was called, which usually happened annually.

4. This change of title is unexplained.

5. Berzelius, Jöns Jacob (1779–1848). A famous Swedish chemist.

6. Lyell, Sir Charles (1797–1875). A Scottish geologist. Repeatedly president of the Geological Society, and president of the British Association in 1864.

7. Agassiz, J. L. R. (1807–73). A Swiss naturalist.

8. Renan, Ernst (1823–92). A French philologist who was destined for the Church, but became unable to accept traditional Christianity.

9. Strauss, David Friedrich (1808–74). A German theologian whose *Leben Jesu*, which raised a storm of controversy, was translated by George Eliot.

10. Mill, John Stuart (1806–73). An English philosopher and radical reformer, in whom Strindberg was deeply interested.

11. Buckle, Henry Thomas (1821–62). Author of the *History of Civilization in England* (1857–61) which Strindberg possessed in a Swedish translation.

12. Taine, Hippolyte Adolphe (1828–93). A French critic, historian and philosopher.

Chapter IV

1. The Swedish flag.

2. Dannebrog. The Danish flag.

Chapter V

1. Gustavian bed. Made or built during the reign of Gustav III (1771–92) during which time Swedish culture blossomed.

2. Mora. A small town in central Sweden, famous for its grandfather clocks of peasant design.

3. Långholmen. A prison in Stockholm for male offenders.

4. In the past Swedish ladies were addressed by the feminine version of their husband's title on the principle of prince–princess, but greatly extended. The title of the old lady's husband was *Kammarråd*, and thus hers was *Kammarrådinna*, which is virtually untranslatable into English.

5. The White Christ. So-called in Old Norse because of the white garments worn by those who allowed themselves to be baptised.

6. Aesir. The Aesir were a group of Norse gods which included Baldur, who was so fair that he shone. The adjective '*ljus*' used by Strindberg can also mean 'fair' when applied to hair.

Chapter VI

1. Blekinge boat. A sailing boat with a single mast, spritsail and foresail, used in Blekinge, a province in southern Sweden.

2. 'The White Mare.' Strindberg painted four pictures of a white navigation mark on a dark cliff above a stormy sea.

3. *The Voice of the Dove* was a Christian children's periodical founded in 1848. *The Pietist*, a religious periodical founded in 1842, is still published.

4. Henry II of France (1519–59).

5. Marieberg. Faience made at the Marieberg factory in Stockholm (1758–88), famous for the use of red and green made possible by a muffle furnace.

6. Nevers. A town on the Loire, famous since the sixteenth century for its faience.

7. Hélène de Genlis (usually known as Hélène de Hangest). The Hangests were the Seigneurs de Genlis. She was the châtelaine of the castle of Oiron near Thouars (Poitou) in the early part of the sixteenth

century. Her potter was François Cherpentier, also patronised by her son, Claude Gouffier. Henri II faience may have been made here, but this is disputed.

8. Frederick I, King of Prussia 1637–1713.

9. Order of Vasa. A Swedish order usually given for services to the State.

10. Bohuslän. A province on the west coast of Sweden, north of Gothenburg.

11. Ansgar. A Benedictine monk who took Christianity to Sweden in AD 829. Created first archbishop of Hamburg in AD 831.

Chapter VII

1. Titan. The Titans were a family of giants, the children of Uranus (Heaven) and Gaea (Earth) who contended for the sovereignty of the heavens, and were overthrown by Zeus.

2. An old folk-tale about a girl who trod on a loaf of bread to save soiling her fine shoes and sank into the underworld. Included by H. C. Andersen in *New Fairy-tales I*.

3. A widespread folk-motif used in a folk-ballad called *Little Karin*. This version is to be found on p. 12 of the commentary to *Svenska folkvisor* by E. G. Geijer and A. A. Afzelius (1880) which Strindberg possessed.

4. The Roman Campagna is the flat country south of Rome.

5. Arholma. A place on the east coast of Sweden about fifty miles north-east of Stockholm.

6. Arabia Petraea. Part of north-west Arabia and the Sinai peninsula which became a Roman province in about AD 106.

7. Carrageen alga. A kind of seaweed called 'Irish moss', also found in Brittany. It yields a jelly used for food and medicine.

8. The blessed thistle. *Cnicus benedictus*, a native of the Mediterranean and Near East, much used as a tonic and cure for gout. Sometimes called *Carduus benedictus*, the name Strindberg gives it.

9. A reference to Delilah, who deprived Samson of his strength by cutting off his hair.

Chapter VIII

1. This is a puzzling sentence. Strindberg seems to mean that Borg still addressed respectfully the woman whom Maria was treating as her child.

2. Revelations 6, 12–15 (Authorised Version).

Chapter IX

1. Roslagen. The coastal area north-east of Stockholm.

2. I Samuel 10, 11 (Revised Version).

3. Revelations 22, 14–15 (Revised Version).

4. Second sight (*OED*): 'A power of internal vision which enables you to see things before they happen.' Strindberg has not understood the meaning of the words.

5. A reference to John Stuart Mill's infatuation with Harriet Taylor, which worried Strindberg, as Mill was one of his heroes.

6. Deny their Paul. I Corinthians 14, 34–35. A reference to Paul's injunction that women should be silent in the churches.

Chapter X

1. This does not make sense as there are no balls in the game of throwing the discus. It should be 'leant back to throw her discus', but this is not what Strindberg says.

Chapter XI

1. The Farnese Hercules. The statue of Hercules from the Farnese collection in Rome, now in Naples. Hercules is resting his weight on his left leg. Consequently the right hip projects slightly.

2. *Cicisbeo* (*OED*): 'The recognised gallant of a married woman.'

Chapter XII

1. Matthew 14, 17–21.

2. Matthew 17, 20.

3. *Ett ungt fruntimmers historia* (1888), by the Danish authoress Erna Juel Hansen, the sister of the Danish poet, dramatist and novelist Holger H. Drachman.

Chapter XIV

1. Hälsingborg. The town on the south-west coast of Sweden nearest to Denmark. Strindberg must mean six hours from Stockholm.

2. Djurö and Nynäs. Places on the east coast north and south of Stockholm.

3. Norrbro and Slussen. Two bridges under which the fresh waters of Lake Mälaren stream into the salt waters of the sea. Slussen is also the isthmus linking North and South Stockholm, and is today a complicated traffic junction.

4. Trosa Bay. Trosa is a seaside town about fifty miles south of Stockholm.

5. All these are Catholics who, for religious or political motives opposed Gustav Vasa (1523–60). Vasa introduced the Reformation into Sweden and unified the country. Only Nils Dacke, the farmer agitator, was caught and killed. Most or all of the others died in exile in Rome.

6. Gone to Canossa. A reference to Bismarck's unsuccessful struggle with the Vatican, called the *Kulturkampf*, and his final surrender to the Pope. 'Gone to Canossa' is a figure of speech and refers to the humiliating surrender of the Emperor Henry IV to Pope Gregory VII in 1077 at the castle of Canossa near Parma (cf Strindberg's *Inferno* (Penguin, p. 253)).

7. A reference to the Franco-Prussian war of 1870. Strindberg is comparing the Prussians to the Huns, the barbarian hordes from the East, who overran Europe in the fifth century AD.

8. Office work. A reference to the records a Swedish parson is required to keep of every detail of every aspect of his parishioners' lives.

9. Ellipsoid. A curved body with three axes so constituted that every plane-section through the axes is an ellipse.

10. The homunculus. A tiny human being produced with the aid of magic or alchemy.

11. Archimedes (*c.* 287–212 BC). A Greek mathematician and mechanical genius. He was thinking in terms of a lever resting on a fixed point by means of which he could move the earth. For Strindberg the fixed point outside himself was something in which he could believe, i.e. God.

12. Dejanira, Hercules' wife, was tricked by the centaur Nessus into believing that his blood was a love-potion. When she suspected Hercules of being unfaithful she steeped a mantle in Nessus's blood, but this proved to be a fatal poison.

13. In a fit of madness, Hercules killed his friend Iphitus and as punishment had to serve Omphale for three years. Some sources say that during this time he behaved strangely, spinning, and wearing the dress of a woman.

14. The pain from the poisoned mantle was so excruciating that Hercules had a funeral pyre built on top of Mount Oeta, laid himself upon it, and commanded Philoctetes to set it alight.

15. The change from Hercules to Heracles is significant – Strindberg distinguished between the two. Hercules was the Roman hero, Heracles the Greek one. The former was an athlete but also an object of derision, the slave of Omphale. The latter was a symbol of true greatness. In a letter of 5 December 1895 Strindberg says: 'The Romans made an athlete of Heracles, but the Greeks kept their Heracles as a symbol, for they could see beyond what lies on top.'

16. Heracles was the son of Zeus and Alcmena.

MORE ABOUT PENGUINS, PELICANS, PEREGRINES AND PUFFINS

For further information about books available from Penguins please write to Dept EP, Penguin Books Ltd, Harmondsworth, Middlesex UB7 ODA.

In the U.S.A.: For a complete list of books available from Penguins in the United States write to Dept DG, Penguin Books, 299 Murray Hill Parkway, East Rutherford, New Jersey 07073.

In Canada: For a complete list of books available from Penguins in Canada write to Penguin Books Canada Ltd, 2801 John Street, Markham, Ontario L3R 1B4.

In Australia: For a complete list of books available from Penguins in Australia write to the Marketing Department, Penguin Books Australia Ltd, P.O. Box 257, Ringwood, Victoria 3134.

In New Zealand: For a complete list of books available from Penguins in New Zealand write to the Marketing Department, Penguin Books (N.Z.) Ltd, Private Bag, Takapuna, Auckland 9.

In India: For a complete list of books available from Penguins in India write to Penguin Overseas Ltd, 706 Eros Apartments, 56 Nehru Place, New Delhi 110019.

Also by August Strindberg in Penguin Classics

INFERNO AND FROM AN OCCULT DIARY

Both of these works are based on a diary Strindberg kept between 1896 and 1908 – undoubtedly the most troubled period of his life. *Inferno* is an intensely powerful record of the author's mental collapse; by the time Strindberg wrote *From an Occult Diary*, he was suffering the first pangs of a fatal cancer, and this work conveys an anguish and a pathos beyond the scope of fiction.

THREE PLAYS

Passionate and powerful, the three plays collected together in this volume represent Strindberg at his best. Acute psychological analysis and total mastery of the power to create unforgettable dramas of human life and love: these elements have here combined to make Strindberg, as Eugene O'Neill said, 'the most modern of the moderns'.